# KITTY HAMILTON

HARLEIGH BECK

*To Vicky Jewell,
I hope you enjoy Kingsley's dirty talk ♡
With love,
Harleigh Beck*

This is a work of fiction. Names, characters, organizations, places, events and incidents are either products of the author's imagination or are used fictitiously.

Copyright © 2022 by Harleigh Beck

All rights reserved.

No part of this book may be reproduced in any form or by any electronic or mechanical means, including information storage and retrieval systems, without written permission from the author, except for the use of brief quotations in a book review.

Editing: Chris Williams

Proofreading: Paula Hevia Riveiro.

Proofreading: Nisha at Nisha's Books and Coffee.

*Not suitable for readers under 18

*For Chris, who edited this lil' baby. I couldn't have done it without you!*

# PROLOGUE

How I first met my future husband is quite a humorous story. It happened in a coffee shop of all places.

I hold my freshly brewed cappuccino in one hand and my phone in the other. Hazel and Becky are busy gossiping about Kingsley, one of the most popular boys at school who also happens to be awfully boring. I know because he's in my class, and the only thing on that boy's mind is sex, alcohol, and his precious BMX bike. I don't think he has more than two brain cells, and it's as if they have packed up and gone on holiday.

Where was I? Oh right, I'm busy scrolling through Instagram when I walk into a hard and rather muscular wall. That isn't the worst part of this story. No, most tragically, I spill my coffee all over said muscular wall.

"What the fuck?!" a deep and gravelly voice growls, awakening my slumbering feminine parts.

I look up, up, and up again until I meet the stormy cobalt blue eyes of the most handsome man I have ever seen. Now, this is the moment where I should woo him with a flirtatious smile, but I'm dumbstruck and stare at him like he is the Greek God Apollo.

"You need to fucking watch where you're going!" he growls, shaking his wet hands. Drops of coffee fly everywhere.

I finally snap into action and grab a handful of paper napkins from the dispenser on the desk and begin patting him down, secretly admiring his hard chest. "Oh god, I'm so sorry!" I blurt, but it's a blatant lie, and now I'm just groping him instead of drying him off.

He's dressed in distressed jeans and a t-shirt, which used to be white but is now brown. Usually, I like my men in finely pressed suits, but I'm sure I can get this fine specimen of a man to improve his dress sense with some careful coaxing.

"I'm Katherine," I smile, patting him awfully close to the groin area. He looks at me like I belong in the local mental asylum and bats me off. "Whatever, just watch where you're going next time!" He storms out, and I stare after him like a lovesick puppy.

Becky and Hazel squeal behind me. "Oh my god! Oh my god!"

I turn and look at them quizzically. They begin talking at the same time. Hazel giggles and gestures for Becky to tell the story.

"Do you not know who that was?"

I look between them questioningly. "My future husband. Should I know who he is beside the obvious?"

Becky looks like she's about to burst at the seams. "You live under a rock. That's Hunter Wood. Only one of the most famous pornstars around!"

I furrow my brow. "Hunter Wood? Terrible name for a pornstar, don't you think?"

Hazel grins and winks. "But he's sure got some wood."

Becky laughs as I scoff and discard the napkins in my hand.

"What is he doing here anyway?"

The bell over the door chimes as we walk outside. I squint in the bright sunlight, shielding my eyes with my hand.

Hazel puts her phone back inside her purse and says, "Apparently, there's a porn convention in town."

*Aha!* I grin at the girls and pull my sunglasses down off the top of my head. "I'm changing my career plan."

Hazel cocks her head. "But what about college?"

We set off walking down the main street. It's rather busy for this time of day.

"I never wanted to pursue a career in law. That was my father's wish, and he's not here anymore. I could take a year out, pursue my future husband, and enjoy a rather adventurous career path in the meantime. How hard can it be?"

"Wait a minute!" Hazel says.

Becky takes a sip of her coffee.

"What are you going to do?"

I eye Becky's coffee longingly and reply, "I'm going into porn."

Becky sprays her beverage and stares at me in disbelief with coffee droplets on her chin.

I cringe, motioning to them. "You've got a little something there."

She wipes her chin, still staring at me.

Hazel scrunches her cute button nose. "But why?"

I steal Becky's coffee and take a sip. It tastes like coffee heaven, and I moan as I meet Hazel's inquisitive eyes. "Because I'm going to make Hunter my husband."

Becky snaps out of her stasis and laughs. "You are crazy!

He's a thirty-year-old pornstar, and you're an eighteen-year-old high school student."

"So?" I ask and hold her coffee out of reach as she makes a grab for it. "Nope, you're not getting it back until you tell me what your point is."

Becky sighs. "Kath, don't take this the wrong way, but look at you."

I do. There is nothing wrong with my fitted dress and Louboutin heels.

Becky rolls her eyes, waving a hand at me. "You're so… pristine."

"Pristine?"

Hazel sniggers, and I shoot her a look. She holds her hands up placatingly.

"There's not a wrinkle in sight. Your legs look oiled and shit."

"Oiled and shit?" I echo, staring down at my legs.

Becky seems at a loss for words before she replies, "Well, only celebrities have such perfect legs."

My mouth opens and closes. Her logic makes no sense. "So, I can't be a porn actress because I have nice legs?" I take another sip of coffee heaven.

Becky groans, blurting, "You're a virgin!"

I choke on the coffee and thump my chest. "What has that got to do with anything?"

A group of boys wolf-whistle as they walk past. Becky flips them off and then turns to me and says, "You need sexual experience to work in porn."

"That can easily be arranged."

Becky stares at me. "You're still a virgin. That's like rare gold at our age. Don't you think you should save it for someone special?"

I shrug. I'm not waiting to have sex per se. I have just

not been interested in anyone until now. There's not a lot of choice in this small town.

Hazel stops in front of a store window and eyes up a pretty dress.

"So, let's say you go through with this master plan of yours. What exactly *is* the plan?"

I hitch my purse higher onto my shoulder. "I don't know yet. Let me think about it. The first place to start is the convention." I tap Hazel on the shoulder. "When is it?"

"Saturday."

That's in two days. I have so much I need to do before then. Manicures, pedicures, a haircut. Suck a cock. The last thought makes me snigger.

Becky enters the store, calling over her shoulder, "Let's get you a new dress. Something less modest. You need to turn heads."

# ONE

"I'm leaving for the day, miss," Geoffrey, my butler and my late father's right-hand man, says in the doorway to my bedroom.

I pull on my fluffy pajama jumper and stick my head out of the walk-in wardrobe. "See you in the morning, Geoff."

"Bunnies?" He can barely suppress his amused smile.

I look down at the pink bunnies on my pajama jumper. "What's wrong with bunnies?"

"Nothing. Except Easter has been and gone."

I give him a droll look and close the door to my walk-in wardrobe. "I happen to think it's cute."

"What happened to the Kermit pajamas you refused to part with?"

"You know," I say as I tie my hair up. "That is an excellent question. What *did* happen to my Kermit pajamas, Geoffrey?"

"Oh, look at the time!" Geoffrey replies, inspecting the expensive watch on his wrist. "I must get going."

I'm highly amused by our banter. "I will get to the

bottom of it!" I shout after him as he makes his escape downstairs.

His voice carries up the stairs. "Your detective skills are subpar, miss. It'll remain a mystery for all of eternity."

I chuckle as the front door closes.

The first part of my research starts online, so I cozy up on my bed, grab my laptop and reach for my trusty coffee on my bedside table. Mr. Boomer, my three-year-old Sphynx cat, lies curled up on the end of my bed, purring like an engine. His blue eyes watch my every move.

"Let's see your wood, Mr. Wood," I snigger, searching his name online. He's not exactly difficult to find. Becky was right—he's a big name in the business. I click on an x-rated website and stare wide-eyed at the many videos of Hunter. I'm not starved for choice.

Mr. Boomer stretches his legs as I press play and take a sip of my coffee.

Hunter, dressed in a suit, is sitting on an office chair with his legs spread when a voluptuous receptionist walks in and drops a file on his desk.

I cringe when she talks. The acting is terribly bad.

Hunter loosens his tie and sweeps his eyes down her body in a way that's highly inappropriate in the workplace but makes me throb in unspeakable places.

"Naughty, naughty, Mr. Wood," I whisper as the receptionist drops to her knees between his legs and the desk. I think I could enjoy this if it wasn't for the cheesy background music.

Mr. Boomer yawns, stretching his cute little paws.

I lower the screen and hiss, "Don't judge me!"

Mr. Boomer lifts his head. He stares at me lazily and flicks his ear.

When I look back at the screen, the receptionist is sucking on Hunter's Wood.

*Ha! See what I did there?*

My mouth drops open. Hunter is huge! Jesus, he's an Adonis! Screw Apollo! Hunter is the Hades to my Persephone. I bite my lip and groan, ignoring Mr. Boomer's judging blue eyes. He may be a cat, but he's totally judging me right now. The loud moaning coming from my laptop is not helping my case either.

I click out of the video and select the next one in my recommended playlist. Jeez, I've watched the first ten minutes of one video, and I already have a playlist recommended to me.

I fast forward until it's midway through and press play. Hunter is fucking a girl from behind on a luxurious love seat, and her surgically enhanced breasts bounce in time with his powerful thrusts.

I cock my head and try to imagine myself in her place. If I pursue a career in porn to get close to Hunter, I'll have to practice the perfect facial expressions and sounds. I study the girl. Her mouth hangs open, and her eyes are at half-mast. She looks convincing. *Or maybe Hunter is that good?*

I suck my bottom lip between my teeth and sweep my eyes over his big hands, gripping her slim hips. The receptionist's ass is already red from repeated slaps. As I watch, he lands another loud spank before fisting her hair. He pulls it back and growls in her ear, whispering things that make me blush and close the laptop.

I'm shamefully aroused. My clit throbs like it has its own heartbeat, and it's not a feeling I'm used to. "Not a word," I whisper hiss, glaring at Mr. Boomer, who flicks his ear.

I open my laptop again and google how to suck dick. I

never thought I would abandon my academic studies on a Thursday night to research the technicalities of fellatio. My father would turn in his grave.

~

Mr. Adams, my English teacher, is an awfully boring man. His voice is monotone, and he wears the most horrid shirts that never fit him properly. It's no wonder he's still single. His glasses are always askew, so it's impossible to take him seriously.

My mind wanders while he drones on about things that I used to find fascinating but don't anymore. My mind is too preoccupied with the thought of how to gain enough experience to convince an executive producer to hire me. It's not like I can tell them about my non-existent expertise. I haven't even kissed anyone. My seven minutes in heaven with Joel in sixth grade doesn't count. It lasted two seconds and was sloppy. His tongue poked my cheek more than my mouth.

A sudden raucous laugh to my left rips me from my thoughts and disrupts the class enough to earn a glare from Mr. Adams. I stare at Kingsley as he runs a hand through his already disheveled brown hair. He's still laughing. If there is anyone more suited to be my teacher at this school, it's him. He's already slept with most girls here, and he is not the clingy kind who expects commitment. He can show me what to do. Then we can go back to ignoring each other. It's perfect.

Becky nudges my shoulder. "Why are you staring at Kingsley with a creepy smile on your face?"

I treat her to my best Cheshire cat smile. "Seek, and it

shall be provided, my friend. I love it when a plan falls into place."

"Huh?" Becky furrows her brows.

A shadow falls over my desk, and I lift my head. Mr. Adams is staring down at me with a deep crease between his eyebrows. "You're usually my best student Katherine. Is there anything you wish to share with the class?"

My eyes flick over to Kingsley, who looks amused by my discomfort. I shake my head. "No?"

Becky giggles next to me.

Mr. Adams harrumphs. "No talking in class, ladies." He points to Kingsley's table. "Katherine, go sit with Kingsley. Becky, you're with Sam. The rest of you split up into pairs.

"Why don't we get to pick who we sit with?" Becky whines, pushing her chair back.

"Let this be a lesson to you." Mr. Adams walks back to the whiteboard and begins writing down the task.

"This sucks," Becky groans, grabbing her bag.

Kingsley sits one table over from mine, so it's not exactly a trek to the Alps and back. He scoots out the chair next to him with his foot and gestures to it. "So, I'm graced with the presence of her royal highness, the unattainable Katherine Hamilton."

Okay, so maybe I will need to lower my standards a lot. *Remember, Katherine, he is the expert on sexual misadventures, not you.*

I straighten my skirt and take a seat. Kingsley sits spread out in his chair like he hasn't got a care in the world, his elbows on the back of it and his legs spread wide like he's ready to accommodate his latest conquest. Images flash through my mind of Hunter and the receptionist.

The nuisance throbbing between my thighs starts up

again. Before I can stop my treacherous eyes, they flick down to the visible bulge in Kingsley's jeans.

"See anything you like?" he drawls with a healthy dose of amusement in his voice.

My cheeks flush. I reach for the zip on my bag. "As a matter of fact, I have an arrangement I would like to discuss with you." I put my book on the desk and open it to page 143.

Kingsley leans forward, resting his elbows on the desk. I can smell him. It's a masculine smell that reminds me of leather and bonfires.

"An arrangement?"

I highlight a passage in my book and studiously ignore how nice he smells.

Mr. Adams walks past, placing a sheet of paper on the desk. I wait for him to be out of earshot and then face Kingsley, noting the slight smirk on his lips. He's amused by my obvious discomfort. "I need you to teach me something." I sweep my eyes over the room for listening ears.

"Go on," Kingsley drawls. He's smiling now.

I stare at his white teeth, then shake myself off and say, "I have decided to pursue a new career path. You're the most experienced one here. You have two days to teach me."

He laughs. "Well, are you going to tell me what *it* is? I'm not sure what knowledge I have that's of any interest to you. I don't see you being interested in BMX." He chuckles at his own joke. It's a well-known fact that Kingsley competes in freestyle BMX. When he's not at school, fucking or partying, he practices tricks on his BMX bike.

I roll my eyes. "I don't have a death wish."

Mr. Adams points to the whiteboard. "This is what we're working on today. I want you to read the three texts on the sheets of paper that I gave you and try to see if you can figure out which famous author wrote what. We have covered these authors this year, so if your memory is better than that of a goldfish, you should have no problem solving it together."

I read over the first passage, tapping the pencil on my lips. "Well, this is easy. It's Jane Austen," I mumble.

When I look at Kingsley, he sits smirking with his fingers linked behind his head.

"What?" I ask.

He shrugs. Then wets his lips and says, "You're cute when you concentrate."

I roll my eyes. "Oh please, stop that."

Kingsley laughs. "Stop what?"

I gesture to him. "The flirting. I'm not one of the bimbos at this school. I'm not going to fall to my knees because of some smooth pick-up line." I feel like a hypocrite telling him this when I've already decided to let him teach me all things sexual. Regardless, I need him to know that I'm not turned to butter by some carefully chosen words.

He shrugs, grinning. "Can't blame a guy for trying."

"Are you going to help with this?"

He leans forward, invading my space and I'm once again hit with his intoxicating smell. He turns the sheet and scans his eyes over the text. "George Orwell," he says, pointing.

"What? No." I lean forward and read the text. Sure enough, it's George Orwell.

Kingsley raises an eyebrow. His annoying smile is still intact. "The last one is John Keats."

My mouth drops open. "How?" I blurt, searching his face. Maybe his brain cells multiplied to four?

The bell rings. Kingsley leans down and grabs his cap from his backpack. He puts it on, twists it backward, and picks up his bag. "You shouldn't be so quick to judge people."

I watch him walk out of the classroom. I'm still in shock. Before he disappears out of sight, I grab my bag and chase after him. "Wait," I call out, pushing past students.

Kingsley stops and looks over his shoulder as I come running up to him. I grab his elbow and steer us towards a quieter part of the school.

"Where are we going?" he asks when I push him into a bathroom and lock the door behind us. It's not one of the bathrooms with cubicles but a single toilet, perfect for what I have in mind.

Kingsley gives me a questioning look as I take in his face. He's quite handsome with his brown eyes, sharp jaw, and straight nose. Wisps of dark hair peek out from beneath the cap. The effect is not bad on the eye at all. It's a shame his personality hasn't got more to offer.

"I'm locked in a bathroom with Katherine Hamilton. Did I hit my head this morning?" Kingsley mumbles under his breath, scratching beneath the trim of his cap.

I snap my fingers. "Attention, Kingsley." He looks adorably confused. "You're here because I need you to teach me sex."

Kingsley chokes on air. His mouth opens and closes. "Teach you sex?" he blurts.

I roll my eyes. "Come on, you've been with half the school. Who better to teach me than you?" I straighten my skirt and fluff my hair. "So, how do we do this?"

Kingsley's eyes bug out before he starts laughing incredulously. "What the fuck is happening right now?" he whispers, looking around the small bathroom. His eyes find mine again, and he says, "You need to explain it to me because I'm so fucking lost right now."

I walk over to the small sink and root through my bag for my lipstick. I reapply it, watching Kingsley through the mirror. "I met a man the other day who I want to marry. The only problem is that he's a famous pornstar. I've decided to land myself a role in his next movie, hence my problem—I'm a virgin. I need experience to get hired for the part."

Kingsley stares at me, not saying a word for once. First time for everything. "You want to get a role in a porno so you can make the male lead fall in love with you and marry you?"

"Oh, don't say it like that." I roll my eyes and smack my lips in the mirror. "It's an ingenious plan. Couples meet and fall in love at work all the time."

Kingsley laughs. It's a full-on belly laugh that seems to go on forever. Tears stream down his face when he finally composes himself enough to take a breath. "You have a great sense of humor," he chokes out, wiping tears from his eyes. His cap is askew.

I drop the lipstick into my bag before closing the small distance between us. "I don't think you understand." I take off his cap and place it down carefully on the sink. His laughter dies in his throat when I sink to my knees. I run my hands up his jeans-clad legs, squeezing the strong muscles in his thighs. "I've never been more serious, Kingsley."

He gulps.

I dig my nails into his thighs and sweep my tongue over my bottom lip. The truth is I haven't got a clue what I'm doing. I'm starting to think I should've watched more adult entertainment the night before. Maybe I could've learned a thing or two from the women in those clips. I think back to what the receptionist did and channel her energy. Her confidence. She took what she wanted without apology.

When I undo his belt and start on his buttons, Kingsley makes a choked sound in his throat, one so unlike him, but before I have a chance to lower his zip, he stops me with a hand on mine.

I look up at him questioningly. He guides me up by my elbow. Then quickly tightens his belt and rubs his hands over his face. He blows out a breath. "Fuck." He sounds tortured.

"Did I do something wrong?" I ask, staring at him. Strangely, my eyes prick with tears.

He shakes his head and drops his hands. "No, you did nothing wrong. It was perfect."

"Then why did you stop me?" I ask, furrowing my brow.

"Look," he begins, then stops. His heavy hand lands on my shoulder and he dips his head. "You don't want your first time to be in a bathroom at school."

I scan my eyes over the cracked tiles and flickering fluorescent lights. "Why does it matter? It's not going to mean anything."

He closes his eyes as if begging for patience. In a soft voice, he says, "Trust me, it matters."

"Look, if you're not willing to help me, I'll ask someone else. I'm sure Sam won't say no."

Sam is Kingsley's best friend. He's a manwhore of the worst kind, but I can't be picky right now.

Kingsley's grip on my shoulder tightens. "I'll help you, okay. Just not... not here."

I search his eyes. He looks sincere enough. "Okay, when?"

His hand falls away. He picks up his cap and puts it back on. *Why does he insist on wearing it backward?* "I'll meet you after class. We can go to your place if your parents aren't home?"

"Sure." I don't tell him that I live alone because my father is dead. And I never knew my mom.

"Okay. Great." Kingsley looks at me for a full minute, then leaves the bathroom.

The door clicks shut behind him.

I stare at my reflection in the mirror. I look like my usual put-together self, but on the inside, I feel strangely vulnerable.

∽

"Where did you go?" Becky asks in the lunch hall when I plop down in my usual seat.

I open the yogurt pot, dip my spoon in, and place it in my mouth, moaning like the porn actress I aspire to be.

Hazel laughs. "Good attempt."

"Thanks," I grin, then turn to Becky. "I secured the best sexual education available around here."

Becky drops her sandwich. "You did what?!"

"I said I secured the best sex—"

"Yes, I heard you, but what does that mean?" She picks her sandwich back up and bites into it.

I lick my spoon and find Kingsley across the room. He's leaning back in his chair, laughing at something Sam tells him. Girls flock around him like pigeons to bread. It's awfully predictable. Olivia, his most insistent admirer is nowhere to be seen for once. "It means I got Kingsley to agree to teach me his tricks."

Becky chokes on her food, and one of the guys at our table kindly thumps on her back. She thanks him and sets her sandwich down. "You did what?" she squeals.

"She got Kingsley to agree—"

"Yes, Hazel, I heard what she said. Thank you!" Becky growls.

Hazel and I share an amused glance.

"Why Kingsley of all guys?" Becky asks.

I lick my spoon. My eyes collide with Kingsley's across the room, and I make a show of sucking my spoon like the receptionist sucked Hunter's cock.

Hazel laughs. Even Becky joins in as she follows my line of sight. It looks like the mighty Kingsley is blushing.

"Kingsley has more experience than anyone here. Just look at him. Girls flock to him like he's the messiah."

Becky cocks her head, scrunching up her nose. "But he's a manwhore."

I nod, unwrapping my sandwich. "He certainly is. It's precisely why I picked him to be my mentor. He'll teach me what I need to know, and then we'll go our separate ways. No feelings involved. No drama."

Becky looks unconvinced but lets it go. "Just be careful, okay?"

"Yes, sir." I salute her.

She rolls her eyes and throws the sandwich wrapper at me, making me laugh.

Hazel takes a sip of her juice. "I did some research. Hunter produces his own movies, and there's an audition in the next town over for one of his productions in two weeks."

I quirk an eyebrow. "An audition?"

Hazel nods before taking another sip. Her bottle is almost empty. "Yes, I figured you've got more of a shot at landing a role in his movie the traditional route than you have of convincing him to hire you at the porn convention."

It's genius. I smile a genuine smile. "Thank you, Hazel."

She shrugs. "Anytime."

"Wait a minute," I whisper, furrowing my brow. "I

guess it's not like a traditional movie audition where you perform lines and squeeze out some fake tears?"

Becky scoffs, scrolling on her phone. "It only just occurred to you?"

I ignore her jibe. "What will I have to do?"

Hazel leans forward. "I heard one girl was asked to masturbate as part of her audition."

I scrunch up my nose. "Masturbate?"

Hazel nods, linking her fingers on the lunch table.

Becky hums before she steals my drink and takes a sip. "They'll want to see you naked. You might get groped and asked to perform in some way."

"In some way?"

"I don't know. Probably a blowjob," Becky says tiredly and a little loudly. Two of the boys on our table look over.

I find Kingsley again. He's typing on his phone with a girl hanging off his arm and whispering in his ear. I have a lot to learn if I'm going to stand a chance at landing this role.

# TWO

As promised, when I leave the school building at the end of the day, Kingsley is waiting for me outside. He's leaning on the small brick wall next to the bike rack with his BMX at his side and his helmet in his hand. The bike looks like a death-trap. He's dressed in a slightly loose gray t-shirt and black ripped jeans which hug his legs like a second skin. There's enough definition in his arms to make me curious what the rest of his muscles look like underneath his t-shirt.

As I approach, he looks up from his phone and runs his eyes down my body.

I gesture to his bike. "So this is her?"

He looks down at his bike and strokes the handlebars affectionately. "The only woman worth my time."

I cover my laugh with a hand over my mouth.

Kingsley looks up, and there is a sparkle in his eye. "Have you ever ridden one of these?"

I laugh and point to myself. "Do I look like I ride bikes?"

Kingsley sweeps his eyes down my body in a slow caress. Then shakes his head. "Sorry, but no. You look like you attend state dinners and host garden parties."

My mouth drops open. "Take that back!"

He chuckles as he pushes off the wall and fingers the strap of my fitted navy dress. It's strangely intimate. "Do you want me to lie, Katherine Hamilton?" He drags my name out. I never knew it could sound so sensual on a man's lips.

I roll my eyes. "I didn't choose my name. Kingsley."

He chuckles a rich and deep sound, gesturing for me to lead the way.

"Are you offering to let me ride your bike?" I ask even though I know the answer. For some reason, I find myself drawn to his laugh.

"Not a chance," he grins. "No one rides her but me."

We fall silent. The school is behind us now.

"How did this all come about?" Kingsley asks.

I raise an eyebrow in question.

He clears his throat. "This pornstar you want to meet. And marry." The last bit comes out choked.

"Oh, Hunter Wood? I ran into him at the local café the other day and spilled my coffee on his t-shirt."

Kingsley's eyes bug out. "*The* Hunter Wood?"

I side-eye him. "You watch porn, Kingsley?"

He clears his throat, looking sheepish. "Well, don't we all?"

I watch him rub his neck. "I didn't until last night."

Kingsley pauses in his step. We're standing in the middle of the path. "You're a virgin, and you never watched porn until last night?"

I smile at an elderly man who walks past. "Sorry about that, my friend here has no filter," I tell the man and look at Kingsley pointedly. "Maybe say it a little bit quieter next time, so the whole town doesn't find out."

He pretends to zip his lips up. We start walking again. "Are you saving yourself or something?"

I give him a droll look. "I asked you to educate me sexually so I can enter the porn industry, and you ask me if I'm saving myself for someone?"

He shrugs. "Well, you're good-looking. I don't see why you haven't got laid already if you're not saving yourself on purpose."

My brain latches onto the first part of that sentence. One by one, I squash the butterflies that spring to life in my belly. "I haven't been saving myself for someone special. There hasn't been anyone that I'm interested in. The standards in this town are subpar."

Kingsley laughs. "So, what made you pick me? It can't have been for my standards."

"I told you. You're the most experienced guy at school."

He gives me a look that tells me he doesn't believe me. "So my looks have nothing to do with it?"

I pause. "Are you fishing for compliments, Kingsley?"

A bus driving by drowns out his response. He tries again, "I guess I don't get it. I'm no Hunter Wood."

I scoff. "You don't have to look like Hunter to teach me how to give awesome blowjobs."

Kingsley trips over his feet.

"How come you don't have a girlfriend?" I don't know why I'm curious.

Kingsley snorts and gets on his bike, riding alongside me. "Too much hassle."

I laugh. "Hassle? Really?"

Kingsley stands on the front peg and moves the wheel along using his foot to roll the wheel. "They always want something," he says.

I pause in my step and watch him. "What's that trick?"

He jumps off his bike and smiles. "Gyrator."

"Gyrator?" We start walking again.

Kingsley waves to a car that beeps as it drives by. "It's the name of the trick. Gyrator."

"Oh..." I study his profile. He's got such a chiseled jaw. "What do you mean when you say girls always want something?"

Kingsley seems to weigh his words. "Girls are manipulative. They want you based on what you can do for them rather than for who you are. Popularity. Money. It attracts women like moths to a flame. It's shallow." He shrugs. "Fucking is easy."

"Fucking is easy," I parrot as he jumps back on his bike. He rides ahead and then stands on the pegs and kicks the frame around while rolling. He makes it look so easy. The muscles in his forearms are pulled tight, there are beads of sweat on his forehead, and those wisps of brown hair that stick out from beneath his cap have a certain allure to them. I feel drawn to him as I watch him on his bike. Passion is sexy, and Kingsley is passionate about perfecting his tricks. For the first time, I can kind of see why girls flock to him despite his apparent lack of brain cells.

"What's that trick?" I ask when I catch up with him.

"It's called a whiplash," he replies with a grin. "So, Katherine Hamilton. How are you going to win over Wood?" He high fives some guy we walk past.

"A friend of yours?" I ask.

"We ride together sometimes." He nudges me. "So?"

I tuck my hair behind my ear. "I haven't thought that far ahead yet. I figured it would happen naturally when we work together."

Kingsley doesn't comment, but I can see the amusement in his eyes.

"Go ahead and laugh," I say, nudging him back.

He sucks his lips between his teeth, shaking his head. "Nope.

"That's me," I say, pointing to my townhouse.

Kingsley jumps off his bike and whistles under his breath. "Impressive."

I climb the stairs and root through my bag for my keys. It's a luxurious townhouse in the most affluent part of town, but I'm used to it. Seeing it through Kingsley's eyes makes me uncomfortable.

My father was a successful man with an even more successful business. He left it all in my name, and the first thing my lawyer helped me with was to sort it all out so I wouldn't have to lift a finger. I'm eighteen years old and own a large company. It's a scary thought.

Kingsley carries his bike inside, and I gesture for Geoffrey to put it away for us.

Kingsley stares after him. "You have paid servants?"

I kick off my shoes and wiggle my toes. Heels are beautiful things, but also modern torture devices. "That was Geoffrey. He's my butler. I also have a chef and a cleaner who comes in a couple of times per week."

Kingsley follows me into the large kitchen. I open the fridge and take out the freshly cooked spaghetti Bolognese that Maureen, the chef, made this afternoon.

Kingsley watches me heat it up and place it on the island before reaching for bowls and cutlery. I plate the food and hand him a bowl. "Eat."

I twirl pasta around my fork and bring it to my mouth. It tastes like heaven.

"How long have you lived here?" Kingsley asks around a mouthful.

I finish chewing before answering him. "Since I was five. We lived out in the countryside before then, but my dad wanted to live closer to work. What about you? Where do you live?"

Kingsley looks uncomfortable. His fork scrapes loudly against the bowl. "Here and there."

I lift my head. "Here and there?"

He shrugs, chewing loudly. "I couch surf."

"Couch surf?"

Kingsley brings his now empty bowl to the sink and rinses it off. "My dad is a dick, so I left home. I stay at Sam's place some nights, and girls let me sleep over most of the time when I can't stay at Sam's."

I stare at him. It explains his oversized backpack. I swallow the food in my mouth and join him at the sink, rinsing my own bowl.

"It won't be like this next year when I'm at college. I'll have my own dorm room."

I put our bowls in the dishwasher and dry my hands on the hand towel.

"What was it you said about subpar standards?" he says in a low voice.

I raise my head. I didn't realize how close we were standing. "That's not what I meant," I reassure him. I can feel his warm breath on my face—that's how close he is.

"Now you know why I don't do the girlfriend thing. I have nothing to offer."

I grip the counter behind me. Kingsley follows. I'm not sure if it's intentional or not on his part. "You have plenty to offer," I whisper.

He reaches up, tucking my hair behind my ear. It's a tender touch. "No, I don't, Katherine Hamilton."

I ignore how much I love the sound of my name on his

lips. "If that's true, then why do girls throw themselves at you at school?"

His eyes drop to my lips before he takes a step back and shoves his hands in his pockets. "It's not like I've told anyone. Sam is the only one who knows. And now you. The girls at school only like me because I win competitions. It's skin deep. They won't give me a second of their time if they find out that I sleep on my friend's couch."

I feel honored that he trusts me with his truth. "I won't tell anyone."

His answering smile is vulnerable.

"Shall we?" I ask, pointing a finger over my shoulder just as Geoffrey walks in and bows low.

"I'm done for the day, miss. Is there anything else you require before I take my leave?"

I chance a look at Kingsley and say to Geoffrey, "No, that's okay, Geoff. Get yourself home. I'll see you tomorrow."

When he's gone, Kingsley bursts out laughing, and I join in. It feels good to laugh.

"Come on," I nudge my head to the hallway. "I'll show you my room."

Kingsley follows quietly behind. His brown eyes bug out as he scans over the large paintings on the walls as we walk up the sweeping staircase.

"This is my room." I hold open the door, so he can step inside, then close it behind us even though we're alone in the house. It's more out of habit than anything else.

Kingsley turns in a circle in the middle of the room. "Wow, this is something else."

He stands out amongst all of the creams and muted pastels with his grungy style. I always thought my room was big, but it looks small with him in it. I'm not entirely sure if it's his body or simply his presence.

I feel myself blush when he looks at the neatly made four-poster bed.

He walks over to my music collection and begins rummaging through my LPs. "I didn't take you for a fan of classic rock."

"I'm not. It was my dad's collection."

Kingsley looks up. His eyes roam my face, but he doesn't comment. "Can I put something on?"

I nod. "Sure, help yourself."

I watch him pick a record and place it on the turntable. Soon after, a rock ballad begins to play. His eyes meet mine across the room. I'm nervous. More so than I ever anticipated.

He walks up to me and puts his hand on my waist. His touch is firm and confident, but there's a hint of something else in his eyes. He looks nervous, but that can't be true. He's the experienced one here.

"What do you want to happen here tonight? he asks.

His question takes me aback. I haven't given it any thought. "Shouldn't you tell me that?"

His eyes drop to my lips, making my heart beat faster. "It's your first time. You need to tell me what *you* want to happen."

I swallow thickly. "Becky told me I will probably need to perform a blowjob as part of the addition."

"What previous experience do you have."

"I told you. I have no experience."

Kingsley grows still. "You must have some experience? Has no one gone down on you?"

I shake my head.

"How many guys have you made out with?"

I blush. "I haven't kissed anyone."

Kingsley falls silent. I look up and find him watching me closely with a crease between his brows.

"You've never been kissed," he whispers.

I thought this tutoring business sounded like a great idea, now I'm not so sure. I feel stupid.

He strokes his fingers over my cheek, and his warm touch makes my breath hitch. "Then that's where we need to start," he whispers, leaning in.

Our noses brush a second before I feel his soft lips on mine. I have no idea what I'm doing. All I know is that my whole body comes alive the instant our lips connect. I've never felt anything like it before.

Kingsley's hands are in my hair. He cradles my head as he guides the kiss, and when his tongue strokes against mine, I moan a soft sound I've never heard before. I reach up to fist his t-shirt, creasing the soft fabric.

Kingsley swallows my sounds with greedy kisses and bands his arms around my waist, bringing our bodies flush. He deepens the kiss with a groan that makes my toes curl in my shoes. I knock his cap off as I reach up and bury my fingers in his brown hair. It's silky to the touch.

I moan appreciatively, making him smile against my lips. He slides his big hands down my back and cups my ass as he lifts me into his arms and spins us around.

It's as if something ancient has woken up inside me. I wrap my legs around his waist and deepen the kiss. I don't need instructions; my body knows instinctively what to do.

Kingsley carries me over to the bed. My back hits the cool soft sheets, and Kingsley lies down on top of me. Who knew it felt so good to be squashed beneath the weight of a man?

"If you want me to stop at any point, all you have to do

is say," he whispers as he hikes my skirt up around my waist and hooks his fingers in my panties. He slides them down my legs, and air hits my sensitive wet folds a second before he dives down and covers my sex with his warm mouth. I arch off the bed. The sensation is too much.

"Oh fuck! Oh, God, yes!" I pant, surprised to hear myself curse as I sink my fingers in his hair and pull on it until he chuckles deep in his throat. I lean up on my elbows so I can watch him eat my pussy.

Kingsley glances at me from between my thighs and grins before licking me in one long stroke that makes me fall back on the bed and moan his name.

"God, Kingsley! Ahhh!" I cry out, rocking to meet his mouth.

He rises up and watches my tits strain in the confines of my dress while he rubs my clit with his thumb. His lack of brain cells aside, asking Kingsley for help must be the best decision of my life!

He climbs up my body and frees my tits as he yanks my dress off my shoulders. He's rougher than I thought he would be, but I like it a fucking lot. My clit is pulsating painfully.

He leans down and takes my nipple in his mouth. He sucks it between his teeth, watching me fist the sheets by my sides and arch my breast to his mouth. He nibbles and sucks until I don't know my own name anymore before kissing a path over to my other breast.

"I need..." I whimper as I squirm on the bed.

"What do you need, baby?" Kingsley asks in a husky voice, sucking my nipple into his mouth. I don't know what I need. I just know I need something... I need him to touch me and to never stop touching me. I am about to combust!

Kingsley releases my nipple with a pop and settles back

down between my legs. He grabs each of my thighs, spreads them wide, and dives back down, swirling his tongue in steady, hard circles over my clit.

I push against the headboard and thrust my body to meet his tongue. His day-old stubble scratches my thighs deliciously. He picks up speed, licking and sucking, nibbling and kissing, faster and faster until I feel an orgasm cresting.

I make a strangled noise in my throat. I can't even moan coherently now; I'm that far gone in Kingsley pleasure land.

Kingsley reaches up and tweaks my nipple between his thumb and finger as he grins against my sex. I swear he knows I'm close and is prolonging it on purpose. I push on his head in a bid to force him back down, and he chuckles before latching on to my clit and sucking it hard.

My hips buck off the bed, and he pushes my stomach back down with his big hand.

"You like me eating your pussy!" he taunts.

"Stating the fucking obvious there, Kingsley!" I choke out, surprised at my ability to string together a full sentence as I squirm on the bed. I plant my hand on the headboard again. "Kingsley! God! Fuck! Don't stop," I pant, cresting. This time he lets me fall over the edge.

I cry out his name, and Kingsley prods my puckered hole with his finger, adding more sensations on top of my climax. I shudder and shake, moaning his name until there's no air left in my lungs.

When the wave has receded, I lie sweaty and spent, breathing hard.

Kingsley places one last kiss on my clit and plops down on his back next to me. We stare at the ceiling for a long minute.

"That was..." I whisper, laughing incredulously.

Kingsley rolls his head, smirking. His eyes drift down to my naked tits. "Good, huh?"

I don't bother to cover myself. "That was more than good. That was amazing!" I roll over on my side and stare at the hard bulge straining in his jeans. He sucks in a breath when I trail my fingers over it.

I bite my lip. I want to taste him.

Kingsley sits up and climbs off the bed. He adjusts himself and clears his throat, looking uncomfortable. "I should go."

*What?*

I scoot up on the bed. I'm suddenly very aware of my nakedness, so I pull my dress up. "Don't you want me to return the favor?"

He squeezes his eyes shut. "No, erm...when is the audition?"

"In two weeks," I reply, feeling oddly vulnerable. Don't most guys jump at the opportunity of having their dick sucked?

"So there's no rush to take things further just yet."

I go to move off the bed, but he holds his hand up. "Stay in bed. Look, tonight was great. I know you want to learn more, but I don't want to rush you to do more than you're ready for. Let's just leave it for tonight. We can always meet up again tomorrow if you want."

"You don't have to leave. It's a big house. You're welcome to sleep in one of the guest rooms."

Kingsley cringes. "It's a kind offer, but it's not a good idea." He hooks a thumb over his shoulder and says, "I'm off. I'll see you tomorrow, yeah?"

"Okay...Your bike is in the first room to the left as you go downstairs."

With a quick goodbye and a wave over his shoulder, he's

gone. The bedroom door clicks shut. I stare at it for a long moment.

My thighs are tingling where his shaved beard scratched my skin raw.

I feel confused. I can't understand why he ate me out but then turned me down when I wanted to make him feel good? Kingsley is known for taking what he wants when he wants. So why did he turn me down?

∼

"He did what?" Hazel asks, grabbing a handful of popcorn. I rang my girls to meet up at the movie theater. I don't have experience with boys like they do, so this called for an emergency meet-up.

"He left you on the bed?" Becky asks, scrolling on her phone.

I nod and pinch a popcorn from Hazel's bag. "He ate me out and left. He looked like he had fun, so I don't know what to make of it."

"Maybe he wanted to be a gentleman?" Hazel asks.

Becky scoffs, looking up from her phone. "Really, Hazel? A gentleman?"

Hazel shrugs. "Well, why not?"

"Because he's a manwhore who fucks anything that walks. That's why," Becky says, and a couple on the next row up shushes us. "Oh, chill the fuck out, it's adverts!" she growls, throwing a handful of popcorn at them.

Hazel holds her bag of popcorn out of reach when Becky goes to grab for more. "I told you both to get your own popcorn. I didn't pay $8 for you to throw popcorn at strangers."

Becky waves her off and leans in, smiling. "So, was he any good?"

Hazel nods eagerly. "Yes, we need details."

I grin. "It's not like I have anyone to compare him to."

"Did you come?" Hazel asks around a mouthful of popcorn. Becky swipes for the bag, grinning triumphantly when she hits the jackpot and comes away with a handful of popcorn.

Hazel glares at her.

"I definitely came," I boast, puffing up like a peacock.

"My baby is growing up," Becky teases, pretending to wipe tears off her lashes.

"There's still one problem," I point out as I reach for Hazel's diet coke. I take a sip. "While cunnilingus is fun, it won't get me picked for the role. He needs to let me practice my oral skills on him."

"Didn't he say you're meeting up tomorrow?" Hazel asks, reaching for her diet coke in my hand.

"Well, yes..."

"So, let's be patient for one more day and see what happens tomorrow. If he turns you down again, then corner Sam or someone in the bathroom. Sam won't turn you down," Becky says.

"You're right," I reply as the screen widens and the movie starts.

Becky leans in, whispering, "If not, you can always practice on me. I've heard girl-on-girl action is good business." She winks, making me giggle as the couple behind us kick the back of our chairs.

Hazel protectively holds her popcorn out of reach, and Becky flips them the middle finger, shouting, "Just fucking chill, will you!"

# THREE

Mrs. Ackland, the school's career advisor, pops her gum. "Let me get this straight. You don't want help filling out your college application because you want to pursue a career as a porn actress?"

"Adult entertainer," I correct.

Mrs. Ackland pops her gum. Again. "Alright then, you don't want help filling out your college application because you aspire to become an *adult entertainer*."

I don't like how much emphasis she puts on 'adult entertainer.' "I can't help but feel like you're mocking me, Mrs."—I read the sign on her desk—"Ackland. But I'll have you know that I think I can be a very successful adult entertainer."

Mrs. Ackland sweeps her eyes over my clothes, chewing her gum loudly. "Uh-huh."

I look down at my outfit. I'm wearing a pink and cream LK Bennett tweed dress and my favorite pair of black heels. I think I look very presentable. I adjust the pink diadem in my blonde hair and clear my throat. "Have you got something to say about my clothes?"

Mrs. Ackland pops her gum again. It's really starting to annoy me now.

She moves a lock of her unruly hair out of her eyes and shakes her head, leaning back in her chair. "Not at all, Katherine. Your clothes are very *modest*."

There it is again—that tone in her voice! I narrow my eyes, convinced she's mocking me. I gesture to her sign. "It says you're a career advisor, correct?"

Mrs. Ackland puts her feet on the desk and threads her fingers together on her stomach. "That would be correct."

"So, are you going to advise me on my chosen career path or not?"

Mrs. Ackland laughs. She wipes tears from her eyes, drops her legs back down on the floor, and leans forward, elbows on the desk. "Let me level with you, Katherine. I don't think you have what it takes to succeed in the porn industry—sorry, the *adult entertainment* industry. My advice would be to fill in a college application form as a backup to your"—she clears her throat—"fascinating choice of career path."

"You don't think I can succeed? Why? Are my boobs not big enough?" I gesture to my chest.

Mrs. Ackland's eyes fall to my chest. She clears her throat and throws her gum in the trashcan. "There's nothing wrong with your chest, Miss. Hamilton, but it requires a certain kind of girl to make it in such a brutal business."

I scoff. "I'm the daughter of one of the most brutal businessmen this town has ever seen. It's in my blood, Mrs. Ackland."

She quirks an eyebrow, assessing me in a new light. "Maybe there is something in that skull of yours after all," she mumbles under her breath.

I gasp, pressing a hand to my chest. "Excuse me!"

Mrs. Ackland sighs tiredly. "Katherine. Do you really want to suck cock for a living?"

I gasp even louder this time and glance at the closed door. Hopefully, no one is eavesdropping. "Are you suggesting there is something wrong with promiscuous women?" I whisper hiss.

Mrs. Ackland laughs again, shaking her head. "I never said that. But you, Katherine, don't strike me as a "promiscuous woman." She makes air quotes with her fingers.

I stand up and grab my purse off her desk. "I'll have you know I'm very promiscuous. Just last night, I let Kingsley eat me out after school."

Mrs. Ackland's eyebrows hit her hairline. It gives me a small measure of satisfaction to have taken her by surprise.

She opens the desk draw, extracts another piece of chewing gum, and pops it in her mouth. "I don't know what to say to that." She rubs between her eyebrows. "Well done. Congratulations. Go you!" She fist bumps the air, then shakes her head and continues, "No, it sounds inappropriate no matter what I say." She rummages through the open drawer and hands me a stack of papers. "Take these. You don't have to fill them out just yet. You still have a month until the deadline, but read through it and have a think, okay? Don't throw this opportunity away just yet."

I accept the papers in her hand. "Thank you for your time, Mrs. Ackland." I leave the room with my head held high. *I'll show her!* She's wrong to underestimate me.

∽

Becky nudges me as she leans in. I look away from the whiteboard and Mrs. Beechwood's wrinkled blouse.

Becky has a mischievous look in her eyes. "Are you excited for the convention tomorrow?"

I grin and check to make sure Mrs. Beechwood isn't looking this way. "I spent an hour last night deciding how to do my hair."

"Only an hour?" Becky mocks. "Girl, we're going to make you look fabulous!"

Hazel, who sits at the desk in front, tips her chair back, whispering, "He won't be able to take his eyes off you."

I giggle just as a disheveled-looking Kingsley walks in and plops down into his regular seat a couple of rows over. I worried that he wouldn't turn up today when he didn't show for the first lesson.

"Mr. Delanoy, how nice of you to join us," Mrs. Beechwood drawls sarcastically.

Kingsley salutes her. "The pleasure is all mine, Ma'am."

I trail my eyes over his clothing. He's dressed in a creased white t-shirt with a band name on the front and distressed light blue jeans. Around his neck are a pair of black Beats headphones. They're the big obnoxious kind that only guys can pull off. As always, he's got his trusty cap on backward.

"You're staring," Becky whispers.

I frown. "Am not."

"You're definitely staring," Hazel chimes in, twirling a strand of her brown hair.

"Girls!" Mrs. Beechwood groans, turning toward us. "Can we please stop with the chitter-chatter? I am trying to conduct a lesson here."

I feel Kingsley's eyes on me, but I'm blushing too hard to look at him.

"Care to share with the class since all I've heard from you three this morning is giggles and more giggles."

Becky and I shake our heads, but Hazel nods eagerly and says, "We're going to Adultcon tomorrow."

Mrs. Beechwood looks confused.

Becky and I frantically shake our heads, but Hazel is on a roll. "It's a convention for the adult entertainment industry, Mrs. Beechwood. We're hoping to see Hunter Wood there."

The entire class erupts in laughter.

I drop my forehead to the desk with a groan, and Becky pats my back, shaking with laughter next to me.

It takes poor Mrs. Beechwood at least five minutes to get the class to settle down. I still have my head pressed to the table. I might just stay here for the foreseeable future.

"It's not that bad," Becky giggles.

I roll my head on the table until my cheek is squashed against the surface. I stare at her in disbelief. "My embarrassment is no longer of relevance. I'm comfortable here."

Becky pinches my nose affectionately. "If it's of any help, Kingsley keeps looking at you."

I groan and roll my head again. My nose is flattened against the desk now. "No, that's of no help at all. Staring doesn't get me experience. What if Hunter falls madly in love with me tomorrow and drags me into the bathroom or hides me under his desk. I won't know what to do."

"It's not a desk. It's a table, so Hunter can't hide you underneath it. People will see you."

"Thank you, Hazel," I drawl sarcastically. "That's very helpful to know."

"You can always open your legs and invite him to the all-you-can-eat buffet," Becky teases, poking me in the ribs.

"Oh yeah, because I'm now an expert in that," I deadpan as I sit back up and rub my forehead.

"She's awake!" Mrs. Beechwood taunts. She drops a

stack of papers on my desk. "Why don't you hand these out?"

I take one and turn to hand the stack to the person behind me, but Mrs. Beechwood clears her throat.

"By hand."

"By hand?" I ask, my mouth opening and closing like I'm a goldfish in a bowl.

"It should wake you up, Katherine. May I suggest you go to bed earlier from now on."

"But I wasn't asleep!" I blurt, but Mrs. Beechwood has already gone back to her desk. I mutter under my breath as I stand up and walk down the aisle, handing everyone a sheet each.

As I place one on Kingsley's desk, I nearly fall flat on my face when he snakes his hand up my skirt. The desk hides his wandering fingers, but I sure feel them burn a path up my legs before skimming the edge of my panties. His smile is dangerous.

"I'll wait for you in the same spot as yesterday," he whispers in that deep timbre of his. Then his hand is gone, and Kingsley is reading the paper in his hands as if I'm not standing here with my pussy clenching in anticipation.

Ha! In your face Mrs. Ackland, career counselor! Who's promiscuous now?

I sit back down and squeeze my thighs together as images of Kingsley between my legs flash behind my eyelids. God, I need his tongue on me again. And those hands. I sneak a glance. He's drumming a beat on his desk with his pencil. His hands look strong, and now that I've been up and personal with those fingers, it makes a delicious shiver run down my spine. The things he can do with his hands... *The way he can make me feel.*

"Katherine Hamilton!" Mrs. Beechwood hisses. "Are you paying attention?"

I straighten in my seat. "Of course."

"Oh, really? In that case, what is the 9$^{th}$ term of the arithmetic progression." She points to the whiteboard.

I'm clueless as I stare at the numbers in front of me. My mind is drawing a blank.

Kingsley speaks up in lazy a tone, "It's twenty-one."

Mrs. Beechwood beams. "I'm glad someone pays attention. Outstanding, Kingsley."

Okay, I digress. Maybe Kingsley's brain cells have evolved the ability of mitosis. Perhaps he now has eight brain cells?

I stick my tongue out at him and feel flutters erupt in my stomach when he smirks. *Oh god, no, no, no!* Not the dreaded butterflies. I lean in close to Becky's ear and whisper, "Emergency!" She looks at me questioningly, so I point to my stomach and mouth, "Butterflies."

She blinks.

I sigh as I rip out a page in her notebook and write down 'BUTTERFLIES!'

Becky's eyes widen in horror. She leans forward, taps Hazel on the shoulder, and shows her the note.

Hazel gasps out loud, eyes flicking to Kingsley briefly before she looks at me and slides her fingers against her throat, whispering, "Abort mission!"

I shake my head and rip out another sheet of paper. My pen flies across the sheet. I turn it, so she can read it.

*I can't abort the mission. I need him to teach me.*

Hazel cringes, reaching for her own pen. She scribbles a note underneath mine.

*Butterflies are only the beginning. You'll fall in love! Get out while you can!*

Mrs. Beechwood pops up like a jack in the box and tries to swipe for the paper, but I'm too quick for her. I scrunch it up and shove it in my mouth. *Gross!* It tastes terrible. I'm fighting the urge to gag.

Next to me, Becky is in stitches, and Hazel is staring wide-eyed. But desperate times call for desperate measures. If she gets hold of it, Mrs. Beechwood will read our note to the class, so I fill my mouth with as much saliva as possible and chew like my life depends on it.

Mrs. Beechwood is glaring at me with her hands on her hips. She points to the door. "Get out!"

I swallow down the soggy mess and stare at her in disbelief. I've never been thrown out of class before. Ever! I'm an exemplary student. This is why sex ruins lives. I get my pussy licked one time, and look at me now, getting thrown out of class like some working-class delinquent.

If I'm not wrong, even Kingsley is hiding a chuckle behind his hand. I point at him. "It's all your fault!"

Amused, he gestures to himself. "Me, what did I do?"

I scoop up my papers while Mrs. Beechwood watches me like I'm a nuisance. "You know exactly what you did, Mr. Delanoy."

Kingsley laughs loudly, and Mrs. Beechwood turns her ire on him. "Do you wish to join Miss. Hamilton in detention?"

"Detention," I shriek, outraged just as Kingsley says, "No, I'm good." He winks at me, far too pleased with himself.

I point my finger at him as I back out of the room. "One call, Kingsley! One call and Geoffrey will cut your lock, buddy. Watch me ride your bike outside these windows." I motion to the windows that line the far wall and grin like the delinquent I have morphed into. I might as well go down in flames.

Kingsley's mouth falls open. The pen drops from his fingers. "You wouldn't?!"

"Oh, but I would!" I dash out of the room, laughing like a hyena.

∼

"Honestly, I can't believe that you got detention," Becky says around a mouthful of lasagna.

I wipe the stain on my dress where the food decided to jump off the spoon and land. Someone higher up must be having a laugh at my expense today. No amount of rubbing with a crumbling piece of tissue will ever remove this bad boy. Tomato stains are of the devil!

I groan. I really like my pretty tweed dress too. I throw the tissue down on the table and sulk. What's the point anyway? I'm promiscuous. I get thrown out of class. What's a little stain to top it all off like the cherry on the cake?

"I can't believe it either," I reply, reaching for my drink. *Watch me spill it on my lap.* It wouldn't surprise me. I wrap my lips around the straw as my treacherous eyes seek out Kingsley across the room.

Olivia, his most dedicated admirer, sits straddling his lap. Would it be really wrong of me to pull out her cheap hair extensions?

Becky nudges me, and lo and behold, a mouthful of coke spills down my chin. I wipe it off and place the drink down on the table before I end up wearing it. Then turn my glare on Becky. "What?" I bark.

She holds her hands up placatingly. "Don't bite my head off. Just don't... stare so much. You're being obvious."

I grimace. "That bad, huh?"

Becky chews her food, pointing her fork at me. "Oh, yeah. Very!"

I cringe. Fuck, this is bad!

"Besides," Becky continues. "You can't be the jealous type if you're going to lock down the infamous Wood stick."

Hazel giggles next to us. "Did you see what she did there? Wood stick."

I wave her off. "I noticed, Hazel. Trust me," I reply in a droll voice, then turn my body to face Becky. "I'm not jealous."

Becky simply grins.

"I'm not!" I insist, sounding like a squeaking bird.

"Uh-huh."

"God, I hate the sparkle in your eye right now." I lean back and cross my arms. I'm so not watching Olivia whisper in Kingsley's ear. Nope. Not at all.

"I think you should practice your seduction skills," Becky says around another mouthful.

I give her a skeptical look. "My seduction skills?"

She nods. "You'll see Hunter at the convention tomorrow. How are you going to get his attention? It's not enough to just show up. There will be hundreds of women there, all vying for a piece of him."

I stare at her, and she sighs, placing her fork down on her plate. "Have you ever flirted with anyone?"

I think back. "There was the time I smiled at the clerk in Harrods to get a discount."

Becky quirks a brow. "And did you?"

"Well, no. But in my defense, I think he played for the other team."

Hazel butts in, "She's right. I saw him once in town when I was shopping for my grandmother's birthday, and he was dressed in high-waisted pleated pants. The man sure knows how to dress well!"

I turn back to Becky with an 'I told you so' look, which she ignores.

"Don't you want all the experience you can get?"

I narrow my eyes. The little she-devil knows precisely how to hook me. "Fine," I relent and turn in my seat, tapping Caleb on the shoulder. We've sat next to each other for years at lunch. He's part of the debate team, has one of the highest IQs at this school and his mother loves a summer banquet.

He smiles at me tentatively and readjusts his glasses.

Becky clears her throat behind me.

I swallow down my annoyance and look at her with my best sugary smile. "Yes? Can't you see I'm a little busy here?"

She suppresses a laugh as she leans in and points her finger to the basketball players' table to our left. "Not him. Knox."

I stare at her. "Knox?"

Next to us, Caleb shifts and Becky rolls her eyes. "You can turn back around now."

I peek at the basketball players. Knox is tall. Very tall. And athletic. He's got light brown wispy hair and green eyes that always speak of mischief.

Becky's breath hits my cheek as she whispers, "He's perfect for our mission. He's highly popular with the girls but not as easy as Kingsley or Sam. He's more selective. He hooks up occasionally but is more of the loyal kind. If you can catch his attention, then you'll be golden tomorrow."

"You're positively evil!" I hiss, still staring at Knox.

She chuckles against my cheek. "Hey, you're the one who wants to become an adult entertainer. Hooking your audience is the most crucial part. Go see if you can hook Knox."

I scoot my chair back and glare down at her. "I'm only doing this for the experience."

She sucks her lips between her teeth, suppressing another laugh. "Go for it."

"I don't know why I let her talk me into this stuff," I mumble under my breath as I make my way over to his table. I've never spoken to any of the basketball players before. I don't even attend their games.

How exactly do you flirt? I try to remember what I've witnessed in the lunch hall. It's the optimal setting for hormonal teenagers to practice their seduction skills. If you pay close attention, you have a front-row seat to their mating calls, but I never did, which is proving a bit of an issue at this moment in time.

Oh god, I'm close to him now. The back of his head is within reach. If I stick my hand out, I can stroke his hair. Shit, here we go. Incoming in three, two, one.

I plop myself down in front of him on the table, scoot his lunch tray out of the way, and smile my most alluring smile. Or perhaps I simply look deranged. "Hey, Knox." Even my voice is sultry.

The shocked look on his face is almost comical. Almost. I'm acutely aware that I have attracted quite the audience at his table. They all stare at me like I'm an alien from Mars. So, what do I do now? I can't channel 'receptionist girl' and slide down on my knees to suck his dick. Not in a crowded lunch hall with his friends watching. Fuck, why do they make the art of seduction look so effortless in pornos? Just walk right in, rip open your shirt and shove your tits in the man's face.

"Can I help you?" Knox asks, tearing me from my inner dialogue. Fuck it, I'm going for it.

I lean forward and drag my nails down his chest as I bite my bottom lip in what I hope is a seductive manner. "You can most certainly help me."

"Err, okay?" he squeaks before chuckling awkwardly.

Because I feel somewhat reckless and brave, I hike my skirt up and straddle his lap. If Olivia can do it, I can do it.

Knox doesn't object. He's mute, staring at me like he can't process what is happening.

I grin and trace my fingers over his sharp jaw, loving the stubble I feel there. "I think you should take me out, Knox."

"Take you out?" he parrots.

"You know..." I purr. "On a date." I meet his eyes and roll my hips because why not? What is a movie at the cinema without special effects? "In the backseat of your car."

Someone coughs to cover up a laugh.

Before he has a chance to turn me down, I press my tits against his chest and whisper in his ear, "I'm going to come on your face so hard!"

*That sounds like something you would hear in a porno.*

His erect dick twitches in his jeans, and when his hands land on my hips, I know I've won this round.

"You're quite the surprise, Katherine Hamilton."

*What is it with guys and my full name?* I hum in agreement as I play with the wispy strands at the back of his hair.

Knox's eyes are glued to my cleavage. "When do you want me to pick you up?"

I pretend to think about it. "I'll let you know."

He stares after me as I clamber off and make my way back to my laughing friends.

"Fuck, you don't do anything by halves!" Becky chokes out, handing me a chocolate bar. "You deserve a treat."

I rip open the packaging and take a large bite, moaning. "Chocolate heaven!"

"I think you made a certain someone jealous," Hazel whispers with a grin.

I chance a look at Kingsley. He's glaring at me over Olivia's shoulder, completely disinterested in her roaming lips on his neck. I can't help but feel a sense of triumph to have evoked such a reaction in him. I don't know why since he only went down on me once. It's not like we're dating or even know each other that well. We didn't even speak before yesterday. Still, her lips and hands on his body annoy the living daylights out of me. It's an effort to not go over there and rip her off him.

"I think you'll do just fine tomorrow," Becky smiles. "But don't climb the table and straddle Hunter, okay? We don't want to get escorted out by security."

I laugh, throwing the chocolate wrapper at her.

∼

Turns out detention is as dull as it sounds. Not only that, but I'm stuck here with some of the worst troublemakers at school. There's the boy with a shaved line through his eyebrow who sells weed at breaktime. I recognize him because someone needs to gift him a belt for Christmas, so I don't have to look at his boxer briefs with SpongeBob on them every time I turn a corner.

Then there's the girl with the black bob, purple lipstick, and neon yellow lacers, Nina. I only know her because I had the misfortune of walking in on her giving Rhys, the chess nerd, a blow job in the science lab. That's the last time I will ever arrive early for a class again.

Her trusty sidekick April is here too. Apparently, they don't do anything on their own, not even detention.

The chair next to me scrapes loudly on the floor, and Josh, another one of their sidekicks, plops down, dumping his bag on the desk. I stare dumbly, then sweep my eyes around the room. There are lots of empty seats.

"Don't worry, I'm used to privileged princesses who don't like to associate with my kind," he whispers, grinning. His voice is rich and smooth.

I open my mouth to say something, but it remains in an 'O' shape, and no words come out. What is this? 'Everyone, come talk to Katherine Hamilton' day?

He chuckles knowingly as he picks up his phone and scrolls through a group chat.

I stare at him for a full minute until my eyes burn, and I'm forced to blink. "Why did you choose this seat and not one of the million other chairs?"

He lowers the phone and scans his eyes across the room. "I thought you were supposed to be good at maths." He quickly counts the chairs. "I can only see thirty chairs, of which sixteen are unoccupied."

I glare at him.

He chuckles again. "I don't know, princess. You're a new face within these walls, and you look like a juicy zebra amid a lion pride. Call it curiosity."

"Well, be less curious next time!"

He throws his head back with a laugh, and the sudden noise makes the teacher at the front lift her head. She frowns disapprovingly before flipping a page in her romance novel.

Josh leans in, whispering, "So you're saying there *will*

be a next time? Are you thinking of joining the dark side?" He winks, then cups his mouth and shouts, "April!"

She looks over her shoulder.

Josh lifts his hand above my head, pointing down at me. "We're corrupting privileged princesses one at a time. This one wants to come back to detention."

April mimics a high five.

I sit there and feel like I've bumped my head and woke up in an alternative universe. What on earth is happening right now?

I breathe a sigh of relief when we're finally dismissed.

Josh stands up, grabs his backpack, and winks at me. "See you around, princess."

I stare wide-eyed at his broad back as he walks out.

Nina stops by my desk and circles her temple. "He's a bit cuckoo." She laughs at my expression before walking out and leaving me even more dumbfounded. What on earth was that about?

# FOUR

Kingsley is riding his BMX bike at the bottom of the steps. I watch him do a 360° rotation of the bars with the front wheel in the air and the rear wheel on the ground.

"What's that trick?" I call out as I descend the steps.

"His head snaps up. He comes to a stop and plants his feet on the ground. "It's a Chicken Barspin," he says with a smile.

I descend the last step and take my time admiring his chiseled jaw and brown eyes as I walk up to him.

He removes the helmet and snaps it to his backpack. Then motions for me to lead the way. It's another sunny day. "How was detention?" he asks with a barely suppressed grin. He's mocking me.

"Well, I got told I look like a juicy zebra, so I think my science experiment in social behaviors went rather well."

He chuckles, gazing at me before jumping back on his bike and riding alongside me.

"What got you into BMX?"

Kingsley jumps from his rear wheel and performs another barspin. I can't help but be impressed by his sheer level of skill. "When I was five, my elderly neighbor taught me how to ride a bike. My dad spent his days drunk and fucking locals down at the bar. I was left alone a lot with nothing to do. My neighbor... she took me under her wing. She and her husband didn't have a lot. Still, they gifted me a rusty old bike. I kept it in their garden because I knew that if my dad found it, he would kick it to pieces during one of his angry fits or sell it for quick cash. My passion started from there."

I stare at his profile. I don't know how to respond, so I stay silent.

Kingsley rides ahead some distance. He does a small hop, pulls the handlebars toward him, brings the rear wheel up with his legs, and spins the bike 180°.

"Let me guess," I say when he comes to a stop and waits for me to catch up. "A gyrating giraffe?"

Kingsley throws his head back with a laugh. It's a deep and rich sound that makes my toes curl in my shoes as I stare at his long neck and gleaming teeth. He laughs with his whole body. It's contagious, and I can't help but feel drawn in by his light. It shines like the brightest spotlight in the darkest night.

"No, nothing quite as exciting as that. It's called a Manual 180. I'll teach you one day if you want?"

I laugh drily. "I think I'll pass, thank you."

"What about you?" he asks. "You haven't mentioned your family? Any siblings?"

My heart squeezes painfully, but I don't let it show on my face. "Trust me, it's not a topic you want to discuss." I keep my eyes forward but feel him watching me.

"So, Knox, huh?"

I glance at him. "What about Knox?"

Kingsley watches me for a moment, seemingly

searching for something. Then shrugs and says, "I heard he's taking you out."

I guffaw. It's not the kind of laughter I've ever heard bubble out of me before. "Becky challenged me to seduce him as part of my preparation for the convention. I don't have any experience with flirting, and somehow I have to catch Hunter's attention tomorrow in a room full of women far more experienced than me."

"Don't you think that your innocence is what makes you stand out from the crowd?"

I give him a look. "Inexperience is not attractive, Kingsley. He's a pornstar who fucks women for a living. He won't be interested in some eighteen-year-old virgin."

"Even so. You're different. Your innocence is refreshing."

I eye him for a long minute.

He waves to someone across the street.

"You know everyone."

Kingsley laughs. "Not everyone, but when you move in my circles, you meet a lot of people."

I wonder what that feels like. I have precisely two friends, Becky and Hazel.

"Show me another trick and make it impressive."

He smirks, eyeing me, before getting back on his bike. He rides ahead. Then stands with one foot on the back peg, grips hold of the handlebar and front peg, and spins around on his axis. He spins and spins until I feel dizzy just watching him.

The smirk he throws my way when he finally comes to a stop is nothing short of filthy. My pussy clenches like the treacherous little vixen that she is.

"Spin Cycle?"

"No, Time Machine." He grins.

I roll my eyes and walk ahead, but I can't stop smiling, and there is a lightness in my chest that spells trouble.

"Will I meet Geoffrey again today?" he says when he catches up, pulling his bike along.

I shake my head. "No. You can blame my unforeseen adventures in detention land. Geoffrey finishes at four o'clock."

"So we'll be alone?"

*Throb. Throb. Throb.*

I ignore my clit and clear my throat as I rummage through my bag for my keys. My townhouse is just up ahead.

Kingsley hoists his bike over his shoulder and ascends the stairs after me. I'm painfully aware of him behind me. You can fit at least two football players between us, but he still feels like a warm blanket wrapped around my back. Even the exposed skin on my neck is tingling.

I unlock the door, and Kingsley steps through first. He disappears down the hallway to store his bike, and I close the door, kicking off my heels.

No sooner have I managed to free my second foot when I'm lifted off the ground. My back connects with the door, and Kingsley slams his lips to mine, plunging his tongue past my lips. I moan as I knock his cap off and pull at his hair. The world around me spins.

Kingsley's kiss is possessive and dirty. I feel his rock-hard dick against my stomach, and it's all I can do not to beg him to take my virginity against this door. I want to be filled. Oh my god, how I want to be filled! I didn't even know it was possible to feel empty until now.

"Kingsley," I pant as he kisses and nibbles a path down my jaw and neck before sucking on the sensitive skin. He drops to his knees, yanks my skirt up, and lifts my leg up on his shoulder. I'm holding my breath as he pulls my underwear to the side and stares at my pussy.

He wets his lips in anticipation. "So fucking pretty!" He dives in, burying his tongue in my wet folds. My knees buckle, and he steadies me with his big hands on my hips.

"Oh, god!" I throw my head back, mewling and whimpering as he swirls his tongue over my sensitive nub until my whole body feels like it's on fire. I'm growing wetter and hotter with every lick and nibble.

"You taste so fucking good!" he growls against my sex, prodding the tight entrance with his tongue.

I whimper and grind down on him. I feel empty. So fucking empty!

"Please," I plead and feel him smile against my sex before plunging his tongue inside me. I'm tight, and it stings, but fuck, it feels good too. He thrusts his tongue like it's his cock, and his grip on my hips is possessive, bordering on pain.

"Do you want me to fuck your tight little pussy?"

I clench, moaning. My hands are in his smooth hair now, pulling on the short strands.

"Is your virginity mine?"

Fuck, his dirty talk makes me clench his tongue in a vice. "It's yours, Kingsley!" I pant. At this point, I don't know what the hell I agree to. I just know that I need him. His hands. His tongue. *His dick.*

He stands up, spins me around, and flattens my hands on the door.

I arch my ass back against him, seeking something...

Kingsley chuckles in my ear as he grasps the back of my neck possessively. "So eager for my cock!" he breathes, his hot breath on my skin.

The sound of his belt falling to the floor filters through

my lustful haze. I feel him shift behind me before he spins me around and wraps my hand around his big cock. I gasp. He's hard but also smooth. I never thought dicks felt like this. I stroke his thick length once, watching his face contort with pleasure as he sucks in a breath.

He traps his lip between his teeth and groans low in his throat. "Keep stroking."

I tighten my grip and swirl my thumb over the engorged head like I've seen them do in the porn movies.

Kingsley hisses and wraps his big hand around my throat, squeezing lightly. "Good girl," he breathes, staring at my parted lips. "Just like that!"

I stroke him faster, marveling at the sounds of pleasure slipping past his lips. *I'm making him feel this way.*

He puts his hand on my shoulder and applies pressure as he guides me down on my knees. The hardwood floor is cold and unforgiving, but it barely registers as Kingsley strokes my hair off my face. His gaze burns like liquid fire everywhere it touches.

He pushes his fingers past my lips. "Suck."

I wrap my lips around his fingers and suck as if they were his cock. I moan, swirling my tongue. I don't recognize this side of myself. I'm so eager to please. It's like his touch has made something blossom to life.

Kingsley strokes himself as he thrusts his fingers, his eyes glued to my mouth. He pulls out, grabs a handful of my hair, and angles my head. My mouth waters in anticipation when he pushes the hard tip of his cock against my lips. He's beautiful like this, with his brown eyes clouded over with lust and his bottom lip trapped between his teeth.

"Open your mouth," he instructs, his voice dripping with desire.

I do. It's instinctive. He sinks his dick into my mouth,

placing his palm on the door. I try to take as much of his cock as I can like the receptionist did in the movie, but he's big, and I gag when he hits the back of my throat. The grip on my hair tightens.

"Fuck," he groans, then pulls out and slams back in, again and again. Slow at first and then faster and harder until he's pounding my mouth. My knees are aching on the hard marble floor, and I'm clawing his jean-clad thighs. I'm so turned on it's unreal.

"That's it! Hollow your cheeks, baby," Kingsley instructs as he slows down and rolls his hips, grunting low in his throat. I look up at him, meeting his dark gaze. *This isn't so difficult.* Kingsley is taking the lead, anyway.

He puts both palms flat on the door and stares down at me as I suck his cock. I moan around him, my eyelids fluttering. I'm in heaven right now! Kingsley is ruining me slowly but surely with his masculine power and rough touch. I take him deeper and pick up speed, sucking his cock faster and harder.

*I've got this!* I'm going to graduate with first-class honors!

"God, baby! Yes, fuck! Just like that," he groans. His hand lands in my hair again, and he grabs a handful of the blonde strands, guiding me on his thick cock.

I lean back and release him with a pop, stroking his hard length. "I love your dick!" I bat my eyelashes at him for effect, and he groans as if he's in pain, his thick cock twitching in my hand. *Hook your audience.*

"Stick your tongue out, baby," he instructs, fisting his dick. He strokes himself a couple of times, watching me on my knees with my tongue out. I can't stop looking at the muscles in his forearms, how they pull taut with every stroke.

"Fuck, you're such a good girl, taking my cock how I like it!" He slaps his dick against my tongue. Again and again. "Suck!" he orders. "And keep looking at me."

I fist his shaft and lick him from root to tip. Then take him as deep as I can until he hits the back of my throat. This time I go for it, sucking, licking, and moaning around his cock, faster and harder until his whole body goes rigid. His salty cum hits the back of my throat and streams down the corners of my mouth.

*Not too shabby for my first attempt.*

"Jesus fucking christ!" he groans, breathing like he's run a marathon. He loosens his grip on my hair and strokes my head tenderly before stepping back and tucking himself in. "Don't get up just yet," he says, tilting my tear-streaked face back. He brushes the pad of his thumb through my tears of lust, and his eyes fall to his cum on my chin. "Fuck, you look beautiful like this, ruined and covered in my cum."

I'm still throbbing with need as he walks to the kitchen and leaves me behind. I scramble to my feet and chase after him, painfully aware of my soaked panties.

He points to the kitchen island. "Take your clothes off and lie down."

"Wha—?"

"Do you want me to eat your pussy or not? Strip."

I do as he says, shedding my clothes and lifting myself up on the cold, smooth surface.

Kingsley leans against the counter opposite, grips the edge, and crosses one foot over the other. "Touch yourself."

I stare at him. The chill in the air licks my skin, but his gaze... It burns!

I place my heels on the edge of the island and let my legs fall open. I'm grateful in this moment that I keep everything trimmed and neat down there.

Kingsley's eyes fall to my pink pussy lips. "Sink your finger in that tight cunt. I want to watch you fuck yourself."

I slowly trail my fingers down my body, past my aching nipples, belly button, and lower still.

I gasp.

"Spread your lips so I can see."

God, I'm going to come soon if he keeps talking like that.

I slide my fingers through my wet folds and spread them open for him. The heat in his eyes makes my pussy clench.

His nostrils flare. "Do you have any idea how fucking beautiful you are?"

My tits heave with every breath. I can't look away from his dark gaze. My lips part as I slowly work a finger inside my tight heat. It stings, but I'm soaking wet, so it slides with no resistance. I pick up speed, fucking myself deeper.

Kingsley's dark eyes stay trained on my pussy. He pushes off the counter and comes to a stop between my legs. I'm panting, heat building low in my core. He removes my hand, swirls his fingers through my swollen wet folds, and coats them in my juices before slowly inching one inside me until he's knuckle deep. He hooks it, pulls it back out, and plunges back in. Deeper this time. My tits bounce from the force, and I bite my lip, suppressing a moan.

His eyes find mine as he adds another digit. "Does it hurt?"

I whimper, nodding. It burns in all the best ways possible.

"Good!" he whispers darkly and thrusts back in, watching my tits bob. "I want you to feel me tomorrow at the convention when you lust after another man."

Kingsley takes my nipple in his mouth and peers up at

me. It's a possessive gaze that tells me I belong to him. Right now, I do!

He swirls his tongue over the hard nub and pulls it with his teeth before biting down on the sensitive flesh above my nipple. As his warm lips trail lower, I notice a bite mark on my tit. I'm not stupid—Kingsley branded me on purpose, but I don't get to shout at him before his skilled mouth latches onto my clit, and he sucks it hard, swirling his tongue. And then I'm gone. Lost in the universe of Kingsley.

He pulls me down by my hips until my ass hangs off the edge. He licks, swirls, and nibbles, plunging his fingers inside of me faster and harder until liquid fire pools low in my stomach.

"Ahhh! Kingsley, I'm coming!" I pant, moaning and mewling as a force of pleasure hits me like a tidal wave. It courses through my body with destructive power and breaks down my carefully erected walls. I'm left exposed and vulnerable at Kingsley's mercy.

He blows softly on my throbbing, sensitive sex and peeks up between my thighs with a smug grin.

"Holy fuck! Kingsley, what the fuck are you doing to me?" *There I go cursing again.*

He bites the inside of my thigh, and I know by the searing sting that he left another mark. "I'm ruining you!" He smiles and gets up.

"Not so fast," I say, jumping off the counter. "If anyone is ruining anyone here, it's me ruining you!" I push against his chest and guide him into the adjoining living room. His calves connect with the luxurious couch, and he plops down, looking amused by my newfound confidence.

I bite my bottom lip as I sink to my knees between his spread thighs and free his dick. It twitches in my hand when I lean down, smiling against his engorged head. "Tell me, Kingsley, have you been ruined by a woman before?" I take him in my mouth, stealing a piece of his soul for myself before he has a chance to reply.

∽

Hazel twirls another section of my hair around the curling iron.

"How many times did you suck his dick?" Becky asks around a mouthful of chocolate hoop cereal.

"Too many. My jaw aches." I move it, wincing.

Hazel snickers. She meets my gaze in the mirror. "At least you're prepared for the audition."

I hum in agreement and grab a handful of chocolate hoops when Becky walks over and holds the box out for me.

"I'm still a virgin, though. Plenty left to learn. I can't be a virgin pornstar."

Becky throws a chocolate hoop on my forehead. It bounces off and lands in my lap. "You have a week and a half until the audition. Plenty of time to lose your cherry."

Hazel unwinds my lock of hair from the curling iron and grabs another section of hair. "Do you still want Hunter Wood?"

I throw a chocolate hoop at my mouth but miss. "Of course I do. Why wouldn't I?"

"Maybe because you're falling for the manwhore cyclist."

I roll my eyes. "It's called BMX, Becky. And he's not a manwhore."

Becky and Hazel exchange a glance.

"It's worse than I first anticipated," Becky says, staring at me wide-eyed.

"What is?"

"You're falling for him," Hazel says, meeting my horrified stare in the mirror.

I laugh awkwardly. "I'm not falling for Kingsley!"

"And I'm an Olympic gold medalist," Becky deadpans. She points to my chest and the bitemark visible just above my dress. "Kingsley branded you. He wants Hunter to see his mark on you. It doesn't get more alpha than that."

Hazel cringes as she gestures to my neck. "You have a little something there too."

Groaning, I drop my head in my hands. This is just fucking great! "We've only known each other for a matter of days. Why mark me?"

Becky angles her box of cereal, and I gratefully reach in for a chocolate hoop. "Well, you hurt his pride for one."

"What?" I furrow my brow.

Hazel applies a mist of hairspray.

"Babe, you're using him so you can fuck someone else. He feels like he has something to prove."

My eyes widen. "I didn't think of it like that."

Hazel shrugs behind me. "You know what men are like."

I shake my head, staring at her with saucers for eyes. "No, I really don't. What are men like?" I look to Becky for clarification. She simply smirks.

"They want what they can't have. Girls throw themselves at Kingsley, but he's only got your attention because you need him to prepare you for *someone else*. You don't want *him*. Of course he's going to feel intrigued and confused."

I stare at Hazel with my mouth hanging open. "Wow, Hazel. You sound like Becky." I pop another chocolate hoop into my mouth.

Hazel shrugs. "I know what I'm talking about when it matters."

Becky chuckles.

"There, your hair is done," Hazel says, looking like a proud mother hen waving her daughter off to prom.

I inspect my shiny blonde hair. It falls down my back in beautiful waves. "It looks great!"

Hazel preens. "I know how to work my magic."

I reach for my purse and dig out my red lipstick. I pop the lid off and apply it to my lips before eyeing Becky in the mirror. "Are we ready to go?"

Hazel goes to grab her purse, and Becky sprays perfume on her neck. Her brown hair has been straightened and tied up in a high ponytail. She's dressed in a dress too, but hers is slightly more modest than mine. Becky insisted I buy this little black number because, in her words, it's slutty but at the same time respectable. Whatever that means.

I put on my black heels with the red soles and Hazel whistles. She blows out a breath and says, "You have some amazing legs, woman!"

I roll my eyes. "Let's just hope they hook Hunter."

Becky holds the door open for us. "Trust me. When he sees those bad boys—sorry, *girls,* he'll imagine himself suffocating to death between them."

I laugh, stepping out in the hallway. "Is he suffocating or being squashed to death in this scenario?"

Hazel giggles as we descend the sweeping staircase. "Definitely suffocating."

Geoffrey holds the front door open for us, and we step through, squinting at the sunlight like a clan of vampires emerging after millennia beyond the grave.

"Have a pleasant time, ladies."

"Oh, Geoffrey, we plan on having a very *pleasurable*

time." Becky purrs, making us all giggle as we descend the stairs and fall into the town car. Mr. Dundon, my driver, tips his hat and closes the door behind us.

I swipe the screen on my phone as the girls chat about what other famous pornstars are doing signings at this convention.

I have a new message from an unknown number.

Unknown number: I can still taste you on my tongue and hear your needy little whimpers.

Me: Kingsley?

Unknown number: The one and only. Are you sore today, baby?

Me: Do I want to ask how you got my number? And for your information, yes, I am sore!

Kingsley: Good. I can't wait to eat your pink little pussy again!

I blush fiercely.

Becky leans in, reading over my shoulder. "Oh no, girl!" she snatches my phone, and before I know what's happening, she's typing out a response with a shit-eating grin on her face. She hands it back. "You're welcome."

Me: I want you to pound my tight little pussy so hard I can't walk for days after.

My eyes widen in horror. "What the fuck, Becks?"
Another text comes in.

Kingsley: Fuck, baby! I can't stop thinking about your pouty lips around my dick.

It's quickly followed by another text.

Kingsley: Tell me what else you want me to do.

Becky snatches my phone again. I make a swipe for it, but she cackles like the wicked witch and types out another response.

Me: I want you to spank my ass until my skin burns, and I'm begging for your cock.

I stare at her reply. "What the hell, Becks! What the living fucking hell?! Kingsley will know these aren't from me."

"No, he won't. He's too busy jerking off."

My phone pings.

Kingsley: Can I come over tonight?

I don't even fight Becky this time as she grabs my phone and types out a response that I know for a fact I won't like judging by her evil grin.

Me: I can't. I plan on spending the evening on my knees with my favorite wood. Thank you for the masterclass! :)

I gasp. "Becky. That's just cruel!"

She inspects her nails. "I think a little bit of jealousy will do him some good. He's too used to girls dropping everything at the chance to be with him. You're not one of his regular groupies."

I stare at my phone, but Kingsley doesn't reply again. I chew my lip, feeling guilty for reasons that don't make sense to me.

∼

It's busy. I shouldn't have worried that my dress might be too revealing. Not in this place. I'm surprised by the number of middle-aged women here. Is that a thing that happens? You marry, pop out kids, and become a middle-aged bored housewife who spends her days watching porn?

"I need one of these," Hazel squeals and holds up a huge dildo, the kind you don't find on your regular websites. "Look, it sparkles!"

"Yippee-ki-yay!" Becky says drily, then points to another dildo on the table. "Look, Kath. Just what you're after. A dildo modeled after Hunter."

I place the spinning rabbit dildo in my hand back down on the table and walk over to inspect the veiny replica of Hunter's real dick.

"Here, catch!" She throws it at me, and I catch it. Just.

"It looks awfully real, doesn't it," I say, staring at the pinkish mushroom head.

"Careful it doesn't come alive and bite you," the tattoo-covered girl behind the counter jokes.

I blush and place it back down on the table, but Becky shakes her head and hands it to the woman who bags it up and rings it through the register.

"I'm buying it for you," Becky says, winking at me. Leaning in, she whispers, "For when you've popped your cherry and can fit that bad boy inside."

Hazel joins us and proudly holds up her brown paper

bag in the air. "The nice guy behind the counter threw in a pair of nipple clamps as a freebie."

My eyebrows hit my hairline. I look over at the tattooed lady behind the counter, wondering why she didn't gift me something extra.

Becky leans in again. "See, that's how you flirt!"

"Flirt?"

Becky gives me a pointed look. She nudges her head toward Hazel, who's gone again and is now leaning over another table, squishing her tits together. Her loud giggles make me cringe, but it must work because the man behind the desk winks at her and slips an extra item in her bag. She runs over to us and bounces on her heels.

"What did you get this time?"

Hazel opens her bag and holds up a threesome compilation DVD. Next, she pulls out a square cardboard box and squeals, "I got a buttplug!"

Becky unwraps a lifesize cock-shaped rock candy and gives a little lick before taking it fully in her mouth for a suck, pulling in her cheeks, making us all laugh.

I wipe tears from my eyes but startle when a heavy arm drapes around my shoulders.

"Fancy seeing you here, princess. Up to no good again, I see," Josh from detention says, watching Becky suck on her candy-cock.

"Let me guess," I say, rolling my eyes and removing his arm from around my shoulder. "I look like a juicy zebra amid a lion pride?"

Josh sweeps his eyes down my body. He pretends to think. "No, I think Gazelle suits you better." He gestures to the crowds. "These people? All lions! Watch out, princess, or you might find yourself prey to an apex predator."

"Man, there's some fine meat here!" a blonde guy says

as he comes to a stop next to Josh.

Josh smiles and gestures to me. "Matt, meet Gazelle. Gazelle, meet Matt. He's an apex predator who you need to stay well and truly away from." Another guy joins them, looking bored. I've seen him around our school. Mainly because of his brightly colored green hair.

"I lost Dallas over by the helium cock balloons."

"Well shit," Blondie says. "She's lost to us forever."

Becky gives me a look. I try to convey my best 'I don't know what the fuck is going on' face, but judging by her now frowning eyebrows, I don't think I succeeded. "Oh, give me that," I say as I grab her candy cock and suck on it like I'm on a fucking mission to fire it off to Mars.

Josh whistles. "Whoa, we better let Gazelle have some privacy. See you in detention, juicy meat."

Blondie mouths 'call me,' and I roll my eyes, flipping him off with my mouth filled with candy-cock. *Yeah, I can't take myself seriously either.*

"We better get going if we don't want to end up last in the queue. It's not long until the signing," Becky says, tugging on my elbow.

Next to me, Hazel claps her hands excitedly. "Let's chop us some wood."

"Chop us some wood? Really, Hazel?" Becky says, giving her a look.

"What?" Hazel looks confused. She bites off a piece of her breast-shaped marshmallow. "I thought it sounded good?"

"It really didn't," I reply, shaking my head as she offers me the nipple of her marshmallow.

"Let's find us some wood?"

"Much better," I grin, hooking my arm through her elbow.

# FIVE

The queue is a mile long. My tits are sweaty and my feet ache. Not even my cock-candy can cheer me up right now. There are only so many times you can watch women saunter up to Hunter's table and behave like the receptionist lady but without the cocksucking, before you start to lose your sanity. Slowly but surely.

"Turn that frown upside down," Hazel quips, fanning herself with the paper program. "We're nearly there."

"He's never going to notice me," I whine, pouting like a kid.

Becky props her chin on my shoulder. "Remind him of your amazing coffee spilling skills. He'll remember you right away."

"Ha! Ha!" I reply drily.

"It says in here that Hunter has starred in and produced 35 movies. That's a good number, isn't it?"

I blow away a wayward piece of hair from my face. "I really don't know, Hazel. My only experience with porn is the ten minutes I watched the other day."

The woman in front of me who's obscured my vision all this time moves aside, and it's like I'm hit in the chest when I see Hunter fully for the first time since I ruined his t-shirt. Fuck, he's handsome! Dirty blonde hair that curls at the nape of his neck. Cobalt blue eyes. Full lips. *A strong jaw that ticks when you spill your drink on him.* His arms are chiseled. Not that I can see them right now because he's dressed in a fitted black shirt that brings out the blue in his eyes.

As I watch, he swipes his tongue across his bottom lip, his marker pen scrawling over the DVD on the desk. He hands it back to the woman and motions for the next one in line to step forward. I wouldn't say he looks bored exactly, but he definitely doesn't look like he's enjoying himself either.

I love the crows' feet around his eyes when he smiles. They make him look worldly. Experienced.

I'm still sucking on my candy-cock when Hunter motions for me to step forward, and for one agonizingly long minute, I just stand there with my cheeks hollowed like some freak. Becky grabs the candy-cock, hands me my paper bag, and shoves me forward.

"And what's your name," Hunter asks, reaching for my bag as I hold it out for him.

"I'm Kath—Kitty Hamilton."

He pauses, searching my face. "Have I seen you somewhere before?"

I clear my throat and fidget. Wow, so much for my flirting practice. "Well, it's a funny story," I say, chuckling awkwardly. I motion to my chest.

His eyes follow my movements, and he stares at my cleavage.

"I spilled coffee on you last week."

Hunter's eyes flick up. He sweeps his eyes over my face and then bursts out laughing.

Well, this is a surprise.

He motions to his own chest. "I thought you were going somewhere completely different there with the whole"—he clears his throat—"tit pointing."

"Tit pointing?"

He covers up another laugh with a cough and opens the paper bag. It crinkles as he pulls out the replica dildo of his cock. He chuckles again and motions with two fingers for me to come closer.

I lean in, feeling rather confused. This is not how his conversations with the other women went. It was a simple, hi, sign, next.

"Put it in the freezer overnight. It will make you see fucking stars."

I stare at him wide-eyed.

He pulls the cap off his marker pen with his teeth and signs the veiny replica of his manhood.

"I'm auditioning next week," I blurt. Why I say it, I don't fucking know.

His hand freezes midair. He caps the marker pen, drops it on the table, and leans back in his chair. He trails his eyes down my body, lingering on my legs. "Is that so, coffee girl?"

"Kitty. Kitty Hamilton," I correct him, feeling a blush creep up my neck.

"Tell me, *Kitty*," he says, purring my name deliciously. "Do you have what it takes to star in one of my movies?"

I swallow thickly before raising my chin. "Trust me, Mr. Wood. I have what it takes!"

His eyes darken when I call him by his title. He smirks and signals for his assistant.

A woman with a blond bob, dressed in a business suit appears by his side with a piece of paper.

His pen flies over the sheet. He hands it to me but keeps hold of it when I try to take it. "The address and time are on there. I will *personally* audition you"—he pauses, and his lips curve—"Kitty."

I'm trembling as he lets go of the note and hands me the signed dildo.

"I hope you enjoy my cock, Miss. Hamilton," he whispers before leaning back in his seat, motioning to the woman behind me. She glares at me as she walks past.

∽

I try to sleep. I really do, but it's impossible. My mind keeps replaying the day's events... Hunter's breath on my neck as he whispered in my ear. How he undressed me with his cobalt blue eyes.

I growl and throw the quilt back. It's late, and I'm exhausted, but sleep eludes me. On top of that, there's a throbbing ache between my legs.

I switch on my bedside lamp, scoot up on the bed, and reach for my laptop. Mr. Boomer lies asleep at the end of my bed, his cute little paws twitching as he growls. He's probably fighting the street's vicious tomcat in his dream.

I chew on my lip as I start up my laptop. I know I shouldn't search for any more videos. But my own curiosity is a stubborn bitch with an amazing talent for persuasion. Before I know it, I'm watching a video of Hunter in the process of eating a woman like he's a condemned man, and she's his chosen final gourmet meal.

"You want me to finger your tight little pussy?"

I groan. "Yes, Hunter, I really, really want you to do

that!" I reach down for the paper bag I hid underneath my bed. "I want your fingers to do unspeakable things to me, Mr. Wood."

Great. I'm talking to myself.

I fast forward and press play. Hunter is pounding the woman into the bed. Her knees are somehow up by her head, and she's holding onto her ankles as she stares down at Hunter's thick dick, sliding in and out.

I cock my head. How is she so bendy? Can I get my knees up there? I guess with the right incentive, I could probably transform into a circus contortionist too. I start to lift my foot but stop. I don't want to try because with my luck, I'll end up with my foot stuck behind my head and have no choice but to call 911.

I look down at the dildo in my hand and compare it to the real thing on the screen. "It's definitely Hunter's cock," I whisper.

"Fuck me deeper!" the girl growls. Literally growls! I lower the screen and check that Mr. Boomer is still asleep. The last thing I want are his blue eyes judging me right now.

"Ahhhhh! Yes! Yes!"

Nope, still asleep.

I look back at the screen. The muscles in Hunter's stomach ripple as he pounds into the girl while watching her surgically enhanced tits bob with every thrust. Beads of sweat drip down from his temple.

"Yes, oh god, yes!"

I yank my sleep shorts down and bury my fingers in my wet folds. Pleasure floods through me thick and fast, melting my insides as I begin circling my clit.

Hunter slows down, fucking her deep and slow. He pulls all the way out and then slams back in with a groan.

I guide the dildo between my legs and rub the head through my sensitive folds. It's not warm and silky like Kingsley's cock. It's cold and feels plasticky, but just the thought of it being a replica of Hunter's dick makes this moment feel dirty and forbidden. I'm growing warmer and wetter with every stroke on my throbbing clit.

Hunter pulls out, fists his cock, and slaps her glistening pussy.

"Ohhhh!" her mouth is a pursed 'O'

Hunter shifts, so he's on top of her, knees on either side of her face. He prods her lips with his dick. "You want me to fuck that pretty little mouth of yours?"

I rub my clit harder with the dildo, feeling warmth build and spread in my stomach. Hunter grabs hold of the headboard, then fists the woman's hair and smirks as he sinks his cock into her mouth. My eyes roll to the back of my head. Why the fuck is he so hot?

The woman gags, but instead of pulling back to give her a chance to breathe, he holds her to him and thrusts deep in her throat.

I bring the dildo to my lips and dart my tongue out, tasting myself on it. I fill my mouth and imagine it's his cock stretching my lips. God, this feels so wrong but so good! I moan as I suck on the head.

Hunter pulls out, grabs the woman's jaw, and growls, "Do you want more?"

She's crying and sobbing but nods eagerly and opens her mouth. Hunter doesn't need to be asked twice. He plunges back in and fucks her mouth with savage brutality as snot and tears run down her face.

Just when I think I'm about to combust, he pulls out, flips her over, slaps her ass, and begins fucking her from behind. Everything about Hunter is masculine. He takes what he wants. He dominates and plunders.

The woman comes with a long and drawn-out cry that echoes my own as I feel myself coming. I rub my nub until I can no longer take it, and like a wave, it builds power before hitting the shore and slowly ebbing away.

I'm breathing heavily, staring at the ceiling. Everything tingles and pulsates. The bed shifts, and then Mr. Boomer sniffs my face, meowing.

"Not a word, Boomer! Not a single word!"

∽

The gymnasium is buzzing with noise. The school's football team has an important away game this weekend, and the cheerleaders are about to debut their new routine for the first time. Football is a big part of our small town. My dad used to take me to a couple of games when I was younger, but it never stuck. Sport is not my thing, and my dad was never a big fan either, but pep rallies are a weekly thing here at Hedgewood high during football season. It's just one of those things uninterested people have to sit through.

"Isn't he dreamy?" Hazel swoons, biting her bottom lip.

"Who?" Becky asks, looking up from her phone.

"Rick." Hazel's voice has a dreamy quality to it.

"The quarterback?"

Hazel nods.

Becky rolls her eyes, returning her attention to her phone. "He's dated the head cheerleader for the last two years. It's never going to happen, Hazel."

"A girl can dream, can't she?" Hazel counters.

"Or fantasize." I wink.

"I want to hear more about your fantasies," Kingsley says as he plops down next to me.

His friend Sam sits down on his other side. He brushes his blonde hair out of his eyes and grins. "Hi, sweetheart."

I cross my arms and snort. "Sweetheart? Really, Sam?"

He shrugs with a grin.

Kingsley leans in, and his soft lips graze my ear, making me shiver as he whispers, "I can't stop thinking about your tight pussy."

*Throb. Throb. Throb.*

I love how dirty it feels when he whispers such filthy words in a room full of students and teachers. My eyes fall to the sliver of tanned leg peeking through his ripped jeans. I itch to trace the dark hairs and feel his warm skin under my fingertips.

I eye his arms next. They're on full display in a white t-shirt with the sleeves cut out.

When he notices me watching, he smirks and flexes his arm muscle. "You like?"

I lean in and bite his bicep a little bit too hard before whispering in his ear. "I like."

What is this mysterious side of me that keeps resurfacing whenever he's nearby?

Kingsley shivers and moves my hair aside, his touch lingering. He presses his lips against the sensitive skin below my ear. It's intimate, and I'm surprised by his public display, but I can't deny how wet he makes me.

"Hunter is going to *personally* audition Kitty next week," Becky says, grinning like the devil.

I feel Kingsley stiffen before he leans back, and I instantly miss his lips on my neck. "What do you mean by "personally audition?"

Becky shrugs, and her smile widens even more. "He

gave her a note with an address and a time. Then told her to be there and that he would personally audition her. He also signed a replica of his dick and told her to"—Becky makes air quotes—"enjoy his cock."

Kingsley's eyes flick to mine just as the headteacher steps up on the podium and starts to drone on about the importance of school spirit. Kingsley digs in his front pocket for his phone. He pulls it out, swipes the screen, and types a quick message.

My phone vibrates in my hand.

Kingsley: Meet me after school?

I smile before I can stop myself and type a response.
His phone pings.

Me: Only if you show me some tricks.

His thigh pushes against mine. I don't know if it's intentional, but I would like to think it is.

Kingsley: Trust me, babe. I know plenty of tricks ;)

～

"Here, catch!" Kingsley says when I descend the steps after school. He throws me a spare helmet.

I catch it instinctively. If I didn't, it would have hit me in the face. "What's this for?" I ask, staring at the black helmet with band stickers on it.

Kingsley motions to a second BMX bike by his side. "I have this spare one. It's an older model, beaten up, but it'll do for learning on."

I blink.

Kingsley abandons the bikes as he walks over to me and puts the helmet on my head. "You have a small head, so you need to tighten these straps here."

When he's done, he steps back and shoves his hands in his jeans pockets. As if a thought occurs to him, he digs in his back pocket for his phone and takes a picture of me.

It snaps me back to reality. "Why am I wearing a helmet, Kingsley?"

He grins, pocketing his phone. "Rather than show you my tricks, I decided to teach you some."

I laugh. Oh, how I laugh! It bubbles out of me like a volcano experiment at a science fair for $6^{th}$ graders. Kingsley is watching me like I'm some fascinating animal at a zoo exhibition.

I wipe tears from my eyes and gesture to my expensive floral midi dress and heels. "Do I look dressed for the occasion?"

There's a gleam in his eye. He shrugs casually and says, "No, you don't."

Just then, a town car pulls up next to us, and I gasp as Geoffrey steps out and hands me a bag of clothing.

"Perfect timing, Geoff," Kingsley says and high fives Geoffrey, who looks somewhat confused but amused all the same.

I'm staring dumbly with my mouth hanging open. The bag dangles from my fingers.

"Your friend advised me that you're taking up a new hobby, so I went ahead and purchased you some more suitable clothing for the occasion, miss. Flowy dresses and bikes don't go well together."

"Wh—?" I've lost the ability to speak.

"You can change in the car," Kingsley says, guiding me

over with a hand on my lower back. As soon as my butt hits the backseat, he shuts the car door and walks over to Geoffrey.

I watch them converse through the tinted window. Geoffrey laughs. He actually laughs! What on earth is happening right now?

I tear my gaze away and tip the contents of the bag onto my lap. There's a white t-shirt, a pair of black leggings and a pair of trainers. Things I've never worn in my life before. I hold up the t-shirt between my thumb and index finger, dangling it in the air. "What is this?"

After much grumbling to myself, I remove the helmet and get changed. Everything fits perfectly. The t-shirt is a little loose, but it's designed that way.

"I look like I'm going to an underground rap battle," I say as I step out of the car and close the door behind me.

Kingsley's throat jumps when he sees me. Usually, it's the other way around in the movies. The ugly duckling does her make-up, gets dressed up in pretty clothes, and magically turns into a beautiful swan. With Kingsley, apparently dressing down is the way to his heart.

"All we need now is a little bit of breeze to tousle my hair, and then I'll be able to join a punk bank and tour the country." I put my helmet back on, ignoring Geoffrey's quiet chuckles. Secretly, I love to see him laugh.

Kingsley looks at me for a minute longer, then turns to Geoffrey. They do a weird handshake. "Thanks, man."

Geoffrey turns to me, bows low, and takes his leave.

"I really wish he would stop bowing," I mumble under my breath.

Kingsley suppresses a smile. "Really? I thought you liked being treated like royalty?"

I give him a droll look that makes him laugh as he walks over to the bikes. "Have you ever ridden a bike before?"

"Of course, I know how to ride a bike."

"Good, that makes things much easier." He gets on his bike and pedals forward. "Come on, I'm taking you to the abandoned warehouse."

The abandoned warehouse. It's notorious for attracting the troublemakers at school.

I get on my bike and catch up with him. "I heard there's a skatepark in there."

He stands on the pedals and does a little bunny hop. "Sure is. It's where I learned most of my BMX tricks."

"Is that where you learned the Gyrating Giraffe?"

Kingsley laughs. "You mean the Manual 180. No, that's flatland. I practiced those tricks in my neighbor's driveway as a kid. One of my friends introduced me to the warehouse, and that's when I managed to expand and learn tricks that involve ramps."

"You must have spent a lot of hours practicing?"

"I did. It's what kept me sane growing up." He rides ahead, hops on a bench, and does a wheelie. I don't know how he hasn't died yet. If I tried anything like that, I would end up in hospital.

"I hope you don't expect me to learn that anytime soon," I tease as I catch up, riding alongside him.

He looks at me with a smug curl to his lips. "You'll be doing tricks like a pro in no time."

"Did you ever fall off and hurt yourself?"

Kingsley scoffs. "So many times you wouldn't believe. It only made me more determined to land the trick every time I scraped a knee or an elbow."

"I admire you, you know."

His brown eyes meet mine. "Why?"

I tilt my head to the sun, enjoying the slight breeze on my face. "I wish I had your passion." I smile at Kingsley. The wind makes his white t-shirt contour to his chiseled chest, offering me a preview of what's beneath. "It will take you places."

"You're more down to earth than I thought at first."

"Yeah?" I smile. His compliment makes my heart sing for some reason.

He nods and brings his attention back to the sidewalk. I instantly miss his eyes on me, but it's probably for the best before his brown eyes cause me to crash into an elderly pedestrian. Or a bus at a crossing.

"We're nearly there," he comments. "It's just through those buildings over there."

"Kingsley?"

"Yeah?"

"Thank you for this."

His eyes collide with mine, and for a moment, I'm not living dangerously, riding down the street on a borrowed bike—for a moment, it's just him and me.

"Watch out!" he shouts in an alarmed tone, breaking me free from whatever dangerous web he had me trapped in.

I only just manage to swerve around a tree. Why the fuck is there a tree in the middle of the sidewalk anyway? "If I die today, I'll haunt you, Kingsley!" I say, ignoring his deep chuckles.

"And I'll make sure to put on a show worth haunting me for." He winks, then rides ahead, guiding the way.

I stare after him, and a tortured groan slips past my lips. What kind of witchery is this? God, seeing him ride his bike, his muscles pulled tight, his broad back... If I was a nun, I would give up my vocation to worship at his altar. I'm a little ashamed to admit that I'm turning into Olivia or one of his other female admirers. It's inappropriate. I'm just using him. It's Hunter I want and who I plan to capture on my hook and reel in.

We emerge through two buildings, and the warehouse comes into view. It's a derelict building covered in graffiti. Most of the windows are broken or missing entirely. I've never been here before, but I've heard plenty of people talk about it. Apparently, the inside was converted into a skatepark.

I jump off my bike, remove my helmet, and follow Kingsley inside. Sunlight streams in through gaps in the roof, reflecting off puddles. I can hear music, people laughing, and the distinct sound of skateboard wheels on wooden ramps. We step into a large open space. I don't know where to look first. The multitude of people? The various ramps? The graffiti on the walls?

"Yo, Kingsley," someone shouts.

Kingsley fist bumps a guy with an unruly mop of hair underneath his helmet.

"I finally managed to land the Euro Table you showed me. Took a lot of fucking time, man."

"I knew you'd nail it!" They fist bump again.

"What's a Euro Table?" I ask.

The guy with the unruly hair lifts his chin in greeting. "New bae of yours?" he asks Kingsley.

Kingsley rubs the back of his neck. "Come on, man. You know I don't do that shit. This is Katherine." He looks at me and points to his friend. "Katherine, this is Mylo." He turns to his friend. "I'm going to teach her some beginners' tricks."

Mylo's eyebrows shoot up. He eyes me appreciatively, then says to Kingsley. "Cool. You should teach her the Bunny Hop first."

Kingsley shakes his head. "No, we'll start with a Manual."

Mylo nods thoughtfully, then grins. "She asked what a Euro Table is. Show her. She should see it from the pro."

Kingsley blushes. He actually blushes! Rubbing his neck, he says, "I don't think Katherine wants to see me do tricks."

"I do!" I blurt, nodding eagerly. Next to me, Mylo grins victoriously.

"See, bae wants to see you land a Euro Table." He looks at me. "Kingsley can go higher than anyone here."

Kingsley looks comically awkward. "Sure. Okay, why not." He hops on his bike and rides off.

"He's being modest," Mylo says, leaning in. "He's by far the best rider here, if not in the whole area. He takes home a medal in every competition he enters."

I stare at Mylo. He's got kind eyes. They're blue with a ring of green around the iris. "How long have you been riding?"

"A couple of years now." He grins, pointing. "You ready? Kingsley's going for it."

Kingsley accelerates up the ramp, jumps, turns the bars $30°$, and puts his bike parallel to the ground while in the air.

My mouth drops open.

He lands perfectly.

"How?"

Mylo grins. "Practice. Lots and lots of practice."

"But did you see how high he jumped! That was so high!" Am I swooning? I'm totally swooning. Even my voice is high-pitched.

Mylo grins knowingly. Nudging me with his shoulder, he says, "Be good to him. He acts tough, but he's one of the good guys." He stands up.

Kingsley comes to a stop in front of us, removing his helmet. His dark hair is sinfully tousled. "Are you off?"

"I'm meeting up with Adam. We'll be back later."

They do a weird handshake.

"So basically," Kingsley says when Mylo is gone. "A Manual is all about balancing on your back wheel. You want to ride on your rear wheel and not turn your pedals."

I nod along, but I'm distracted, watching his facial expressions and body movements as he explains in detail what to do. His eyes remind me of chocolate. Rich dark chocolate...

*Oh, shut up, brain!*

"...You simply lift the front wheel off the ground, shift your body weight backward and balance with your legs."

"Okay," I reply, dragging the word out.

"I'll show you." He rides forward a bit, leans back, and uses his body weight to lift the front wheel.

I stare. Kingsley makes it look so easy to ride along while balancing on the back wheel. I'll probably die.

He comes to a stop in front of me. "But first, you need to combat the fear of falling on your back. So, to do that, you're going to practice jumping off your bike backward." He demonstrates.

"I can't do that, Kingsley," I laugh.

"You can't right now, but you will soon. Right, try it. Let's see what we're working with."

Another laugh bubbles out of me, and I shake my head as I kick off the ground. "You're crazy, Kingsley. Positively crazy."

"Take it slow to start. Be careful not to catch your legs on the back pegs."

I attempt to pull up on the bars, but it's a lot harder than it looks.

Kingsley laughs. "Good try, but to pull up, you need to lean back steadily, bend your legs and keep your arms straight. Use your body weight to lift the front wheel."

"Uh-huh," I say drily.

Kingsley winks, motioning for me to try again.

I manage to lift the wheel off the ground this time, but the instinctual fear of falling backward has me squealing in fright.

Kingsley rides ahead of me and jumps off his bike backward. "Like that, babe."

Okay, so I really like it when he calls me that.

I look at him skeptically and give it another go. This time I don't lean back far enough, and as a result, I fail to lift the front wheel.

"You have to find the sweet spot."

"Sweet spot, huh?" I grin and wink.

He chuckles deeply. "You have a filthy mind for a virgin."

"What can I say? You're corrupting me, Kingsley."

I try a couple of more times. Kingsley is patient with me. He shows me where I'm going wrong and takes his time instructing me until I finally manage to jump off the bike backward. I squeal in victory like I won an Olympic gold medal and didn't simply manage to jump off the back of a BMX. It's not even the actual trick. It's just a step I need to master to start learning it.

"Now, find your sweet spot."

"What exactly is the sweet spot?"

"It's the point before you overtip and fall. The spot where you can comfortably balance on the rear wheel."

"Oh, okay."

I don't know how many hours pass. All I know is that I'm having more fun than I've had in a long time. I'm wearing clothes I've never worn before, doing something I never saw myself doing.

Mylo returns with his friend Adam and a couple of girls in tow.

"We're heading down to the lake. You coming?"

Kingsley looks at me, and I find myself nodding. "That sounds great."

# SIX

We arrive at the lake and park our bikes by a tree. Kingsley secures the lock and hangs our helmets on the handlebars.

While Kingsley talks to Mylo and Adam, I remove my shoes and socks and wander down to the shore. It's a small circular lake lined by trees. The sand is warm after a full day of sun. We've had a good summer this year, which is unusual for our small town.

I dip my toes in the water. It's cold but pleasant.

"I'm Morgan, and that over there is Paige and Elle," a brown-haired girl with cute freckles says.

"I'm Katherine."

She smiles. "I haven't seen you around before. How do you know Kingsley?"

*Well...* "We go to school together."

She brushes away a strand of hair stuck to her lipgloss. "I live in the next town over."

"That explains why I haven't seen you at school."

She nods. "I know Kingsley through Mylo."

"Have you known him long?" I'm not probing. Not at all. What I really want to ask is if she's fucked him?

"A couple of years now."

*No, Katherine. Do not ask!*

"What's your school like? Any cute boys?" I'm really terrible at socializing with girls I don't know.

She smiles, dipping a toe in the water, looking at me through her lashes. "I think you would like some of the boys."

I laugh. "Oh yeah?"

"Oh yeah!" she nods, grinning. "So, what about Kingsley? Are you trying to reign in the notorious womanizer?"

I shake my head. "No, we're just friends."

Morgan looks over at Kingsley. "I've never known him to bring a girl to hang out with before. He usually just fucks them."

I cough to cover up a surprised laugh. "What about you then? Dating anyone?"

"Adam is my boyfriend."

"Oh." I feel a confusing internal floodgate of relief.

"Let's go for a dip." Morgan pulls off her top.

I open and close my mouth. "But I didn't bring a bikini."

Unbuttoning her jeans, she says, "Just swim in your underwear."

I stare at her neon pink bra. It's unfair how big her tits are.

Kingsley waves a hand in front of my face, his eyes shining with amusement. "I see you've met Morgan's titties. Morgans titties, this is Katherine Hamilton."

"Shut up!" Morgan laughs, throwing her jeans at him.

He catches them one-handed and grins just as Adam comes running over to us in his boxer briefs. He picks up Morgan fireman style and runs for the water. It's followed by the sound of squealing laughter and a loud splash.

Kingsley pulls the back of his t-shirt over his head and

throws it down on the sand. My eyes bug out. I try not to gawk, but it's impossible. The hard ridges of his muscles are mouthwatering, and I marvel at the contours of his cut, tanned chest.

"Are you not getting undressed?"

"Err? What?" I tear my gaze away from his dark happy trail.

Kingsley chuckles. "Strip, or I'll carry you in with your clothes on. It's your choice."

His cheeky threat makes me pull my t-shirt over my head. When I lower my arms, I catch him watching me as I throw my top next to his in the sand. His hands go to his buttons. I shimmy out of my jeans and kick them off. "Speechless, Kingsley?" I smirk as I walk backward to the water.

He tears his eyes away from my white lace balconette bra and swallows thickly.

I know my nipples are visible through the lace, and once I go in the water, there will be nothing left to the imagination. But this was his idea.

"Fuck," he mumbles under his breath as he joins me in the water. His eyes roam my body, so I splash him and run for my life when he grins and starts chasing me further out. I don't get far. Kingsley catches me around the waist, and my loud squealing laughter echoes over the lake as we hit the surface with a splash. I pop back up, spitting water and laughing until my stomach muscles cramp from exertion.

He moves in close, brushing my wet hair off my face. His own dark hair lies plastered to his forehead, and water drips off his nose. "Got you!" he whispers in a tone that makes my heart race.

Water bobs around my chest as the sun beats down on us.

"I can't be caught, Kingsley."

His eyes fall to my mouth. He lowers himself down in the water until it's up to his chin. "Maybe not."

I lower myself down, too, until we're eye to eye with only inches between us. Kingsley's blue eyes flick up, searching mine. There's something in the air between us. Electric energy I haven't felt before.

Water skims my tingling lips. "What about you? Can you be caught?" I whisper.

Kingsley swipes his tongue over his bottom lip, shaking his head. "No."

He's so certain.

"We'll see about that." I wink, then splash him and fall back in the water. I float on my back. The clouds overhead move slowly across the sky. "Have you ever been in love, Kingsley?"

I feel his hand skim mine. He's floating on his back too. "No. Have you?"

My breath hitches as he interlaces our fingers in the water. "No."

We float in silence for a while. Morgan and the others laugh some distance away, but right here, right now, it's just Kingsley and me.

"I never knew my mom. She left when I was a baby, so my dad raised me. He passed away last year."

Why am I telling him this?

"You were wrong," he whispers after a moment of silence.

A bird flies up ahead. I follow its trajectory across the sky.

"Wrong about what?"

His thumb strokes circles on the back of my hand. "You

said your family is a topic I don't want to discuss. You were wrong."

I close my eyes. My chest feels like an open, bleeding wound. "He was sick. Prostate cancer. By the time it was discovered, it was too late. He only lived for another three months."

Kingsley squeezes my hand.

I open my eyes and search the sky overhead. "I miss him every day."

"It's okay to be sad, Katherine. You can't be strong all the time."

My eyes sting. "He would want me to be strong."

Kingsley's hand on mine feels like an anchor right now, like it's the only thing stopping me from sinking into the depths of this lake.

"You can be strong and feel sad. One doesn't have to cancel out the other."

"He was the strongest man I've ever met."

The sun warms my skin as it reappears from behind a cloud.

"You're strong too. Far stronger than you think."

A tear travels down my skin and into the water. "Thank you, Kingsley," I whisper. I don't know how he does it, but he's slowly mending the parts of my soul I thought were lost in an ocean of hurt.

Just then, a splash of water hits me in the face.

Mylo is watching us with a shit-eating grin on his face. "You guys up for some water games?"

"Fuck off," Kingsley growls as Mylo laughs like he knows he interrupted something he shouldn't have but doesn't care.

"What are we playing," I ask, attempting a smile.

"The girls said for you to choose between a chicken fight or Marcos Polo."

I scrunch my nose. "How about a handstand contest?"

Mylo looks at me like I've sprouted a third head.

"You know... handstands but underwater."

"Girl, you're crazy. Let's try it."

They all gather around, and I explain the rules. "The object of the game is to hold an underwater handstand longer than your opponents. The last person to tip over wins."

"I've so got this," Adam says, rubbing his hands together. Next to him, Morgan rolls her eyes.

"Dream on."

Paige and Elle both giggle.

"I'll judge," Elle says. "Okay, are you ready? On three! One. Two. Three."

I dive underwater, plant my hands on the sandy bottom, and push my legs up in the air. Doing a handstand underwater is far easier than on land, but despite my best efforts, I soon topple over. I pop back up and take in a lungful of air. Kingsley and Adam are both out of the game too. It's between Morgan and Mylo. Morgan's feet are straight in the air while Mylo's are bent at the knees, but his feet aren't touching the water, so he's still in the game.

Adam pretends to tickle his feet.

"No cheating," Elle laughs, splashing Adam, who dips down underwater, swims over, and pulls her down by her ankle. She shrieks, splashing wildly.

Mylo finally topples over. He pops back up and flicks his head. "Hey, motherfuckers. Second place ain't bad."

Morgan surfaces, rubbing water out of her eyes. When she realizes she has won this round, she fist-pumps and does a little victory dance.

"How about if we add in a little challenge? Make it a one-finger handstand," I suggest, wiggling my eyebrows.

"I'll beat you this time, babe," Adam says to Morgan, who flips him off with a smile.

"I'll judge," I say. "On your marks. Get, set, go!"

They all dive in the water, and soon their feet are in the air, some straighter than others. Well, almost all. Kingsley wades over and slams his lips to mine, stealing my breath and sanity. My head spins. He tastes of lake water and debauchery. Our teeth clash, his hands are in my damp hair, and my hands explore the planes of his wet muscular chest. I feel his hard length against my stomach, and it makes heat pool low in my belly.

Just as suddenly, he's gone.

Mylo topples over. He pops back up and grabs Kingsley in a headlock, oblivious to the state I'm in or the sexual tension in the air. I can't get enough air. My lungs feel constricted.

Mylo finally looks over at the others. "Who's winning?"

Kingsley pounces from behind, and they wrestle some more.

The others soon topple over, and the gloating winner this time is Paige. She hollers loudly as she jumps on Ella and wraps her legs around Ellas' hips.

"It's good to know that I can beat you at something," Mylo laughs, throwing Kingsley over his head. Kingsley hits the water with a splash but not before grabbing hold of Mylo's arm, pulling him in too.

"Come on," Morgan says, dripping water as she steps up to me. "Let's start a fire. We brought hotdogs and marshmallows."

I follow her out of the water, suddenly very aware of the fact that my nipples are on full display. Morgan doesn't seem to care as she starts collecting firewood, still in her dripping wet underwear.

"I guess no one brought towels," I mumble to myself as I sink down to my knees and start building a fire with the wood that's already here.

Morgan comes back with an armful and helps me out. We soon have a crackling fire.

I can't help but smile to myself. I don't think I've ever done this sort of thing before. Shouldn't all teenagers have experienced bathing in a lake with friends and grilled marshmallows?

I'm rotating my stick in the fire when Kingsley sits down next to me. The sun has finally set, and it's dark. The firelight reflects in his brown eyes.

"Your marshmallow looks burned."

I smile. "I like it burned."

He looks skeptical before rummaging through the grocery bag. He pulls out a marshmallow and pierces it on his own stick. "Are you having a good time?"

I take my stick out of the fire and inspect my marshmallow. "I am, thank you. Are you?"

I feel his eyes on me. "Yeah, it's been a good day. I think you're ready to learn a bunny hop."

I take a bite of marshmallow-heaven and moan. "Easy there, tiger. I'll be a pro in no time, and then you'll really be in trouble when I start beating you in competitions."

He snorts a laugh. "Dream on, lady."

I gasp in mock outrage. "You shouldn't underestimate me, Kingsley. It might awaken the beast in me."

His eyebrows hit his hairline. "The beast?" He asks, his eyes shining with amusement.

I suck sticky pieces of marshmallow off my finger and feel a sense of satisfaction when his eyes fall to my mouth.

"I can be very stubborn, Kingsley. If you don't think I can achieve something, I might feel inclined to prove you wrong."

He turns his attention to the fire and rotates the stick in his hand. His cap is back on. It hides his tousled hair but wisps still peek out at the sides.

Mylo plops down on my other side and wraps his arm around me. "So, Kingsley tells me you're going after Wood?"

I can smell beer on his breath, and because I feel at ease, I snatch the bottle out of his hand and take a large sip. "That I am."

"I know he's a pornstar and all, but aside from his huge dick, what do you like about him?"

I nearly choke on the beer. "A huge dick, you say?" I wipe droplets of beer off my chin.

"Well, yeah. Isn't that a requirement or something? You can't work in porn with a tiny wiener."

I shrug, smiling. "I suppose you're right."

"What's there not to like about Hunter?" Morgan chips in as she takes a seat next to Mylo. "He's blonde, tall, fucking chiseled, and he fucks like a god."

I point to Morgan and grin. "What she said!"

Morgan hands me a beer. I take a sip, glancing at Kingsley.

He's watching me. "So, you like him because of what? His blonde hair?" he asks.

"Well, no..."

"Then why? His chiseled muscles? Is that it?"

I go to answer, but he beats me to it. "Or because"—he makes air quotes with his free hand—"he fucks like a god."

I furrow my brows.

"What's wrong with liking a guy because he fucks like a god?" Morgan asks. There's a challenge in her voice.

"Nothing," Kingsley says, trying for blasé. "Katherine just doesn't strike me as the shallow kind."

*"Girls are manipulative. They want you for what you can do for them. Popularity. Money. It attracts women like moths to a flame. It's shallow."*

His words from a couple of days before echo in my mind. "I don't just like him because of his looks or his skills in bed." My voice is low. Defensive.

"No?"

I shake my head. My hands are trembling. I take another sip of beer, ignoring his dark eyes that seem to want to pick me apart.

"Then tell me one thing you like about him that isn't shallow."

I meet his eyes. "Why do you care, Kingsley?"

He shrugs. "I don't."

Mylo whistles under his breath.

"Great! Then I don't have to justify myself to you!" I throw my stick in the fire. "I need another drink." I stand up and leave them staring after me.

"Don't let him get to you," Morgan says as she joins me, grabbing another bottle of beer.

I pop the cap on mine, side-eyeing her. "I just don't see why he cares."

Morgan watches me over the rim. She shrugs and wiggles her toes in the grass. We're near the treeline, away from the small beach. "I don't think Kingsley always understands his own emotions."

"Oh, please," I say, rolling my eyes. "Spare me the spiel. Kingsley and I are friends. Nothing more."

She searches my eyes. "Are you sure?"

"Very fucking sure!" Why do I swear so much these days?

Morgan lifts her left shoulder and lets it fall. "If you say so."

"How did you meet Adam?"

That makes her smile. She looks over at him fondly. "He joined the track team."

"Oh."

"He hates running. He claims it was the only way to catch my attention."

I laugh, pressing my palm over my mouth. "That's kind of cute."

"Trust me, it wasn't at the time. Adam huffed and puffed like he was about to die. Always came in last. He fainted once."

"Fainted?" I ask, giggling.

She smiles over the rim and takes another sip. I do the same, enjoying the cool sparkles as they tingle my tongue.

My phone vibrates in my pocket. I dig it out and unlock the screen.

Kingsley: You're not shallow.

I look over at him. He's engaged in conversation with Mylo and Adam. His message makes me feel a whole range of emotions. I'm still upset with him, and I don't even understand why he evokes such a reaction in me in the first place. It doesn't matter to me if he thinks I'm shallow or not. All that matters is that I gain the experience I need to do a good job at the audition next week.

But maybe I'm also upset because there's a sliver of truth in his words. I am shallow. I don't know Hunter. I spilled coffee on him and had a physical reaction to his good looks and decided to get to know him by any means necessary. Perhaps it is shallow. Or maybe it's me, taking a chance on something for once in my life.

Even more confusing, Kingsley's text also makes my stomach flutter. I'm smiling. I feel like a little girl who wants to squeal when her parents gift her concert tickets to go see her favorite boyband.

"You look deep in thought?"

I look up. "Huh?"

Morgan chuckles, waving me off. "Never mind. So, are you really going to audition for Hunter?"

I pocket my phone without replying to Kingsley's message. He can wait. "Yes, I am. I really want to try."

"But why?"

I bite my bottom lip in thought. "At first, it was just this thought that popped into my head. It seemed like the best way to get close to Hunter. Now... I've always lived such a boring life. I want to take a chance on something crazy. Everyone keeps telling me I can't do it. It only makes me want to prove them all wrong."

"I think you're brave."

"I'm no braver than anyone else."

Morgan takes another sip, then throws the empty beer in the trash bag. "You are. It's brave to pursue someone like Hunter. He's the leading man in the industry. He's experienced. I don't think I would have the bravery to try."

I know she means well with her compliment, but her words make me break out in a cold sweat. *The leading man in the industry.* And I'm foolish enough to audition for him... Well, didn't I say just now that I want to take a chance on something crazy? It doesn't get crazier than this —little Kitty Hamilton, going after a thirty-year-old pornstar.

Morgan takes my drink, puts it down on the grass, and tugs on my hand. "Dance with me."

"To what music?"

Peals of laughter slip past her lips. She holds up her phone with a grin and picks a song from her playlist. When the tinny music starts to play, she reaches for my hand and moves her hips. "Come on, Katherine Hamilton. This is your chance to not be boring."

I want to smile. But I also want to scowl. Such a complicated mix of emotions. Reluctantly, I begin to move my hips in time to the beat and soon find myself smiling.

Morgan spins me around. "You're a natural."

I throw my head back with a laugh. The sky is littered with stars.

*So many stars.*

She spins me around in a circle, and when she lets go, I find myself dancing willingly. And god forbid, I'm soon singing along too. Morgan screams the lyrics to the stars, which makes me laugh. Paige and Ellen join in, dancing with their hands in the air. Behind us, the fire continues crackling, and the boys cheer us on, hollering and whistling.

"Join us!" Elle yells and then squeals with laughter as Mylo begins moon dancing in a circle around her.

"I've got moves, girl!"

"You're crazy! That's what you are."

"Adam, what are you doing?" Morgan laughs, poking Adam in the ribs.

He grins. "It's the apple-picking dance. Move your hips to the beat, reach your hands up high and pretend to pick apples off a tree."

Kingsley grabs my hand and spins me around until I'm pressed up against his hard chest, lost in his brown eyes. His hands are on my hips, guiding my movements. "You didn't reply to my text." His heart races like the thundering hooves of a stallion beneath my hand.

"I didn't reply because you're right. I am shallow."

A crease forms between his eyebrows. "You're not."

I drop my gaze, staring at my hands on his chest. The fabric is soft and smells of washing powder and bonfire. "It is shallow of me to want to pursue someone like Hunter. I don't know him. But I want to do this for me, Kingsley. I need to do this."

His brown eyes search my face. I don't know what he's looking for or if he finds it. "I know you do."

He lifts his hand and strokes his fingers over my neck, moving my hair aside. I wait for his kiss, but it never comes. He simply holds me and sways us to the beat.

"Have you ever been in love, Katherine?" he asks, his eyes intent on mine.

I blink, tilting my head to the side. "I don't understand. I told you no earlier."

Kingsley swallows thickly. "Me neither."

I fist his t-shirt, struck by the desire to dig my nails into his skin and mark him. As Kingsley tips his head to look at the stars, I stare at his long neck and defined jaw.

"Do you believe there's something else out there?"

I look up. Billions of stars twinkle overhead, many of which burned out years ago. "Yes." My voice is a whisper. The others are loud, but the only thing I can hear is the beat of my own heart.

"I think your dad is up there, looking down."

My grip on his t-shirt tightens. Tears blur my vision and spill over as my throat grows thick with emotion. His eyes come back to mine, following the path of my tears. "He would be proud of you, Katherine."

I look away, blinking rapidly. "Why are you telling me

this, Kingsley?" I'm not ready to feel these emotions. This hurt. Not now. Not ever!

"I'm not trying to hurt you. I just want you to see yourself how others see you."

I scoff, laughing weakly as I step out of his arms. "Kingsley. When people look at me, they see a stuck-up girl dressed in an expensive dress."

He takes a step closer. *Too close.* His voice is low and intimate. "Because that's what you let them see. But I see you. Underneath the mask you put on, there's a girl with the most brilliant smile. A girl who's curious about the world, who wants to explore and take risks. She's funny and adventurous. She has a big heart."

My tears are flowing freely now. I tip my head back and search the stars for a resemblance of control over my emotions that seem to spiral out of control in Kingsley's presence. "Why, Kingsley?" Our eyes collide. "Why are you so hellbent on breaking my shell open? Because that's how it feels. I was intact before you. And now"—I circle my chest—"there's a crack here, and emotions I don't want to feel are seeping out. I can't stop it, Kingsley." My voice is thick with tears.

He palms my cheek, a look of regret on his face. I don't stop him. He wipes away my tears with his thumbs, whispering, "I think your shell needs to be cracked for the real Katherine to shine through."

As I look up at the sky, I see it—a shooting star. I gasp and break away. "Look!"

Kingsley looks up, following its path across the heavens with his brown eyes. Behind us, the fire crackles. It glows dimly in the evening fog, which floats on the lake like a low-hanging cloud.

When his attention returns to mine, it's with an intensity that leaves me short of breath. "Make a wish, Katherine."

My eyes fall closed. I search my heart... The depths of my dreams and desires.

He brushes his thumb over my lips. "What does your heart want, Katherine? What do you long for? What do you crave?" His warm breath hits my face, making my skin erupt in goosebumps.

"I can't tell you. If I do, it won't come true."

His hand falls away. He presses a kiss on my forehead, his lips lingering. "Then lock it away. Keep your dream safe." He steps back and walks over to the grocery bags to grab another beer.

"Just friends, huh?" Morgan winks.

I blush so fiercely it can be seen in the firelight. "Definitely just friends!"

"Uh-huh." She grins. "Keep telling yourself that."

Adam sweeps her up. I look back up at the starry sky, whispering to myself. "Dad, if you're up there, I could do with some guidance right now."

~

Kingsley, being a gentleman at heart, walks me back to my house. The night is quiet. I pull the bike along, too tired and achy to ride it.

"I've had a nice time."

Kingsley keeps his attention on the foggy street. It's a beautiful night, misty and wet, a contrast to the sunny day we enjoyed. "I did too. Thanks for coming along."

"Your friends are great!"

Kingsley chuckles lightly. "They can be crazy sometimes. But yeah, they're good guys."

"I'll introduce you to Becky and Hazel one day. I think you'll like them."

He reaches up to adjust his cap and smiles at me. "I'm sure I will."

I study his profile, feeling a softening within me. "I'm glad I met you, Kingsley."

His eyes slowly meet mine, and we walk along in silence, watching each other. His brown eyes are full of emotions I can't place. His jaw ticks.

I like his lips. They're thin but with enough fullness to make them look soft and inviting. And when he smiles, the way the left side of his lip quirks... His smile is lazy, but his laugh is carefree and raucous. I wish I could see him smile now, but the look in his eyes is intense. Vulnerable even.

He looks away first. "I don't do relationships, Katherine."

I pause in my step, staring after him. *What?* He's so confusing. I start walking again. "You've told me that already."

He stops and sighs. His jaw is tense when he says, "I need you to understand that."

My lips open and close. "I do understand."

"Good." He starts walking again.

What just happened?

"Have you always been this confusing?" I ask him as I get on my bike and ride alongside him.

He laughs this time. "You think I'm confusing?"

"Very."

His eyes meet mine. I lean back, pull at the bar, and squeal in victory when I manage to ride along on the back wheel without pedaling.

His eyes soften.

"I did it! Watch out, Kingsley; I'm coming for your

medals!" I ride ahead, turning the wheel right and left, cycling in an 'S' shape.

He soon joins me, smiling as we do 'S' shapes together.

"I can see why you love it so much."

"Yeah?" his grin is big.

I nod, standing up on the pedals. The foggy night frizzes my hair, but I don't care. "It's freedom."

His eyes are intent on mine.

I wink and cycle ahead, calling over my shoulder, "The last one to my house is a loser!" My heart jolts with happiness at the sound of his laughter behind me. It's a deep, carefree, and delighted sound. My thighs burn as I pedal along like my life depends on it. I fly down dark foggy alleys and past park benches in the local park, empty of laughing children.

Kingsley whoops in victory as he overtakes me, and I can't help but laugh at his glee.

"I'll get you, Kingsley!" I shout.

"No, you won't!" He swerves past a park bench and jumps up on top of another. He rides along and jumps off, landing perfectly.

∽

Kingsley carries my bike up the steps while I unclip my helmet and root through my bag for the keys.

"You can keep this bike to practice on for now, if you like."

"Thank you," I smile, unlocking the door and holding it open for him. Kingsley carries my bike inside and disappears down the hallway. I place the helmet on the shelf above my jackets, then toe off my sneakers and run a hand through my hair. My body aches everywhere.

Kingsley's smile is soft when he returns. He places a kiss on my lips. "See you tomorrow?"

"Are you not staying?"

He shakes his head. "I have to go."

"Where?" I blurt before I realize how insensitive my comment is. Still, where is he going? He has no home.

His lips come down on mine, caressing, seeking. I kiss him back and thread my fingers through his soft hair, knocking off his cap in the process. It lands on the floor with a soft thud.

"I'll see you tomorrow, Katherine," he whispers against my lips before releasing me and reaching down for his snapback. He walks over to the door and throws me one last look over his shoulder. Then he's gone.

I feel strangely disappointed. My house has never seemed more empty. Silent. I take a step backward and then another until my back hits the cold wall. I sink back against it, holding a trembling palm over my mouth, and slide down until my butt hits the hard floor.

My father's smiling face stares back at me from a photograph on the hallway table. I can't stop the tears from falling. Kingsley blew up the foundation to my dam and tore me open. Now my emotions flow freely in my loneliness with no one around to witness me fall apart.

And no one to hold me together.

# SEVEN

I hit the ground hard, groaning and laughing at the same time.

"You're doing great, miss," Geoffrey says, checking his watch. "Another three hours and you should land it."

"Oh, shut up!" I laugh, getting to my feet. "Why don't you try it since you have such a smart mouth. It's much harder than it looks."

"I'm sure it is, miss." He holds up his sandwich. "Mind if I eat, miss? It seems we shall be here a while."

Grinning, I shake my head and get back on the bike. "Go for it. I'm not leaving until I can do a perfect bunny hop. I don't care if it takes me a day. A week. Or a month."

"Fabulous," Geoffrey says drily around a mouthful of food. I like this new side to him. It's fun.

"What do you think I'm doing wrong?"

"Show me again."

I laugh. "You just want to see me fall again."

He takes another bite. "Well, it is proving most entertaining. How else should I amuse myself while sitting on a bench"—he checks his watch—"for four hours."

My eyes bug out. "Four hours?"

"Affirmative, miss. My legs are starting to cramp."

"Jesus Christ," I mumble. "Okay, are you watching this time?"

Geoffrey takes another bite. He's got breadcrumbs stuck in his mustache, but I don't point that out. I get back on my bike and attempt to lift the front wheel again. No matter how much I try, I can't seem to make the jump. This time I don't fall on the ground, but I do squeal.

Geoffrey wipes his mouth. "Try to extend your arms forward and upwards, so you pull the handlebars from under you."

"Like this?"

"Yes. I think the problem is that you try to lift one wheel and then the other. Ride forward slowly, bend the arms and legs and push into the bike. Keep your weight in the middle and try to push off the ground hard with both your arms and legs."

I laugh. "You sound like Kingsley."

"Good, then I know what I'm talking about."

"But Kingsley told me a bunny hop is when you push off the ground with the rear wheel only."

Geoffrey crumbles up the wrapping, stands up, and discards it in the nearest bin. He grimaces in pain. "I feel like a squeaky door in need of oiling." He sits back down. "I don't know the difference between a hop and a bunny hop. The only experience I have with bikes is riding my grams bike with the wicker basket to the corner store for her cigarettes."

I wrinkle my nose, and he waves me off. "Different times. My point is that I think you need to learn how to hop first before you attempt anything else."

I contemplate his words, then nod in agreement. "Okay, what's the worst that can happen?"

"Well, I could grow roots and become part of the scenery. Pigeons could start nesting in my hair."

"Ha! Ha!" I say drily as I ride forward and follow his instructions. It takes me a couple of attempts—okay, lots of attempts, but I eventually manage to do a simple jump.

Geoffrey flips a page in his newspaper at the sound of my excited squeal and says without looking up, "Well done, miss. It seems we have success at last."

"How many hours?"

He sniffs, checking his watch. "Six, miss."

"Not too bad," I note, grinning.

"Maybe not for you, miss. I can't feel my behind and a seagull pooed on me an hour ago."

I hide my laugh behind my hand. "I'm sorry, Geoff."

"It's okay, miss. I quite look forward to my pay raise."

I laugh at his jibe as I get back on the bike and attempt to push off from my rear wheel. Learning new tricks is like taking one step forward and two back. But at least it's another sunny day, and I'm having fun.

Geoff flips another page. "Did you know, miss, it's illegal to hunt unicorns in Michigan? It says so right here."

∽

"Sizing up its prey, the lion crouches and lies in wait, swishing its tail. Then, when the time is right, it pounces." Josh, the detention guy, grabs my shoulders, jostling me. "Hi, gazelle."

I laugh and roll my eyes as I close my locker. I turn to face him. "To what do I owe this honor, detention guy?"

Josh leans his shoulder on the locker next to mine and grins. His eyes follow a cheerleader walking past. "I was on my way to class and saw my favorite steak. Thought I'd say hi."

"Well, your favorite steak is quickly disappearing from view. You should run after her."

Josh tears his eyes away from the cheerleader. "That one?" He scoffs. "She's a piranha. Fascinating to look at, but she'll devour you whole in ten seconds flat if you get too close. Her kind is the ultimate apex predator in this school." He pretends to shudder. "No, thank you, gazelle. I think I'll stay on the other side of the glass." He lifts his chin in greeting as the green-haired guy joins us. "And this here is Ben, who decided against staying on the other side of the glass. With no care in the world for his own safety, this motherfucker jumped in at the deep end. What you're looking at are the skeletal remains."

Ben frowns, then clips Josh on the back of the head. "I don't know what the fuck you're talking about, but we better get going."

Just then, Kingsley walks up, giving us a questioning look.

"Yo, Kingsley," Ben says, and they fist bump. "Haven't seen you at the warehouse in a while."

"I've been around," Kingsley says cryptically. He eyes Josh's arm around my shoulder. *When did that happen?* I try to shrug it off.

Josh seems amused by my attempts. "I like you, gazelle. You're funny."

I pull a face. "Oh wow, that's.. wow, Josh. I'm so pleased."

My dry sense of humor makes him chuckle, and he winks at me before they set off down the corridor. "Don't miss me too much, gazelle."

"I'll try not to, detention guy."

Kingsley clears his throat. "So, you like Josh?"

My mouth forms an 'O'. I throw a thumb over my shoulder. "Him? Detention guy?"

Kingsley watches me closely but doesn't reply.

I laugh incredulously. "Nice to see you too, Kingsley. How are you today?" I set off walking.

"You didn't answer my question," Kingsley says as he catches up with me.

I side-eye him. "Why do you care?"

"I don't. It was just a question."

"Uh-huh." I decide to let the bait dangle mid-air. Who I flirt with is none of his business. Especially as he claims not to care. Truth is, I would prefer to be dragged through the streets tied to the back of a horse than go out with a detention guy, but Kingsley doesn't need to know that.

"I didn't think he was your type?"

"What makes you say that?"

Kingsley rubs the back of his neck. "You know, the black hair, black clothes, piercings, too many tattoos to count."

"And I thought you said I'm not shallow."

We reach the door to my classroom. Kingsley grabs my elbow and pulls me to a stop as I go to enter.

I look down at his hand on my bare skin, then raise my gaze. "You don't know me, Kingsley." My voice is quiet but steady. I leave him to stare after me as I enter the classroom and find my seat.

Becky looks up from her phone. "Is the cherry still intact?"

I blow a strand of hair from my face as I plop down in my seat. "Still not popped."

Becky places her phone down on the desk. "You have five days until the audition."

I groan and drop my head to the desk. "I'm fully aware, Becks. I don't know why he's holding back. What guy says no to sex?"

"It's a fucking mystery," Becky agrees, rubbing my back in consolation.

"I can't be a virgin when the audition comes around. I just can't!"

"And you won't be. Kingsley will take care of it, or we'll find someone else."

"And if we don't?"

Becky shrugs. "Then you'll just have to pop it with Wood's dildo."

I lift my head and laugh. "Now, that's how I've always dreamed of tearing my hymen. A romantic date with my signed dildo."

Becky wiggles her eyebrows. "Well, at least you'll be able to say Hunter Wood was your first—in a roundabout way."

"You slept with the wood?" Hazel asks, sitting down in the seat in front of us.

I groan again, and Becky throws a pencil at Hazel. "Keep up, woman! When would our Kitty here have slept with Hunter? He doesn't exactly live around the corner."

Hazel picks up the pencil off the floor, hands it back to Becky, and shrugs. "I don't know."

"I need a plan of action."

"Your plan of action is simple. Corner Kingsley, drag him into the bathroom, and seduce him."

Hazel crinkles her nose. "That's so unsanitary, Becky."

Becky shoots her a look. "Have you never fucked in a school bathroom?"

"Eww, no!" Hazel looks affronted.

I laugh as Becky shakes her head. "I'm best friends with

a virgin and a woman who's never fucked in a school bathroom. I'll soon turn into a prude by association."

"Who are you calling a prude?" I laugh. "I'd gladly fuck in a bathroom."

"Ooh, look at you, Miss. Promiscuous."

"Ha!" I shout, making a couple of students look over. "Tell that to the career adviser here at school!"

The look on Becky's face is comical. "Why would I tell the career advisor that you're promiscuous?"

"Because she says I'm not."

Becky's mouth opens and closes. "The career advisor told you that you're not promiscuous?"

"Indeed!" I reply.

Becky looks to Hazel, who's busy twirling her pink bubblegum around her finger. "I am so confused right now."

"It's probably for the best, Becks. There's no point in trying to understand."

I Jump in my seat when Mrs. Beechwood slams a sheet of paper on my desk. "Are you going to behave today, or do you wish to land yourself another visit to detention?"

I shudder in horror. No, thank you! I zip my lips close and throw away the key, making Becky snigger next to me.

Mrs. Beechwood glowers at me before she continues down the aisle, handing out sheets as she goes. "You have an hour to complete today's test. I will not tolerate cheating. You can turn your paper over."

I look down at my sheet.

*Solve the following equation:*
$$2x+4x+8x+16x+32x+...=$$

Oh, great...

"Gazelle, what did you do this time?" Josh, the detention guy, asks, looking gleeful.

"Don't, just don't," I say, dropping my bag on the desk next to him. Why did I choose this seat when there are plenty of empty chairs? I don't know.

He nudges me. "For real, juicy meat, what did you do?"

Nina balances her chair on its back legs. "Did you steal something?"

I blink.

"Burn something?"

I look to Josh for help. He's balancing his pen on his nose.

"Did you get caught sucking someone off in the bathroom?" Nina cringes. "Trust me, teachers don't take kindly to that."

"Wha—?"

"Did you key a teacher's car?"

"No?"

"Throw soup at the dinner lady?"

"Why would I throw soup at the dinner lady?"

"Did you escape through a window during class?"

April leans forward. "Did you accidentally drop a Rubik's cube on a teacher's head?"

"Oh yeah, I did that once," Josh says with a sheepish smile as he rubs his jaw.

"You accidentally dropped a Rubik's cube on your teacher's head? How?"

"Don't ask," April sniggers.

"Seriously though, what did you do?" Nina asks, flashing teeth behind her purple lipstick.

I shrug. "I dropped my pen on the floor. Mrs. Beechwood accused me of cheating."

They blink.

April pops her gum. "You dropped a pen?"

"What can I say? Mrs. Beechwood hates me."

Nina nods. "She's a bitch. She once sent me to detention when the mice in the classroom escaped."

April laughs. "Fuck off. The mice didn't"—she makes quotation marks in the air—"escape. You released them."

Josh laughs next to me.

"She can't prove it was me."

April pops her gum again, grinning. "Bitch, you got caught red-handed."

"Like I explained to Mrs. Beechwood. I was in the process of putting the mice back *after* they escaped."

"What? Ten mice?"

"There were fifteen, but I couldn't find the other five."

"Right. Uh-huh." April nods, chewing her gum.

"They live in her bedroom now," Josh whispers, grinning.

"Correction. They live in a cage in my bedroom."

I blink. "How did you get five mice home?"

"Girl, have you never heard of pockets?" She eyes my olive-green shirt dress. "I suppose, where would you put them? In between your tits? What's with rich girls and dresses anyway?"

I look down at my dress. Why does everyone criticize my clothes? "What's wrong with it?"

"Abso-fucking-lutely nothing," Josh grins devilishly. "Easy access, gazelle."

Nina rolls her eyes. "Dude, you're so predictable."

The teacher eyes us over the pages of her romance novel.

"You two should swap clothes for a day," Josh suggests, gesturing between Nina and me.

April chokes on her gum, laughing. "Oh yes, please I would love to see that."

Nina stares at April. "I don't know. I think you can pull off a pretty dress better than me."

I lean down and point at Nina's black combat shoes with neon green laces. "I think I would look good in those."

"Well, I certainly can't walk in your shoes. I'd break an ankle," she replies, eyeing my black high heels.

We're finally dismissed, and Josh points his finger at me. "Don't go dropping any more pens now, gazelle."

I stick my tongue out as I grab my bag and walk over to the window. I open it, throw the bag outside, and look over my shoulder, hands on the windowpane. "What's that you said about joining the dark side?" I smile as I throw my leg over and climb out.

Josh cups his mouth and hollers, "Escapee!"

I drop to the ground and nearly scream when I come face to face with Kingsley.

"Is there a reason why you're jumping through windows?"

I press a palm to my chest. "Jesus, Kingsley. A little warning next time."

"Oh, I'm sorry, do you want me to try again?" He walks over to the edge of the grass, turns, and walks back. "Is there a reason why you're escaping through windows?"

I roll my eyes and pick up my bag. "God, could you be any more ridiculous?"

He laughs, wrapping his arm around my shoulder as we start walking. "Detention again?"

"You're enjoying this, aren't you?"

"Immensely so," he admits. "You're turning into quite the little rebel, Katherine Hamilton."

"I dropped a pen!" I deadpan.

He tuts. "What a disgrace."

I hit him in the stomach, which makes him laugh.

"So, I was thinking..." he says.

I roll my eyes. "Don't strain yourself, Kingsley."

He ignores my jibe as he continues, "You said earlier that I don't know you, so let's change that."

I meet his eye. "And how do you suggest we do that?"

He grins, and it's a smile that spells trouble. "The traditional way, of course. A drinking game."

I snort, sidestepping a group of students and bumping into Kingsley in the process. "I don't have alcohol. Do you?"

We reach the bike stands. Kingsley digs in his pocket for the key. I watch him unlock it, and my eyes roam over his broad back as he bends over.

"I have us sorted. Don't worry." He pulls the bike out and gets on.

"I still haven't forgiven you, you know."

He keeps his attention forward. "For what?"

"For suggesting I'm shallow. Again."

"Come here." He plants his feet on the floor and gestures to his handlebars.

"Where?"

He takes my hand and pulls me to him. Then grabs my hips and lifts me up, so I'm seated on the handlebars. I hold onto his broad shoulders. His grin is both soft and devilish all at the same time.

"You can't see now."

"I can see all I need to see."

A laugh escapes me. "Oh, Kingsley, that was cheesy!"

He lifts one shoulder. "Maybe." He kicks off the ground, and I squeal as we move forward. "Hold on to me."

"This is a very bad idea!" I laugh, digging my nails in his shoulders.

"It is," he agrees. "But what's life without a little danger?"

My heart is beating loudly in my chest. The breeze blows my hair in my face, causing strands to get stuck in my lipgloss.

His brown eyes stay locked on mine. "Are you scared?" he asks. His legs pump us closer to home or closer to disaster. Time will tell.

I shake my head. "No." It's the truth. Somehow, I feel safe with Kingsley.

He swerves us around a tree as if he knew it was there all along, and a surprised laugh escapes me.

I look over my shoulder. "If I die today, Kingsley. I'll haunt you."

"And I'll give you a show worth haunting me for."

My eyes clash with his. We ride, lost in each other. I slowly move my hand down until I feel his steady heartbeat beneath my fingers. "Have you ever been in love, Kingsley?"

His eyes fall to my lips. "No."

"Me neither."

"No?" His eyes flick back up.

"No."

"Crazy fucking kids!" someone shouts, jumping out of our way.

I laugh, burying my face in his neck so that he can see and get us back safely. His deep chuckle vibrates in his chest. I brush my lips over his warm skin and breathe in his smell, and his heart picks up speed, pounding against his ribcage.

"Is this your trick to get girls in bed?" I whisper against his ear.

A shiver runs through him. He shakes his head. "I've never done this before."

I nip his earlobe with my teeth. "Do you expect me to believe you, Kingsley?"

"Believe what you want, Katherine Hamilton. This is a first for me."

*I quite like the sound of that.* I wrap my arms around his warm body, and my eyes fall closed as I nuzzle his neck. If this is what heaven feels like, then I never want to open my eyes again. I'll stay here forever, breathing in his leather and bonfire smell. Lost in him.

～

"Do you have any glasses that don't look like they belong in a museum?" He asks, opening cupboards. His backpack lies discarded on the floor by my kitchen door.

"I'm sorry, is my glassware not up to your standards?" I grin as I open a cupboard to his left and point to the cheap glassware my father hid in the back from the days before he became a powerful businessman. Maybe it was a reminder of his roots, but he never threw them out for whatever reason. "Will these work?"

Kingsley takes one out and pretends to scrutinize it. "Oh yes, nothing beats a $1 glass."

In my best posh voice, I say, "Oh yes, it's most splendid."

Kingsley laughs, placing two glasses down on the island where he ate me out the other day. The memory makes me blush. "You sound like good old Geoff now."

"I've known him since I was a little girl, so yes, I think I can imitate his accent quite well."

Kingsley's brown eyes lock on mine. He smiles as he pours wine in the glass. "I'm getting to know you already." He hands it to me and pours himself one.

"Yeah? What do you know already?"

"Well, I know you suck at BMX."

I throw my head back with a laugh. "Good point!" We clink glasses, and I take a sip, smiling over the rim. "What else?"

He leans against the island and sweeps his eyes over my face. "I know you've known Geoff since you were a little girl. I know you've never known your mother and your father has passed away. You're an only child. You have this crazy idea that you're going to marry a pornstar."

I laugh at that and push on his chest. Kingsley doesn't budge, but he does laugh.

"What do you know about me?" he asks, taking another sip.

I swipe my tongue over a droplet of wine on my bottom lip. "Like me, you're an only child. Your dad is a dick, so you moved out of home, and now, you're drifting."

"Drifting?"

I take another sip. "Yes. You're looking for your place in the world."

"You've got me all figured out, huh?"

I shake my head. "No, not even close."

"So, let's change that," Kingsley says as he refills our glasses. "A question for a question."

I pull myself up on the island. "Okay, who goes first?"

"What's your biggest fear?"

"Wow, starting at the deep end." I take a sip and look down at the glass in my hand. "I guess my biggest fear is to be alone in the world. After my dad died, I haven't felt close to anyone." *Until you.* I meet his eyes.

He watches me steadily.

"How about you? What's your biggest fear?"

He takes a slow sip as he contemplates his answer, and my eyes roam over his white t-shirt, stretching tight over his chest. "I'm scared of failure... of not making something of myself."

"You will," I reply instantly. I've never been more sure of anything in my life.

"Are you into Josh?"

I burst out laughing, jostling my drink, and spilling some in the process. "I should have known that was coming. No, Kingsley. I'm not."

He grins. "Good."

"Is it?" I ask quietly, searching for something I don't yet know what it is.

He shrugs. "Sure."

"Are you into Olivia?"

He scoffs, tipping the last of his drink back. I watch his neck move as he swallows. "Hell, no."

He reaches for my glass and refills it. "What's your favorite food?" He hands me the drink, picks up his own, and we clink glasses.

"Scallops."

He chokes on his drink. "Scallops? Really?"

"I laugh lightly. "What's wrong with Scallops?"

"Nothing."

I laugh again and take another sip. "When did you have your first kiss?"

Kingsley steps between my legs. He takes a sip of his drink as he runs his free hand up my thigh. "I was thirteen.

We played seven minutes in heaven, and my bottle stopped on Hailey."

Now it's my turn to choke on my cider. "Hailey, the cheerleader?"

He puts his drink next to me on the island. Then leans in, brushing his lips over mine. "Did I surprise you, Katherine Hamilton?" He grips my jaw and plunges his tongue into my mouth, and I respond, kissing him back. He tastes like alcohol and bad decisions.

I'm breathless when we break for air. "I didn't think you hang out with that crowd?"

"I don't. It was a school dance. Where were you, Katherine Hamilton?"

"Keep saying my name like that," I whisper against his lips and feel him smile right before he kisses me again. Deeper this time. He slides his hands up my back until they tangle in my hair. His stubble is scratching my skin, and his breath is hot on my lips as he pulls on my tresses until I arch my neck. He trails scorching kisses along my jaw and down my neck, biting, licking, and nibbling. I breathe his name. I need more…

He leans back and takes another sip of his wine.

I can barely see him through this lustful haze. "Why did you stop?"

"We're not done yet." He fills up my glass. "I already know who your first kiss was." He looks smug about that. "What's the sexiest and least sexy name you can think of?"

"Wha—?" I begin, then burst out laughing.

He grins over the rim of his glass. "Answer the question."

I take another mouthful, enjoying the coolness on my tongue as I think of a reply. "I suppose the sexiest name I can think of is Mckenzie."

He laughs at that. "McKenzie? Really?"

I chuckle along with him. "Yes! What's wrong with Mckenzie? I like it."

"Nothing at all," he replies, looking amused. "What's the least sexy?"

"Bob or Ernest."

"Ernest..." he laughs, shaking his head.

"How do you feel about pineapple on pizza?"

Kingsley sucks in a breath. "Oh, it's getting serious now! I don't like pineapple on pizza. It's disgusting."

My mouth falls open. "But it's the best!"

He chuckles deeply and takes another swig. "It really isn't! What would be the creepiest thing you could say while passing a stranger in the street?"

"Wow, putting me on the spot today." I take another sip even though I am starting to feel the effects of the alcohol. "Have you ever dated a cannibal?"

He chokes on his drink.

"Did I surprise you, Kingsley Delanoy?" I ask, echoing his words from earlier.

He wipes his chin, nodding. "Yeah, you could say that." He grabs our glasses and the bottle. "Let's go sit down."

I jump off the island and guide the way to the living room. Not that he needs me to since it's open-plan.

We plop down on the couch, and Kingsley shifts so he's facing me. He sweeps his eyes over the big room. I do the same.

I take in the gray walls and silver framed prints of my dad and me. It's my whole life on one wall. There I am, on my first birthday blowing out candles with my dad smiling behind me.

My first day at school—I have my hair up in pigtails. I'm

gripping the straps of my oversized princess bag, and my dad is crouching next to me, pointing at the camera.

And there I am, ten years old, throwing a frisbee to my dad at the beach; he's mid-jump, laughing.

I look at the next photograph. I'm fifteen years old, standing beside my father at an important business dinner.

I swallow past the thick lump in my throat.

"If you could talk to your dad right now, what would you say?"

I spin my glass in my hands. "I would ask him for advice."

"What advice?"

I don't look up. I can't. I feel too much right now. "I don't know... I just know I could do with his wisdom and guidance. He always had the answers."

He takes my hand in his and strokes his thumb over the back of my hand. We sit in silence. How can he break me open like this and piece me together at the same time?

"What are you looking for in a girl, Kingsley?" I whisper as I raise the glass to my lips. I don't know why I am so curious.

"Nothing. I'm not looking for a girl."

"I know," I reply. "It was a rhetorical question." It's hard to imagine Kingsley with anyone. Girls flock around him, and I've seen him make out with girls at school before, but to imagine him with a girlfriend? He's so adamant it's never going to happen. I can't help but think the same too.

"What about you? Apart from pornstar quality."

I laugh weakly. "I honestly don't know. I want someone loyal."

"And you think a pornstar fits that box?" A look of regret crosses his face as soon as the words are out, but he can't take them back.

I pull my hand away. "Why do you criticize me at every turn, Kingsley?"

"I don't." He brushes his warm fingers over my cheek. "Look, sometimes I say stupid shit. It means nothing. I'm sure someone like Hunter can be loyal too. It was a dickish thing to say."

"Kiss me, Kingsley."

He looks taken aback.

I lean forward and press my lips against his, thieving a piece of him for myself—a piece of us. I break away, and he watches me unbutton the front of my dress. I shrug it off and dive back in, stealing another kiss. Then another until my lungs scream for air, and all I can feel are his hands on my body. His lips on my skin. Gone is the pain.

I brush my fingers over his abs beneath his t-shirt, exploring the smooth skin and hard ridges. Kingsley groans into my mouth, his muscles pulling taut at my touch.

I shove the hem up. "Off!"

He pulls the back of his t-shirt over his head and discards it on the floor before sliding his hand into my hair and kissing me hungrily.

He's on top of me now, guiding me down on the couch.

"Kath," he whispers, nipping my jaw with his teeth. He hooks his fingers in my panties and slides them down my legs.

I whimper as cold air hits my throbbing sex. "More... I need more!" I beg as Kingsley skims his hands up my legs and spreads my thighs.

He lowers himself down, taking his time kissing along the inside of my thighs. "You want more, baby?"

My eyes flutter shut. His stubble scratches my skin deliciously as he inches closer to where I ache for him. His hands roam my body, squeezing my tits through my bra.

"Kingsley," I breathe, sliding down the straps of my dress, exposing my breasts to the cold air and his hungry eyes. "Kingsley...Please!" My voice shakes with need. I'm burning up. He finally latches on to my throbbing clit with his hot mouth, and I cry out. He holds on to my bucking hips and loves me with his tongue, licking, sucking, and nibbling until I'm moaning his name like the holiest prayer.

"Fuck, you're so beautiful!" he whispers against my sex before placing a tender kiss on my clit. "Does it feel good, baby?"

"Please don't stop!" I moan, burying my hand in his hair. The roof is spinning, everything is fading, and all I feel are his lips on my pussy.

"What do you want, baby?" He licks me in one long stroke and then swirls his tongue over my tight entrance.

I cry out, grinding against him, fisting his short hair. "I want you!"

He sucks on my clit and pinches my aching nipple with his fingers. "I'm right here. Feel me, baby."

"Oh, god! Oh, fuck!" I rock against him. My climax is cresting on the horizon. I'm so close!

"I love watching your beautiful tits bob. I love it when you arch your neck and raise your hips to meet my mouth. Do you want my tongue inside you, baby?"

"Please, Kingsley. Please..." I can't take this sweet torture much longer. I am going to fall apart and shatter into a million pieces.

He plunges his tongue inside me and takes me like he's starving—as if he'll die if he can't have me.

"Ahhh!" I grip hold of the couch.

"It's okay, baby. I've got you." He places one last kiss on my throbbing nub before crawling up my body and lying down next to me. He unbuckles his belt, lowers his zipper, and gets his dick out. "Here." He guides my hand to his hard cock, and I shift onto my side. We're nose to nose, our breaths becoming one. He rubs my clit in firm, fast circles while I stroke his hard cock, feeling it swell and grow impossibly harder. My eyes flutter. God, I'm so close! So, so close.

"Open your eyes, baby."

I do. I blink my eyes open.

His are on me. "You're so wet for me!"

"Kingsley," I whimper. I'm drowning in his dark depths.

"It's okay." He works a finger inside me until he's knuckle-deep, and I open my legs wider, moaning into his mouth. Kingsley snatches up my bottom lip between his teeth as he plunges his finger all the way in.

I break away, gasping.

"I'm here with you, baby. Feel me."

I keep my eyes locked on his, jerking him harder and faster. "I feel you, Kingsley."

He smiles lazily—this dirty tug to the left side of his lips that has me clenching around his finger. He pumps it, fucking me slowly. "Does it hurt?"

I shake my head. "No."

He steals another kiss and my breath, stroking his tongue against mine. "Good! Keep your eyes on me."

I pant. My eyelids are growing heavy. "I won't look away."

He smiles again, and it's one I would sell my soul to keep on his lips. "Katherine Hamilton," he whispers against my lips. It's sensual. Intimate.

I swirl my thumb over his tip, making him groan. "Am I doing it right?"

"It's perfect. You're perfect... keep going!"

I stroke his big cock faster. His breath is growing choppy, wafting over my lips in short bursts. His body tenses, our noses brush, and a bead of sweat trails down his temple.

Kingsley moves his finger inside me and strokes his thumb over my clit, faster and harder until I finally explode around him. He swallows my moans, claiming kiss after kiss until I'm dizzy. But before I have a chance to come down from my high, he stiffens, and his warm cum spills on my belly. I keep milking him until he pulls me close and buries his face in my neck. He breathes me in, rocking his still hard cock against my sticky stomach. We're slick with sweat, but right now, I couldn't care less.

I stroke my hand through his sweaty and tousled hair, feeling his warm breath against my neck. "God, that was…"

"Amazing? Life-changing?"

I laugh and push on his shoulders playfully, but he doesn't budge. "You're so full of yourself sometimes."

He hums low in his throat, tracing patterns on my bare hip with his fingers.

My eyes are growing heavy. "Don't go yet. Lie here with me for a while."

"Sleep, Katherine," he whispers, placing a featherlight kiss on my shoulder.

My eyelids flutter shut.

# EIGHT

"That tickles!" I blink my eyes open to find Mr. Boomer sniffing my face, so I scratch him behind the ear before bolting upright and cringing. Fuck, my head is sore! I'm in my bed. I don't remember going to sleep.

I stiffen at the sound of soft snoring to my left. Kingsley is asleep on his front, and the sheet lies pooled around his waist, exposing his tanned back. His dark hair is even more tousled than usual.

Mr. Boomer is purring loudly and kneading my lap. I stroke him absentmindedly while I try to piece together the previous night. We drank too much alcohol, asked each other questions, and got each other off in the living room. I remember that much, but the rest is hazy.

I freeze as a thought occurs to me, I am still a virgin, aren't I? I carefully shift Mr. Boomer to the side and lift the sheet. I'm naked. Very naked. "Boomer," I whisper hiss. He keeps on purring, pushing his head against my cheek as I lean down. "What if I let him pop my cherry last night and don't remember it? I should be sore, right?"

*Purr. Purr.*

"You're of no help, Mr. Boomer," I sigh, flopping back on the pillow, staring at the streaks of sunlight flooding in through the window. I roll my head when I hear another soft snore.

Kingsley looks boyish in his sleep as if all the troubles weighing him down during the day are gone. He's lying on his front with his hands under the pillow. I run my eyes over his tanned back and the muscles in his arms, recalling how good he felt last night.

Mr. Boomer, seemingly bored with me, sniffs Kingsley's ear.

"Boomer," I whisper hiss. "No! Bad kitty!" But it's too late. Mr. Boomer is now meowing and kneading Kingsley's back.

Kingsley groans, stirring.

Meow. *Purr. Purr.*

"Mr. Boomer! I hiss sternly, lifting my head off the pillow. Boomer's ear twitches, but he pays me no mind, kneading Kingsley's back with even more enthusiasm. "That's it, Mr. Boomer, no more catnip for a month! And I won't put on your favorite bird show ever again! No more virtual birds for you, Mr. Boomer! You can forget about tweeting Robins and Bluebirds. Oh, and those Goldfinches you like so much. Gone. Poof!"

Another ear twitch. More kneading.

"Oh, god!" I groan exasperatedly, rubbing my hands over my face. That cat is in big trouble!

Kingsley groans again, shifting on the bed. "Wha—? Why is a cat sniffing my face?" His voice is laced with sleep.

I roll my head on the pillow. "Hmm? Oh, that's Mr. Boomer. He wanted to personally wake you up this morning. I threatened to cancel his tv time and not let him have any catnip, but he's a rebel at heart. Always living dangerously."

Kingsley scratches Mr. Boomer behind the ear. Mr. Boomer, pleased to have been successful in his mission to wake Kingsley up, meows.

I watch Kingsley fuss with Mr. Boomer. It feels intimate to wake up next to him naked in my bed with morning hair and pillow creases across his cheek. I've never shared a bed with anyone. Never mind a boy who makes my chest feel too full.

As if he can feel my eyes on him, he looks over and smiles softly. "How's your head this morning?"

"Bad. And my mouth tastes like a brewery."

He laughs. Mr. Boomer is now begging Kingsley to scratch his belly.

Traitor.

"You're a lightweight," Kingsley jokes, grinning up at me from beneath his dark lashes.

"In my defense, we drank a lot."

Kingsley hums in agreement, and for a minute, the only sound is Mr. Boomer's loud purring.

"Did we...?" I ask, blushing fiercely.

"Did we what?" He looks amused, as if he knows exactly what I mean but wants to see me squirm.

"You know what I mean, Kingsley. Don't make me say it," I groan.

He plasters on a look of faux innocence. "I really don't know what you're talking about, Katherine. You will have to explain it to me."

"Did we have sex?" I rush out on a breath like a blushing bride. It makes him laugh.

Kingsley leans down and rubs Mr. Boomer's tummy. "I'm on your side, buddy. No more bird shows? She's cruel."

His eyes meet mine. "What do you think? Do you think we did it?"

"Well, no... but we're naked." I gesture to his chest and my own naked body, hidden beneath the sheet I'm clutching over my chest.

"You fell asleep last night, so I carried you upstairs. Should I have dressed you first?"

A breath of relief whooshes out of me. I do want to remember my first time.

"How old is he?" Kingsley asks, ignoring my burning cheeks.

I smile fondly as I lean forward to scratch Mr. Boomer under the chin. "He's two."

I feel Kingsley's eyes on me before he gets out of bed stark naked.

He scratches the back of his neck. "Do you mind if I take a shower?"

I sweep my eyes down his body, and his abs tense as I trace my gaze lower, past his dark happy trail. His hard length stands proud in the morning light. My cheeks heat. I swallow thickly and shake my head. "I don't mind."

He lingers for a moment longer, looking unsure, before he turns and walks into the bathroom, leaving the door slightly ajar.

The shower turns on.

Mr. Boomer bumps his head against my chin, purring loudly. I stroke his head. My heart is pounding against my ribcage as I stare at the door.

*"I need a plan of action."*

*"Your plan of action is simple. Corner Kingsley, drag him into the bathroom and seduce him."*

Becky's words echo in my head.

"I'm doing it, Mr. Boomer. It's now or never." I place a

kiss on his furry head, lift him off my lap, and get out of bed. The door looms up ahead. My body trembles with nerves as I walk with tentative steps toward the bathroom. *He's naked and wet behind that door...* One step closer. Two steps. My fingers brush the door. I inch it open and step inside.

The steam hides his form behind the glass panel. I can only just make him out as he scrubs his fingers through his wet hair with his back to me.

I drag in a breath and then join him in the walk-in shower. My mouth goes dry at the sight of water and soap running down his muscular back. He's washing his hair, unaware of my presence behind him as I place my palm on his back. His body stiffens beneath my touch.

"Kingsley," I whisper, pressing my lips to his wet shoulder and feeling a shiver running through him.

He slowly turns. His hair lies plastered to his face, and water drips off his lips and nose. "Katherine?" His voice is a question and a warning all in one.

I sink down to my knees, my eyes locked on his as I run my palms up his thick thighs. How I feel right now is so unlike the previous times. I feel vulnerable like the man before me has the power to crush my heart into a thousand tiny pieces and blow their scattered fragments on the breeze.

I fist his cock and trail kisses up the hard length. "I want you, Kingsley," I whisper before taking him in my mouth, my heart fluttering in my chest.

He squeezes his eyes shut with a groan and his fingers tangle in my wet hair.

I love him with eager sucks and licks, relishing my name on his lips and the pleasure I see on his face. I want to make him feel good and steal a piece of his soul for safekeeping.

Kingsley is a drifter in the world, not tied to anything, but at this moment, he belongs to me.

"Fuck, Kath," he groans, pulling me up by my elbow. He slams his lips to mine as my back collides with the tiled wall.

I kiss him back and sink my nails into his shoulders. I hold him to me like I never want to let him go.

He grabs my hips and lifts me up, pressing me against the cold tiles before diving down and trailing kisses down my neck. His lips come back to mine, swallowing my moans. I can't breathe. I can't think.

"I need you, Kingsley," I plead between kisses, sliding my hands down his shoulders and muscular arms.

His eyes collide with mine, and we watch each other as water pours down our bodies. He leans forward, pressing his forehead to mine and squeezing his eyes shut. "Kath…"

I bury my fingers in his wet hair and hold him to me. Before I know what's happening, we're moving. I keep my eyes locked on his, my heart thundering in my chest.

My back hits the soft sheets, and he slides his palm over my leg as he crawls on top of me and settles between my spread thighs. He doesn't need to say a word; his eyes speak for him.

He palms my tit and squeezes it with his big hand while I run my hands up his chest and over the back of his neck.

I bury my fingers in his damp hair. "Make love to me, Kingsley!" I whisper as he skims his lips over my jaw and down my arched neck.

A tortured sound rumbles in his chest. He kisses a path down my body and buries his nose in my wet slit, breathing me in. I can't stop myself from moaning when I feel his hot breath on my most sensitive parts.

He pulls me down by my hips and licks me in one long

stroke, groaning deep in his chest. "I love how you taste!" He nuzzles my pussy.

I fist the sheet as he sets to work, licking and sucking until I'm writhing on the bed and moaning his name in the morning light that filters in through the curtains. He sinks a finger inside me and latches on to my clit, humming against my aching sex. I grind down on him and fist the sheets in a death grip. The sensation is too much and not enough at the same time.

"Come for me, baby." He sucks my clit between his teeth and inserts another finger, stretching me open.

As if he's the master of my pleasure, the captain of my ship at sea, I come hard, crying out in pleasure. My hips lift off the bed, my pussy meeting his eager tongue and thick fingers.

He climbs on top of me and settles between my trembling thighs. Leaning down, he roots through the pockets of his discarded jeans on the floor. He digs out a condom, and his eyes meet mine as he tears it open with his teeth and sheaths his cock.

I feel him at my entrance, big and hard. My eyes threaten to flutter shut as a breath rushes past my lips. I need him inside me.

Kingsley settles back down on his elbows. His eyes search mine as he whispers, "Are you sure?"

I reach up and skim my fingers over his stubbly cheek. His brown eyes shine with emotion. He looks as vulnerable as I feel—as if we're two souls about to cross dangerous waters together.

I nod, feeling his shaky breath on my face. "Yes, Kingsley. I'm sure."

He swallows thickly, and the muscles in his arms strain

as he slowly thrusts forward, inching his hard length into my tight canal.

My breath catches in my throat.

He stills, searching my face. "Are you okay?"

It hurts. "I'm okay," I breathe, digging my nails into his shoulders.

"I'm sorry, baby," he whispers, pressing his forehead to mine before slamming his hips home, causing me to cry out in pain. My eyes prickle with tears. I breathe through my teeth, bruising his arms with my tight grip.

He holds still, placing soft kisses on my cheeks and lips. "You're doing good, baby."

It feels so strange. It's unlike anything I've felt before. I'm filled with him, and it hurts, but it also feels strangely good, like I never want him off me again.

His body trembles with restraint. "You feel so amazing!"

"Move," I whisper, lifting my hips exploratively.

A breath rushes past his lips and wafts over my tingling lips. He pulls almost all the way out, grips the headboard, and slams back in. My body rocks on the bed. God, I can't look away from his eyes. He pulls back, traps his bottom lip between his teeth, and takes me again. My breasts bob. This time, I grip his back for leverage.

"Does it still hurt, baby?"

It does. But I don't tell him that. No, I don't want him to stop. Ever! I shake my head, and his back muscles tense as he pounds into me again. And again.

"Fuck," he curses, dropping his chin to his chest, his eyes squeezing shut. I pull him down to me by his neck and kiss him hungrily. I never want this moment to end. He responds, cradling my jaw and plunging his tongue against mine.

"Don't stop," I breathe between kisses as I wrap my legs

around his waist. The headboard bangs against the wall with every powerful thrust of his.

His eyes come back to mine. "I won't."

I watch him move on top of me. His hair is in his eyes, and his jaw is clenched. He's inside me, on top of me—he's everywhere. As are his hands. They explore every part of my body, gripping and squeezing.

"Does it feel good, baby?" he asks, palming my breast and tweaking my nipple.

It does. It still stings, but my chest is so full I feel like I might explode any moment. "Yes, Kingsley. It feels good." My eyes flutter shut when he reaches down between our bodies and rubs my clit.

"Look at me," he whispers, slamming into me, making my body rock on the bed.

I open my eyes and gasp as he pinches my clit. He dives down for a kiss, our teeth clashing. My pussy clenches around him, and he breaks away, breathing heavily. "I can't hold on much longer. You feel too good!"

"It's okay," I whisper, tasting his lips. I swallow his groans as he grips the headboard again and begins to slam into me harder and faster. His face contorts with pleasure, and his movements become jerkier.

"Shit," he curses.

*Thrust.*

"Fuck, I can't..."

*Thrust.*

He pounds into me a couple more times before he buries his head in my neck and stiffens with a deep groan. My heart aches with happiness as I hold him to me. His weight on top of me makes it difficult to breathe, but I welcome it. I can feel his heart hammer against mine like the wings of a hummingbird.

His breathing slowly returns to normal. He leans on his elbow and stares down at me with a soft smile. "Are you okay?"

"I'm more than okay," I whisper as I brush my fingers over his stubbly cheek.

Kingsley rolls off me and discards the condom. Then lies back down, resting his arm behind his head.

I roll over on my side and study his handsome profile, wondering what he's thinking about. He's staring at the ceiling, and I'm tracing my fingers over his bare chest.

"You stayed the night."

He swallows thickly, his eyes still on the ceiling. "Yeah, you were drunk."

I trail my fingers lower and explore the hard ridges of his stomach. "Thank you."

This time he meets my gaze. "It was nothing."

*Oh, but it was.*

Mr. Boomer jumps up on the bed and kneads his paws on Kingsley's stomach. I laugh, shooing him, but Mr. Boomer ignores me and continues to purr loudly.

Kingsley's smile is soft. He scratches Mr. Boomer affectionately behind the ear.

I lift the sheet. "Oh my god!" I whisper, mortified, as I spot the smeared blood between my thighs and on the sheet.

Kingsley simply laughs and looks smug in the way only men can.

"I'm so embarrassed," I say, palming my cheeks.

Kingsley's smirk grows into a full smile. "Why? It's natural."

"Natural or not, it's still embarrassing."

Kingsley shakes his head. "It's not. I bet I can make you even more embarrassed." His grin is mischievous.

I cross my arms and quirk an eyebrow. "Yeah? How?"

Kingsley sits up, scoots back on the bed, and shifts Mr. Boomer off him. I watch in horror as he leans over the side of the bed and pulls out my signed replica of Hunter's dick. He holds it up with a cheeky grin on his face.

I eat my words. I'm beyond mortified.

"I bet I can make you come with this," Kingsley says in a devilish voice, and I squeal with laughter as he pounces.

～

"Oh, my god!" Becky laughs, waiting for me by the steps outside school. "You so got laid!"

Hazel's eyes widen. She removes her sucker. "Did you pop your cherry?"

I bite my bottom lip to suppress my smile and shrug. "That obvious, huh?"

Becky grins. "Oh, yeah. You're glowing."

"Glowing?" I laugh, shaking my head as we ascend the steps.

Hazel smiles around her sucker, then removes it and says, "You've got that 'just fucked' glow." They high five over my head, and I roll my eyes as I open the front door.

I hold it open for them to step through. "You're as crazy as each other."

Becky flips off a guy who whistled. "So, how was it?"

I duck my head, blushing. "It was good."

Becky and Hazel exchange a glance over my head.

"It's too late," Hazel says to Becky, who nods and wraps her arm around my shoulder.

"What's too late?" I ask, bouncing my gaze between them.

We reach our lockers, and Becky inputs the code for

hers, glancing at me as I open mine. "You're in love with Kingsley."

I bristle and scan my eyes around the hallway for listening ears. "I'm not in love with him." My chuckle sounds as awkward as it feels.

Becky lifts an eyebrow. After closing her locker, she leans her shoulder on it and crosses her arms. "Keep telling yourself that. Meanwhile, Hazel and I will make sure to keep the freezer stocked with ice cream for when he breaks your heart."

I close my locker. My bag is much lighter now that I've removed some of the books. "I'm not in love, okay? It's just sex!"

"Denial is the first step to recovery." She looks at Hazel, who's reapplying her nude lipstick in the mirror inside her locker. "Kath can't see it herself yet. We have to be patient until she's ready."

I roll my eyes. "I'm right here. And I can't see it because it's not true."

"So not true..." Hazel puts the lipstick in her bag before closing the locker. She grins at me.

I roll my eyes and start walking. "I'm not in love with Kingsley!" How many times do I need to say it to make them believe me?

"If you say so," Becky replies. "So now that you're officially a woman... The audition is in two days. How do you feel?"

"Hunter isn't going to make me fuck him at the audition, is he?"

Becky raises an eyebrow. "Would that be a problem?"

I sense a trap. "Why would it bother me?"

"Oh, I don't know," Becky says, inspecting her nails. "Maybe the thought of fucking another man makes you feel uncomfortable? Perhaps you feel like you would betray a certain someone with dark hair, brown eyes, and a passion for BMX bikes if you rolled around in the sheets with Hunter?"

I laugh and shake my head. "Whatever, Becky. Think what you want."

I'm not in love with Kingsley. I can't be, can I?

Becky and Hazel come to an abrupt halt, and I nearly bump into Becky's back.

"Why did you stop?" My heart freezes in my chest as I lift my gaze.

Kingsley is leaning his forearm above Olivia's head on the locker, and their heads are bowed close together. Their noses nearly touch.

"They look chummy," Hazel says, removing her sucker. I don't miss the look she throws my way, eyes brimming with sympathy.

I shake myself off and hold my chin high. I push past her. I will not let my friends see me weak.

"Kath..." Becky whispers as she catches up. She hikes up her bag higher onto her shoulder.

"What?" I ask, ignoring the concerned look she shares with Hazel.

We're getting close. Olivia is running her palms up his chest and laughing. *Urgh!*

"Are you sure you're okay?" Becky asks, placing her hand on my back between my shoulder blades.

It makes me prickle. I don't like being touched when I feel weak and torn open like this. What is so fucking funny anyway that she has to laugh such a grating fucking laugh? "Of course I'm okay. Why wouldn't I be?"

Another shared look between my friends. Am I that obvious?

"Maybe they're just talking?" Hazel says around her sucker.

"Yeah, because friends nuzzle each other's necks," Becky says drily.

Hazel looks perplexed. "I hug you all the time."

Becky comes to a stop, glaring at Hazel as if to say, 'Choose your fucking moments.'

"What?" Hazel asks, looking genuinely confused.

"First of all. Very few people are as cuddly as you, Hazel. Secondly, you don't pop someone's cherry and then hug other girls at school the next day."

I throw my hands up. "It doesn't fucking matter, okay?!"

They blink, staring at me as I walk off.

"Good morning, Kingsley," I call out in the most cheerful voice I can manage while my heart lies bleeding on the ground. I don't stop. His head snaps up, but I keep walking.

"Kath, wait up!" I hear him shout, but I don't. I take a left down the next corridor, lock myself in the nearest empty classroom, and sink to the floor, the door at my back.

My heart hurts. *It fucking hurts!* What are we doing? Why am I letting myself get this involved? It was only supposed to be a bit of fun to gain experience. But, here I am, crying in an empty classroom while my heart bleeds all over the worn floor. My soldiers are frantically assembling their army, scrambling for any and all available weapons to defend its breached fortress from further harm.

# NINE

I soap my hands up and stare at my red-rimmed eyes in the mirror. I've reapplied my make-up the best I can, but the evidence of my emotional breakdown still shows.

The door behind me opens, and Olivia joins me in the bathroom, but instead of locking herself in one of the cubicles, she joins me by the sinks. She roots through her bag, eyeing me in the mirror. I ignore her as I rinse my hands under the faucet.

She reapplies her pink lipstick, then smacks her lips in the mirror and puts the lid back on. She drops the lipstick in her bag and turns to me. "You don't think he actually wants you, do you? You're just a shiny new toy."

I ignore her as I rub my hands vigorously. It's starting to hurt, but I might punch her in her perfect teeth if I don't keep rubbing.

She steps even closer and smiles tauntingly. "Ask him where he sleeps at night when he's not at Sam's."

I stop rubbing, staring at my raw hands. As if Olivia can sense that she's got to me, she twists the knife in further by whispering, "Ask whose pussy he licks."

She steps back and fluffs her blonde hair in the mirror before glancing at me. "No amount of make-up is going to hide your puffy eyes, bitch. Just admit that you lost this round and stay the fuck away."

When the door shuts behind her, her sickly perfume lingers in the air. I'm still staring at my red-raw hands under the running faucet.

∼

"Mind if I sit here?"

Knox looks up from his plate and stares at me in surprise. Then shakes himself off and pulls out the chair next to him. "Take a seat."

I can feel my friends watching me, but I can't find it within me to care.

"Katherine, right?" Jackson, one of Knox's friend's asks.

I nod as I move my food around the plate. "The one and only."

"Do you like basketball?"

I really don't. "Sure." I smile, fighting the urge to look over at Kingsley's table.

Knox places his arm on the back of my chair. A very subtle but deliberate move. I pretend I don't know what he's doing as I reach for my drink. I take a sip and smile at him over the rim.

He smiles back, playing with strands of my hair. "Still want me to take you out?"

I nearly choke on my drink. Nearly. I place it down on the table and twist the bottle between my fingers. "Convince me that it's a good idea, Knox."

He seems amused by my reply and leans in close,

brushing his lips over my ear as he whispers, "I can make you feel really fucking good!"

So can Kingsley. *Urgh!*

I search his blue eyes. "Have you ever been in love, Knox?"

He seems taken aback by my question but soon recovers and smiles. "Once or twice. Have you?"

"No."

The hand toying with my hair falters for a brief second before he leans in and places a kiss below my ear. I shiver, surprised by how forward he is.

"Can I talk to you, Katherine?"

Knox lingers with his lips on my neck as I lift my gaze and meet Kingsley's stormy eyes.

"Hi, Kingsley."

"Do you mind, Knox?" he growls.

Knox places one final kiss below my ear and leans back. He looks smug. "What's up, Kingsley?"

Kingsley narrows his eyes. His hands are fisted by his sides. "Can we talk?" he asks me, still looking at Knox.

I shrug, dropping my fork down on the plate and scooting my chair back.

"I'll see you later, Katherine," Knox calls after me with such dark promise I can't stop myself from looking over my shoulder.

Kingsley mutters under his breath as he steers us out of the cafeteria. The door has barely closed when he corners me against the wall. "What the fuck was that?"

A student walks past. I wait until she's out of earshot before I meet his fiery eyes. "What's wrong, Kingsley?"

He stares at me for a long minute before narrowing his gaze and leaning in close. "What's wrong? What is this?"

I laugh bitterly. "So I can't talk to Knox, but you can fuck Olivia?"

"What the fuck are you talking about?"

"Don't, Kingsley!" I say, shaking my head. I hug my schoolbook close to my chest like a shield. "Remember this morning? Or have you forgotten already how I caught you with your nose in Olivia's neck?"

He pushes off the wall, staring at me in disbelief. "Olivia is my friend. She's having a rough time right now. I gave her a hug."

I scoff as I walk off, but he scrambles after me and grabs my elbow. "Is that what this is about? You think I'm fucking Olivia?"

"Aren't you?"

He opens and closes his mouth, his eyes flicking between mine.

*"Ask him where he sleeps at night when he's not at Sam's."*

I squeeze my eyes shut. "Where do you sleep at night?"

"At Sam's. What is this, Katherine?"

"And the other nights? You said you only sleep at Sam's some nights. Where do you sleep the other nights?"

*"Ask him whose pussy he licks."*

His eyes darken. He sniffs, laughing bitterly. "What is this? The Spanish Inquisition? Are we a thing now, Kath? We fucked, and now we're a couple? Is that what you're saying?"

I slap him. I don't think; I just react. My hand stings from the impact, but I get a small sense of satisfaction from seeing his head snap to the side. "Fuck you!" I hiss, taking a step back as he stalks forward.

He forces me back against the wall. "I already did that, remember?"

His words are a slap in the face. He doesn't need to hit me for real to feel the impact. But it's my heart taking the hit and not my cheek. I swallow thickly, my eyes pricking with tears as I push past him and join the stream of students leaving the cafeteria. I feel his eyes on my back, but he doesn't follow.

*Well, fuck him.* Fuck him and his fucking perfect smile and brown eyes. Fuck him for making me feel this way.

~

"I thought I would find you here, miss," Geoffrey says, dropping down next to me on the grass.

"Yeah?"

Geoffrey sweeps his eyes over my father's headstone before leaning forward and placing a bouquet of flowers on the ground. "You've been gone all day. Your driver told me he dropped you off at the park this morning, but you weren't there when I went to check on you." He looks at the headstone again. "This was my next guess."

I'm staring at the setting sun in the distance.

"Do you want to talk about it, miss?"

I look back at him and drop my gaze, shaking my head. "No. I guess I just feel lost right now."

Geoffrey hums under his breath. "Your father would be proud of the young lady you're growing into."

I huff a laugh and tear at the grass. "I don't think so, Geoff. He was always so sure of himself. I'm not." I sigh. "I'm lost. I don't know who I am or what I'm doing."

Geoffrey pulls me into a rare hug, whispering against my hair, "We are all lost sometimes, miss. So was your father, especially toward the end. The answers will come to you, miss. When you're ready." He squeezes me and nudges his head to the bike by my side. "What trick did you work on today?"

I breathe him in. He smells of kindness and family. "I'm trying to learn a 180°."

Geoffrey hums in thought. "I don't know what that is, miss. You're going to have to show me."

"It's a 180° degree spin, but alright, I'll show you," I say as I get to my feet and brush off my knees. "I'm warning you though, we might be here a while."

Geoffrey wraps his arm around my shoulder, and we walk in silence. The setting sun casts an orange glow over the graveyard. It's peaceful.

"I trust you're not going to make a habit of skipping school? Your father might strike me down from the other side." He pretends to shudder, making me laugh.

I shake my head, my eyes on the grass as we walk. "No, I just needed a day to think."

"This doesn't happen to have something to do with a certain boy?"

I shrug and kick a rock. "Boys are confusing."

Geoffrey laughs, squeezing me. "You'll figure it out, miss."

"Are you ready?" I ask as we enter the nearby park. It's a small one, popular with elderly dog walkers, which is my main reason for choosing this place to practice in private. I don't know why I keep coming here in every spare moment, but how I feel when I land a new trick is unlike anything else. It brings me a surprising amount of satisfaction and makes me understand why Kingsley has such a passion for the sport.

"I'm ready, miss," Geoffrey says. He sits down on the bench. "I feel like this bench and I are best of friends." I smile as he strokes the backrest and says, "How are you bench? Did you have a good week? My week was splendid, thank you for asking." He winks at me.

I laugh as I put on my helmet and mount the bike. "Right, let's do this," I say and kick off the ground. I ride ahead some distance and then hop and rotate, landing it with a whoop and a cheer. It's far from perfect, but it's a 180° nonetheless.

"Bloody marvelous, miss."

I take a bow. My smile is impossibly big. "Thank you, Geoffrey. You should use such posh but foul language more often."

Geoffrey laughs a rare laugh and then stands up and walks over. He pulls me in for a hug. "Katherine Hamilton. Don't ever let a boy wipe that precious smile off your face."

I clutch his suit jacket. Tears wet my cheeks as the sun dips below the trees. "Thank you, Geoff."

"Anytime, dear. Now let's get you home. I believe you woke the slumbering mother beast inside of Maureen. She spent three hours cooking your favorite meal when she found out that you didn't go to school."

"I should skip school more often," I tease, pulling my bike along as we walk back to his car. The streetlights have come on.

Geoffrey harrumphs, his beard twitching. "I think I heard a fly buzzing."

～

When I close my bedroom door, I pause. Kingsley is sitting on my desk chair. There are shadows under his eyes, and his hair is tousled as if he has run his hands through it repeatedly.

"Why didn't you come to school today?" he asks, rising from the chair.

I watch his slow approach with my heart in my throat. "I needed a day to think."

He comes to a stop in front of me and searches my eyes.

"What are you doing here, Kingsley?"

"I needed to see you."

I don't reply.

"I'm sorry." He takes my hand in his and swallows thickly. "I shouldn't have said what I did. It was wrong."

Now it's my turn to swallow past the thick lump in my throat. "It was."

His fingers travel up my arm and past my shoulder. He cradles my jaw and takes a small step closer, his eyes glued to my lips. "Let me kiss you, Katherine Hamilton."

When he leans in slowly and brushes his lips over mine, my eyes flutter shut, and my hands come up to fist his t-shirt. I know I should be angry, but I can't stop myself from responding. I'm powerless to his kiss. He deepens it and grabs me more firmly.

Our exploring hands and breathless moans heal the bleeding wounds inflicted by our hurtful words. With one touch, he tears down my walls and steals yet another piece of my heart like thief in the night.

He lifts my t-shirt off, and his dark eyes meet mine before he takes my mouth and skims his warm hand over my bare stomach.

I break away from his lips, panting as he trails kisses down my neck. "What are we doing, Kingsley?"

His lips leave my skin. He pulls the back of his t-shirt over his head, and then his hot mouth is back on my body, kissing and nibbling. I'm left breathless.

"I don't fucking know!"

I grapple with his belt and zipper, but my hands tremble too much. He leans back and takes over. The belt soon lands on the floor, and he pulls the zipper down. His eyes are hot on mine as I strip out of my leggings. Then his tongue is in my mouth, and his hands are in my hair. I tug my panties down my legs, meeting his tongue stroke for stroke as we stumble to the bed. He sits down and pulls me on top.

I straddle his lap and sink my fingers in his hair. The strands are sinfully soft. I move in for another kiss, but Kingsley tears a condom with his teeth. He sheaths his cock and guides me onto his length, groaning low in his throat as I sink down.

My lips part and a breath rushes out of me. "Kingsley," I whimper. I'm never going to get used to this full feeling. It's heaven and hell. It's almost too much and not enough at the same time. When I've taken all of him, he guides my hips on his length. Up and down. Faster and harder. I seek his hot mouth, kissing him slow and deep.

He rips his lips away, and his brow comes down on mine. "You're so tight! You feel so fucking good, baby!"

My head falls back, and my long hair tickles my lower back as I roll my hips. "Kingsley," I breathe. I'm cresting. He feels so good. So fucking good!

He guides me down to his waiting lips, kissing me hungrily, moaning my name every time we come up for air.

I come with a cry, and he swallows my mewls and moans with violent kisses that leave me light-headed as the world around me spins.

Kingsley breaks away from my mouth with a grunt and his body stiffens as he comes. He thrusts shallowly from below, his hands clutching my hips in a way I know will bruise, but I welcome it. I want his pleasure—*I want him!*

I keep rolling my hips until he falls back on the bed and chuckles. He rubs his hands down his face. "Fuck, Kath…"

I don't want to climb off him. I want him inside me for as long as possible.

He squeezes my thighs gently. He doesn't say anything; he simply stares at me. "Have you ever been in love, Katherine Hamilton?"

I smile and shake my head. "No. Have you, Kingsley Delanoy?"

He grins, then shakes his head too. "No."

I reluctantly climb off him and lie down next to him, watching him discard the condom before lying back down. I roll over and trace my fingers over his chest. His heart is racing beneath my touch. "I'm auditioning tomorrow."

Kingsley stiffens.

I hold my breath as I stare at his profile.

Kingsley's jaw is pulsing. He rubs his hands over his mouth and blows out a breath. "What will happen at the audition."

I drop my gaze to my fingers on his chest and trace the word 'love' on his skin. I don't think he notices. "I don't know. I'll probably have to strip naked." I hesitate, flicking my eyes up to his handsome face. He's staring at the ceiling. "Becky suggested I might have to perform a blowjob."

This time he sits up and puts on his boxers. "I need the bathroom." He leaves me on the bed.

When the door clicks shut behind him, I scoot back on the bed and pull the sheet over me. My heart aches. *Why does he care?* He's fucking Olivia. He said it himself; we're not in a relationship.

"I should go," he says when he returns and grabs his clothes off the floor.

I watch him get dressed in silence while my heart crumbles to dust and blows away on an imaginary wind. *Why does he keep doing this?* "Where are you going?" I whisper, clutching the sheet to my chest.

He pockets his phone and puts his cap on backward, not meeting my eye. "I don't know. Probably Sam's."

"You can stay." My voice is barely a whisper.

"It's not a good idea. Good luck tomorrow. I hope I taught you something useful."

Then he's gone.

I stare at the door for a long minute before falling back on the bed and squeezing my stinging eyes shut. I will not cry over Kingsley. Not again!

"Fuck you, Kingsley!" I whisper as a treacherous tear slides free.

*"I already did that, remember."*

◈

*"Do you want me to fuck your tight little pussy harder? Are you going to be a good girl for me?"*

Hazel pops another popcorn in her mouth, staring avidly at the laptop screen.

"Did you see the technique she used when she sucked his dick? That's what you need to do if he asks you to suck his. Flatten your tongue, keep eye contact, and lick him from shaft to root. It's all about eye contact." Becky says.

I listen carefully. They have come over this morning to help me with last-minute preparations. I've showered and exfoliated. I don't think I have a single body hair left. I'm as ready as I'll ever be. Hazel did my hair, and Becky did my make-up. We've spent the last hour watching enough Hunter porn to last me for a lifetime. I feel like I know his every tell by now, and I haven't even touched him yet.

Hazel compared it to company research for a regular job interview. Only this time, the company to research is Hunter.

*"Squeeze my dick with your pussy. Yeah, just like that!"*

I snigger. Watching porn with your friends is awkward as hell.

Hazel reaches into the bowl and grabs a handful of popcorn. "How long until you need to be there?"

I check the time on my phone. I'm too nervous to eat popcorn. "Forty-five minutes."

Hazel tips the bowl to Becky, who shakes her head, eyes still glued to the screen.

"When his nostrils flare, it means he's getting close. Don't go for the jackpot just yet—draw it out, make him your bitch!"

I laugh. "I might not even be asked to do anything physical."

Becky gives me a droll lock. "Don't be naïve, Kath."

"Kitty," Hazel corrects, making me chuckle.

*"Oh yeah, ride my dick, you dirty slut!"*

"My point is," Becky says, waving a hand in my face to get my attention when it drifts to Hunter's cock on the screen. "You're auditioning for a role in a porn movie. It's not going to be enough to simply say, 'My name is Kitty. I'm eighteen years old, and I've slept with precisely one person. Twice. Please, hire me.' You need to show him why you're the best choice for this role. Why are you different from all the other girls lining up to suck his dick?"

*"Take my cock. That's it! Nice and slow, all the way in. Ah, yeah!"*

"I know you're trying to help, but you make me feel like I have failed already."

"You have an advantage over all the other girls," Hazel says around a mouthful of popcorn.

"Yeah? What's that?"

"You spilled coffee on him."

I throw my head back with a laugh. So does Becky. "Thanks, Hazel. I'll make sure to drop that into a conversation."

Becky winks. "A conversation that you'll never have because your mouth will be filled with cock."

I blush.

*"Fuck, baby, you like it when I slap your pink little pussy?"*

We burst out laughing, knocking over the popcorn bowl and startling poor Mr. Boomer, who was asleep on the bed.

# TEN

Kingsley: Ditch the audition. Come and hang out at the lake. Mylo says he's up for a handstand rematch.

I pocket my phone without replying and ignore the ache in my chest as I enter the building. I don't know what I expected when I came here, but certainly not this posh office building with glass walls and plants in the reception area. I feel like I'm here to ask for a loan and not audition for a porn movie.

A smart-looking receptionist smiles at me as I approach the desk. "Welcome to Hunter Wood productions. How may I help you today?"

My eyes bug out. I think I would have felt more comfortable if the audition was in a dingy, smoke-filled basement full of sweaty men. Or in a warehouse in the middle of nowhere. This woman with her too-tight bun and sparkly smile is stressing me out.

I grip the edge of the tall desk for something to hold on to and return her smile. "I'm Kitty Hamilton. I'm here for an audition."

Miss too-tight bun taps away on the computer. Her smile is still intact. "Oh yes, here you are. Mr. Hunter is personally auditioning you." She winks at me. "Let me phone him to let him know you've arrived."

I try not to fidget as she picks up the phone.

"Hi, Mr. Wood. Your two o'clock appointment is here."

Two o'clock appointment? What is this? The dentist? Is my mouth going to be filled with cock or new veneers?

Too-tight bun grins even wider, then puts the phone back down. "Mr. Hunter will see you now. Right through those doors"—she points—"you'll find an elevator. Mr. Hunter's office is on the third floor."

She dismisses me and begins tapping away on her computer. When she notices me dawdling, she raises her perfect eyebrows.

"Thank you," I breathe shakily and walk over to the elevator. I step inside, press the button for the third floor, and watch the doors close. My reflection is judging me, telling me to pull myself together.

"Easy for you to say," I hiss through a smile, so I don't look entirely unhinged in case there are surveillance cameras in here.

I'm wearing a little black number that Becky picked out after I stood staring at the clothes in my walk-in closet for over half an hour. What *is* appropriate attire for a porn audition? Do you come dressed in smart-casual, or are you supposed to come dressed in a trench coat with your best underwear on underneath or what? These things don't come with a handbook.

According to Becky, my legs are my best feature and need to be the focus, or as she put it, the feature on my living room wall—the first thing you see. Hence this barely-there dress.

The elevator pings, and I nearly jump out of my skin when the doors slide open. I pop my head out first and inspect the long corridor. When it dawns on me that I probably look like a British spy infiltrating the enemy's lair, I casually step out and roll my shoulders as if preparing myself for battle.

"I'm not awkward. I'm not awkward. I. Am. Not. Awkward!" I whisper under my breath as I walk quickly, scanning the doors until my eyes land on one with Hunter's name badge on it.

I stand there for a moment, contemplating if now is the time to just fucking run and never look back, but my hand has a life of its own, and before I know it, it knocks on the door. Not once but three times. I cringe, staring disbelievingly at my hand.

"Aah, Miss. Hamilton. I wondered if you would show up."

I tear my gaze away from my hand and smile what I think is a normal smile, but at this point, I can no longer tell. Hunter doesn't seem to think my smile borders on serial-killer crazy because he holds the door open and watches me step inside.

I sweep my eyes over the vast room. There's a desk with a smart-looking laptop at one end and an oversized couch with a TV mounted to the wall at the other. There's even a minibar.

"Not what you expected?" he asks, walking over to the desk.

I spin in a circle. Framed movie posters line the walls. "Not at all."

"Clarissa, I am not to be disturbed," Hunter says into the desk phone, following me with his eyes as I run my fingers over a glass shelf filled with award trophies. Not a speck of dust. He puts the phone down and walks over to me. His eyes burn my skin everywhere he looks. "What did you expect?"

"A dingy basement, more like."

He laughs, side-eyeing me. I'm struck once again by how incredibly handsome he is with his blonde hair and those cobalt blue eyes that crease at the corners when he smiles. "It might have started out that way, but I've built my empire from the ground up. Why don't you take a seat." He gestures to the oversized couch.

When I'm seated, he walks over to the minibar and proceeds to fill up two whiskey glasses.

I accept mine with a smile, watching him as he sinks down next to me. He rests his arm on the back of the couch and spreads his legs wide like he's the king of his domain.

I take a small sip, wincing.

He chuckles into his glass. "So, tell me, Kitty. What brought you here today?"

*You.* I clear my throat. "Do you want my rehearsed answer or the truth?"

He lowers the glass from his lips. His smile is blinding. "The truth, Miss. Hamilton. Always the truth."

Well, I am not exactly going to tell him that I'm here because I spilled coffee on him and decided he's the man I want to marry. Still, I can tell him part of the truth about why I'm sitting here next to one of the biggest pornstars in the country.

I swirl the amber liquid, watching it splosh against the sides. "The truth, Hunter, is that I have always lived by the rule book. I'm fucking fed up with being confined. I want to spread my wings. I want to do something that surprises not only those around me but also me. I want to look back at my life when I'm an old lady and be able to say, 'I did that.' I want to fucking live, Hunter. And I want to live free."

He takes a sip of his drink, watching me for a long moment. "You're young."

"Your point?" I ask, throwing back my drink, relishing the burn.

"The porn industry can be a fucking ugly business for young women such as yourself. It uses them up and spits them out. Did you know that the average porn career for a woman is three months? What makes you think you'll last any longer than all of those other hopefuls?"

I get up, walk over to the minibar, and pour myself another drink without asking if it's okay. "You want one?" I ask, tipping the bottle in his direction, and he shakes his head. He's amused. I take a big gulp, wincing. "I'm a Hamilton, Hunter Wood. I'm my father's daughter. I never lose when I set my mind to something." I walk toward him slowly, holding his gaze. "Now you tell me, Hunter. When was the last time a woman took *you* by surprise?"

I straddle his lap and ignore the fact that my skirt is now hiked up around my waist, flashing my black lace panties. Hunter has seen worse. Fucking is his job, after all, and it's freeing not to have to worry about my modesty.

I tip the bottle back and take a sip, then hold the amber liquid in my mouth as I lean in and coax him to open his mouth, which he does without protest, humor glinting in his blue depths.

He swallows the amber liquid, then smiles against my lips and takes the bottle from my hands. "I don't trust you with drinks, coffee-spiller."

I grab the lapels of his suit jacket and kiss him, tasting the bitter alcohol on his tongue. He's hard under me, and it's all I can do not to grind myself against him.

Before he has a chance to take things further, I plop back down on the couch and smile. "Any other questions, Hunter?"

He stares at me open-mouthed for a moment before chuckling and shaking his head. "Are you always this full of surprises."

I sweep my eyes over the big room. "You could say that. So what usually happens now at these auditions?"

Hunter places the bottle and his glass down on the circular coffee table. His blue eyes burn my skin. "Well, we usually talk about your ambitions. What you know about Hunter Wood Productions and your knowledge of the porn industry in general. What you hope to achieve by working for my company.

"Apart from orgasms?"

A surprised laugh bubbles out of him, and he shrugs. "Well, that's a perk of the job."

"And what happens next?"

He smirks. "You undress, so I can see the product."

"The product?" I reply, quirking an eyebrow. "So professional, Hunter." I rise from the seat. "You want to see me?" I slowly slide my straps down my shoulders, one by one. His hot eyes burn a path over my skin when my dress falls to the floor, pooling around my feet. "Eyes on me, Hunter," I whisper, unhooking my bra. It soon joins my dress. So do my panties. I step out and kick them aside, my nipples hardening under his piercing gaze.

He lifts his big hand and circles his finger in the air. "Turn. Slowly."

I do. My heart is jackhammering in my chest but fuck it, I feel alive.

When I meet his eyes again, he leans his head on the

back of the couch and stares at me from beneath lowered lashes. His big cock strains against his suit pants.

"What happens now?" My voice betrays my innocence.

He raises an eyebrow and sweeps his tongue over his bottom lip. "Now you convince me why I should hire you instead of all the other girls."

I swallow thickly as he smirks and begins unbuckling his belt. I can't deny that he turns me on. *God, does he!*

"Come here," he says, beckoning me over as he lowers his pants.

I walk over with tentative steps, feeling very much like I'm approaching the lion's den.

"Drop to your knees."

My clit throbs at his demand. I sink down between his spread legs. The hardwood floor is hard and cold beneath my knees.

"Good girl." He traps his bottom lip between his teeth and guides me down on his big cock with a hand pressed to the back of my head. "Nice and slow. Eyes on me."

I do as he says, exploring his thick head with my lips and tongue. I can tell he's aware of my innocence and gets off on it. It gets me off too, seeing the hunger in his eyes, but a small part of me screams at me to stop. Images flash in my mind of dark hair and a set of brown eyes—a smile that has the power to crumble my defenses.

I push down all thoughts of Kingsley and fist Hunter's dick because I can't take it all. It's too big. I suck him eagerly, moaning around his hard length.

He shifts and digs in his pocket for his phone. He pulls it out and swipes the screen. "You don't object, do you?"

I shake my head before sinking down further on his cock and taking him deeper. It feels weird to be filmed giving head, but I better get used to it if I'm going to star in one of his movies.

Hunter holds the camera up with one hand. He fists my hair with the other, guiding my movements. "Fuck, you have pretty lips!" he groans, bending my head back so he can get a better angle with his camera.

*Flatten your tongue, keep eye contact, and lick him from shaft to root. It's all about eye contact.*

Becky's words echo in my head. I look Hunter in the eye as I flatten my tongue and slap his cock over it.

He hisses between his teeth. "Good girl, just like that!" He pushes me back down until his dick hits the back of my throat. I gag and pull back, but he holds me in place until I have no choice but to swallow around his thick head.

"Fuck!" he groans, thrusting shallowly down my throat. Tears are streaming down my cheeks and ruining my carefully applied make-up. "Fuck, Kitty. Take it!"

God, his dirty talk makes my pussy clench.

"Look at the camera, beautiful," he says as he pulls out and fists his thick shaft. "Good girl, open your mouth." He rubs the head of his cock over my lips and grins behind the camera. "Suck on the head. Make sure to purse your lips."

"Bossy!" I tease, then do as instructed, tasting his salty precum. "Does it feel good, Hunter? I bet you wish you could fuck my pussy?" I grin against his tip, enjoying this new side of myself. I love watching Hunter squirm. It makes me feel powerful.

"Would you like that?" he smirks, fisting my hair painfully. "Do you want me to pound your tight little cunt?"

I grin and swirl my tongue around his head, pumping his long shaft. "No, Hunter. You can't have my pussy."

He laughs a surprised laugh and lifts his head off the

back of the couch, watching me work his cock with eager bobs of my head.

"Why can't I have your pussy?" He grunts, brushing away strands of hair stuck to the tears on my cheeks.

I swallow him down again, moaning around his cock, then pull back and place a kiss on the head, batting my eyelids for full effect. "Because you haven't hired me for the movie. You don't get to try the goods before purchase."

He groans, sounding tortured. Then forces me down on his dick again as if to punish me. "Fuck, such a cocktease!" Hunter guides me up and down on his cock hard and fast. He pulls out and orders me to stick my tongue out.

I stare at the camera while he strokes himself until his warm cum coats my tongue and cheeks in quick squirts. I can't quite describe the multitude of emotions inside of me right now. I am so turned on; it's painful! I also feel a sense of shame, but even worse—the shame turns me on more. It feels so wrong but so fucking good at the same time! The dirtier it gets, the more I want.

Hunter tucks himself back in and reaches for the glass on the coffee table while I pull my panties back on. He doesn't offer me a tissue or anything to wipe his cum off my face. He simply leans back on the couch and stares at me over the rim of his glass. I can't help but feel like this is a test. He wants to see if I get unnerved.

My lips curve. I dart my tongue out and lick his cum off my lips. *Fuck, my clit is pounding.* I steal his drink off him and down it before taking a seat on his circular coffee table and knocking over his expensive bottle of whisky in the process. I kick my heels off and place a foot on the edge. Hunter's eyes flick up from my black lace panties, and he hides his amused grin behind his thumb as he rubs the corner of his lips.

I run my fingers down my body, stroke my hand over my pussy, and grind down with the heel of my palm. "You don't mind if I help myself, do you?" I ask, moving my panties aside, plunging two fingers inside my soaking wet pussy. I'm so aroused it won't take much at all.

"Not at all," he grins, motioning for me to continue.

I let my head fall back as I begin fucking myself until my thighs tremble and my breasts heave. "Oh, fuck, Hunter!" I breathe, biting down on my lip until I taste blood on my tongue. I pull my fingers out to rub my clit in firm circles. Faster and harder until I explode and cry out in pleasure. The orgasm holds me in its grip until the whole world spins. I gasp, my chest shaking with aftershocks.

Hunter is watching me when I blink my eyes open, and his sparkle with amusement. "Feeling better now, Kitty?"

I try to go for nonchalant like I didn't just get myself off in front of a fucking pornstar. "Much better, thank you. Will that be everything, Mr. Hunter?"

He chuckles heartily. "Unless there is anything else you would like to discuss?"

*Discuss.* As if we did any discussing today. I stand up and get dressed. "No, I think we covered everything, Mr. Wood. I look forward to working with you."

Hunter simply grins as he watches me saunter out of his office.

The moment I close the door behind me, I press a palm to my lips to silence the hysterical laughter that bubbles up. What the hell happened in there? Wait until Becky and Hazel hear about this! They'll never let me live this down.

"You did what?" They squeal in unison as we sit on Becky's bed, eating candy and watching a crap movie.

"I got myself off on his coffee table."

Becky sniggers. "Look at you, miss adventurous, and here I thought you were the stuck-up one in this friend group."

I laugh around the sucker in my mouth, then take it out and say, "Gee, thanks, Becky."

"What did he say when you had finished?"

I shrug. "He didn't say much. He looked amused and asked me if I had any more things I would like to discuss."

"And what did you say?" Hazel asks, reaching for a cola candy.

"I told him that I look forward to working with him and then left."

Their eyes bug out.

"What?" I ask, placing the sucker back in my mouth.

Becky shrugs, biting off a piece of her jelly candy. "You surprise us."

"Yeah? How?"

"I don't know. You're usually so... Well, you don't step out of line."

I nod in thought, removing the sucker. "Which is exactly why I want to do this!"

"Have you heard from Kingsley?" Becky asks as she grabs another jelly candy.

I shake my head. I haven't replied to his last text yet.

They exchange a glance.

Hazel chews her cola candy, then says, "Are you going to accept the part if you get it?"

I nod as I twirl the lolly in my mouth. "It's the perfect way to get Hunter to fall in love with me."

"Is that what you really want? For Hunter to fall in love with you?"

I furrow my brows. "Why wouldn't I?"

They exchange another glance before Hazel shrugs and says, "We thought that with everything that's happened between you and Kingsley that maybe—"

"Maybe what? I would change my mind? Well, I haven't."

"Okay," Becky says placatingly. She reaches for my hand. "It's just that you don't know Hunter."

"But I will get to know him." I move my hand away. What don't they get? I *need* to do this for myself.

Becky's eyes flash with regret, and she attempts a smile. "We just want you to be happy."

"Let's pretend for a minute that I'm in love with Kingsley...."

Hazel nods. "Yes, let's *pretend*."

I glare at her. "Even if I was in love with him, he's made it perfectly clear that he isn't interested in a relationship. We said right from the start that it was only a bit of fun to help me gain some experience. Nothing more."

"And did you feel experienced today?" Becky winks, lightening the mood.

I shrug one shoulder and bite down on the lolly. When I finish chewing, I say, "I think I made an impression."

They both laugh and throw candy at me.

I pick up a handful of my lap and throw it back with a mischievous smile.

"I'm jealous," Hazel sighs longingly as she unwraps another cola candy. "You sucked off Hunter Wood."

Becky chuckles, pushing Hazel's shoulder. "Girl, you're crazy!"

Hazel grins. "Kath has us beat! She's the one who auditioned for a part in a porn movie today. What can we possibly do to top that?"

"We could always corner the headteacher in the office and involve him in a foursome." Becky winks. "I think that will be up there with Kath's crazy."

"Ewwww," Hazel laughs, throwing a sucker at Becky. "Make that a threesome. I'm going nowhere near him."

Becky shrugs, grinning. "Suit yourself. Kath and I will just have to rock his world by ourselves." She picks up a red and white, circular rock-candy lollypop and licks it enthusiastically, moaning all the while.

"You've got the technique all wrong," I jest, stealing it off her. "You've got to flatten your tongue. It's all about the eye contact."

I shift on the bed, so I'm lying on my belly. I bring the lolly to my lips and look up at Becky as I purr, "You want me to suck your cock real good, daddy?"

I pretend to give the huge lolly a blowie, making Becky and Hazel laugh until tears stream down their cheeks. It's too big to take in my mouth, so I'm mostly licking it and moaning, but it makes my friends laugh. "Oh yeah, daddy. You like that, don't you?"

Becky wipes tears from her eyes. "You're fucking crazy!"

I wink, handing her the lollypop. "Now, you try."

∼

I close the bedroom door and nearly have a heart attack when I spot the hunched figure on my desk chair.

Kingsley lifts his head as I turn the light on and drop my bag down on the floor by the door. He looks like a wreck with dark lines under his eyes, disheveled hair, and wrinkled clothing. My room reeks of alcohol.

I hesitate for a moment. "You're drunk."

He throws his head back and laughs miserably. "Maybe just a teeny tiny bit," he says, demonstrating with his fingers. He rises from his chair and stumbles over, knocking over my desk chair in the process. "You didn't reply to my text this morning."

"I've been busy."

He sniffs before pulling at his dark hair, staring up at the ceiling for a long moment. His eyes come back to me. "How did the audition go?"

I push past him as I walk over to my desk and right the chair. "It went well."

"Yeah?"

I meet his stormy and hazy eyes. "Yes, Kingsley," I say carefully. "What are you doing here?"

He laughs bitterly. "What? You don't want me here anymore?"

"I didn't say that, but you're drunk, Kingsley." And angry, but I don't say that.

"I don't fucking know what I'm doing here," he says, staring at the moon's silvery glow on my wooden floor, his face scrunching up as if in pain. He stumbles over and comes to a stop in front of me. "What happened at the audition?"

I try to take a step back, but the desk is behind me. I can't escape the fire in his eyes, and the shame I felt earlier today has now taken on a sickening feeling. It clogs my throat and makes it difficult to breathe. "Let it go, Kingsley."

His eyes, like fire, keep me rooted to the spot. "I don't think I will." His voice is deadly silent, like the calm before the storm. "Did you fuck him?"

I shake my head, feeling tears of shame pool in my eyes. My voice is thick as I whisper, "No."

"What happened, Katherine? Or should I call you *Kitty?*" He spits the name.

I place a shaky palm on his chest to soothe him, but he grips my wrist in a tight grip. It hurts.

"Tell me the truth, *Kitty.*"

I shake my head, and my tears spill over as I try to tug my wrist free with no success. "You're hurting me, Kingsley!"

"Did he see you naked?"

"Why do you care, Kingsley?"

He finally releases my wrist, and I stumble back against the desk, knocking over books and a mug. They crash to the floor, and the sound is deafeningly loud in the silent night.

Kingsley reaches forward and shoves my dress down past my shoulders, snapping the strap in the process. I don't stop him. My breast pops free, and he palms it roughly, burning me with his eyes. "Did he see you naked?"

I'm trembling. "Yes..."

His eyes collide with mine. I feel so exposed right now as he continues kneading my sensitive flesh. He's rough, unlike the other times he touched me. There's no love in his touch, only anger.

He tweaks my nipple between his thumb and index finger, whispering darkly, "Did you suck his dick?"

A sob breaks free. I push his hand away and cover my body. The left strap is broken, so I'm forced to clutch the front of the dress to hide my nakedness from his angry eyes. "You need to leave, Kingsley."

He nods slowly, swaying on the spot. "I had this sick feeling inside me all day. I couldn't fucking stop thinking about you. I wanted to punch something every time I thought of that man's hands on your body."

I stay silent, watching him rage.

His eyes collide with mine again. He steps forward and grabs my jaw in a rough grip. "Did you suck his dick?"

My breathing is out of control. I don't answer.

Kingsley jostles my jaw, and I feel more tears trail down my cheeks. I hate the hurt in his eyes. I put it there.

"Answer me, goddamnit!"

"Yes," I whisper, dropping my gaze.

He lets go of me like he's been burned and stumbles backward.

"It didn't mean anything, Kingsley!" I reach for him, but he pushes me off and fists his hair.

His words are slurred and laced with pain as he says, "That's rich coming from you who accused me of fucking Olivia because you saw us hugging."

"You knew I was auditioning for this role. I told you right from the start. What do you think will happen if I get offered the part?"

"SHUT UP!" he yells as he picks up a book off the floor and throws it at the wall. "Just shut the fuck up!"

How is it possible for shame to feel so good one minute and so fucking wrong the next? I've never felt this dirty before. The disgust in Kingsley's eyes hurts more than a physical punch to the stomach.

"Where are you going?" I stupidly ask when he grabs his backpack and stumbles over to the door.

"I got you a rose," he whispers brokenly, pointing to the bed. "I don't know why the fuck I bothered."

"Wha—?"

He leaves.

I'm still staring at the blood-red rose on my bed when the front door slams closed.

*He got me a rose?*

Another sob breaks free. I press my shaking hands over my mouth. The pain in my chest is suffocating. I scramble over to the bed and pick up the flower. The thorns are prickly, much like the walls surrounding Kingsley's heart. It's impossible to get close to him without getting hurt in the process.

# ELEVEN

I spin my head to the left and twist my body around, landing perfectly. I'm ready to start practicing on the 360°.

"What the fuck are you doing?" Becky asks, and I snap my head up, surprised to see her here.

I remove my helmet and hang it on the handlebar. "I'm practicing tricks. What are you doing here?"

Becky opens and closes her mouth like a fish while Hazel grins around a sucker.

"You weren't at school again. We got worried. Geoffrey told us to come here, but he didn't mention"—she gestures to the bike—"that. When did *that* happen?"

I squint against the sun and shrug. "A while ago. Kingsley took me to the skatepark at the abandoned warehouse one day."

"The leggings?" Becky gestures to my t-shirt next. "And the top. Wow, I never thought I would see the day."

"I like it," Hazel says, removing the sucker. It's apple-flavor today.

I gesture to my bike. "Want to have a go?"

Becky laughs so hard she has to clutch her stomach, but

Hazel shrugs and puts on the helmet. "Sure, why not. What do I do?"

"Well, we'll start with something as simple as a bunny-hop."

"Simple, you say?" Becky sniggers and I wink, remembering when I thought it looked complicated. It's amazing what you can achieve when you put your mind to it.

∽

"I think I did well," Hazel says when we take a seat on Geoffrey's favorite bench. Becky has gone to buy ice cream from the parked ice cream van that drives by religiously at this time every day.

"You certainly did." I high-five her.

Becky returns with three ice creams and hands us one each. She takes a seat next to me on the bench. "Talk to us."

I lick off the melting ice cream dripping down the side of my cone. "Kingsley was in my room when I returned home last night."

"Never!" Becky says, wide-eyed.

"He was drunk."

Hazel brushes a strand of hair away from her face and tucks it behind her ear. "What did he say?"

I cringe. "He demanded to know what happened at the audition."

"Ouch. Did you tell him?"

I nod, my eyes pricking with tears. No amount of hours practicing on the bike can remove this sick feeling in my gut.

"What did he say?" Becky asks quietly. Her voice is thick with sympathy.

I watch an elderly lady feed a dog treat to her Cocker

Spaniel. "He didn't say much. He tore my dress off and threw one of my books at the wall."

"He tore your dress off?"

Fuck it sounds so bad. "Yes. He was hurt. He pushed it down, palmed my breast, and asked if Hunter saw me naked."

"Fuck, I'm sorry!" Becky says and Hazel rubs my back.

My bottom lip trembles. "I deserved it."

Becky rears back. "Fuck, no! Don't say that!"

"But I hurt him. I didn't realize that he would care."

They stay silent for a while before Hazel says in a quiet voice, "We tried to tell you."

I wipe my cheeks. The dog is now running after a ball. "He left a rose on my bed."

"Oh, god..." Becky breathes.

"I know." I kick at the ground with my trainer. My ice cream is melting. "I couldn't face him today."

"Why the fuck did I bother with ice creams?" Becky mumbles, echoing my thoughts.

Hazel inspects hers. "I don't know, but we can salvage this. If we hurry up, it'll be like eating a solid milkshake."

"Solid milkshake?" I say, laughing through my tears.

"Well, it's runnier than ice cream but more solid than a milkshake."

"Trust you to lighten the mood," Becky laughs.

"Let's eat our ice creams as fast as we possibly can. The first one to get a brain freeze loses."

"Sure, why the fuck not." Becky grins.

"On three."

"Three." Becky nudges me with her shoulder.

Hazel grins. "Two."

They both look to me, ice creams at the ready.

"One."

I drop my application down on the career adviser's desk. "I followed your advice."

Mrs. Ackland looks up from her laptop and pops her gum. "You came to your senses then?"

"Oh no, my senses are very much intact. I am still pursuing porn. But you told me to have a backup plan." I tap the file on the desk. "This is my backup plan."

Mrs. Ackland moves the file toward her and reads through it. She pops her gum, places the file back down on the desk, and leans back in her chair. "A smart choice."

I try not to preen.

"Are you aware, Katherine, that if you enter the porn indu—sorry, *adult entertainment* industry, it might limit your other options going forward? For a man, it's relatively easy to move on from adult entertainment, but there is a certain stigma attached to it for women. You might struggle to find real work after." She holds a hand up when I go to protest. "Before you get all huffy and puffy. I am not suggesting that sex work isn't 'real work.' But suppose you decide to take on a more active role in your father's company—now *your* company. In that case, you need to be prepared to meet some obstacles along the way if you also pursue porn. You're a woman in a man's world."

I plant both my hands on the desk and lean in close. Mrs. Ackland pops her gum a breath away from my face. "I am a Hamilton. I will take on the porn industry and succeed, and I will take my father's company to further heights. There is no failure in my name, Mrs. Ackland. When I say I want to succeed at something, I do. Don't underestimate me because it only makes me try that much fucking harder!"

*Pop.*

"In that case, Miss. Hamilton. You can't do it. You're going to fail." She winks, making me smile reluctantly.

"Watch me, Mrs. Ackland!" I say as I walk over to the door. I open it and step out, but before I leave, I pop my head back in. "And it's Kitty—Kitty Hamilton."

∾

*Kitty's bucket list:*

- *Marry Hunter.*
- *Take on the porn industry (and be successful).*
- *Beat Kingsley in a BMX competition.*
- *Take on a more active role in my father's company.*

I chew on my pen as I stare at the list. The history teacher rambles on, and it's not long before my treacherous eyes seek out Kingsley. He sits playing on his phone, hunched in his seat. His backward cap hides his normally tousled hair, but it's grown longer and peeks out from the sides and back. He's also more tanned than usual, as if he spent the last couple of days by the lake, bathing in the cool water. We haven't spoken since he left my bedroom that night. I miss him. I miss his smile and his deep laugh.

I take my phone out of my bag and send him a text.

> Me: X-Up. A rider turns the handlebars 180° while in the air. The X-Up is spun toward your front leg. If you spin in the opposite direction, it's known as an X-Down.

There's no biting back my smile when I spot him grinning as he reads my text.

He types out a response.

Kingsley: Talk dirty to me, baby.

I duck my head, my cheeks growing warm.

Me: Crankflip. A Bunny Hop in which you turn the cranks backward 360°.

Kingsley: I'm getting hard.

I laugh, causing Becky to raise her head from her paper. She looks at me questioningly.

My fingers fly over the screen.

Me: This might make you come… Tailwhip: A 360° rotation of a frame around the front end of your BMX.

Kingsley: Fuck woman, such a cocktease!

Me: The tailwhip is an advanced trick, one of the hardest basic tricks out there. Can you do it?

Kingsley: Name a trick I can't do.

Me: Show it to me sometime?

Kingsley: If you're a good girl.

I bite my lip, groaning quietly. My clit is already throbbing like the little traitor she is.

Me: I can be a very, very good girl, Kingsley.

Surely sexting is good practice, right?

Kingsley: Trust me, I know first-hand just how good you can be ;)

I worry my bottom lip.

Me: I'm sorry, Kingsley...

He doesn't reply, and when I chance a look, he's staring at the phone in his hands. His jaw is pulsing.

Me: I loved the rose.

Kingsley: I shouldn't have done what I did. I was a dick.

Me: You can make it up to me later ;)

Kingsley chuckles, and we share a smile. Something passes between us—an understanding. We both have prickly thorns that cut deep and draw blood. We can't come away from this thing between us without scars.

～

I collapse onto his bare chest, slick with sweat and breathing like I've run a marathon. "God, Kingsley, that was... wow!"

Kingsley chuckles and slaps my ass. "Make up sex is the best sex for a reason."

I chuckle as I roll off him. "Say that again. We need to argue more often."

A deep laugh rumbles in his chest. "So, you memorized BMX tricks?"

I move onto my stomach and smile at him. "I learned a lot more than that, Kingsley."

He traces his fingers over my cheek, his eyes flicking between mine. "Yeah?"

I nod, biting my lip. "I've been practicing. I can do some more tricks now."

Kingsley rolls over on his side and slides his warm hand down my slick back. "I haven't seen you at the skatepark."

"I went to a different park."

He grins as he palms my ass cheek and squeezes.

"I told you I'm coming for you, Kingsley. You better watch out!"

He chuckles, kneading my ass. "I would love to see you try."

"You shouldn't underestimate me, Kingsley."

"So you keep telling me." He slaps my ass.

"I'm going to beat you in a competition one day. It's on my bucket list."

He crawls on top of me and nuzzles the back of my neck. His slick chest sticks to my back, but fuck if I care. "Bucket list?" He chuckles, nipping at the sensitive skin with his teeth.

"You know... Things I want to accomplish before I'm an old lady."

Kingsley pushes my leg up by my side and sinks inside my tight pussy. I bite back a loud moan, fisting the sheet.

"Talk to me some more about how you're going to beat me."

*Thrust.*

I whimper. "Trust me, Kingsley. I won't give up trying. I'll practice until I'm ready to take you on."

"Is that so?" he says, amused, and slams into me hard.

"Fuck," I groan, arching my ass up like a cat in heat.

He grasps the back of my neck firmly. "What makes you think you can beat me?"

*Thrust.*

I'm panting. "Anyone can win if they practice hard enough. I'm a Hamilton. I never lose."

"Never lose, huh?" He says, tightening his hold on my neck.

*Thrust.*

"We shall see about that."

"Ahh, fuck!" I moan, and Kingsley smiles as he moves his big hand around to the front of my neck and wraps fingers around my throat.

He bends my head backward, whispering against my temple, "You've got it all wrong, Kitty Hamilton. I always win!"

He takes me harder and faster, fucking me into the mattress and leaving me breathless.

"I never lose." He grinds his cock deep, pulls out, and plunges back in, spearing me with his hard dick. "I always conquer!"

I chuckle before a particularly punishing slam of his hips makes me groan. "If you say so, babe. But this time, you've met your match."

Kingsley's chest rumbles. He tightens his grip on my throat, whispering filthy words in my ear. He owns me, body and soul. I'll never recover from the onslaught of his love.

I come for a third time that day, moaning his name. I'm shaking and trembling as Kingsley pulls out with a groan and milks his cock until his warm cum coats my back.

When he's done, he collapses next to me, looking

sinfully wrecked. "You're killing me, woman!" He rolls onto his side and strokes his fingers through the cum on my back. I watch him. My chest feels like it's going to pop like a balloon, as if there's not enough room inside me to contain all of these emotions.

He is watching me too, eyes flicking between mine.

Our moment is interrupted when my phone rings. I keep meaning to change the ringtone, but for now, it's this annoying old-fashioned ring that reminds me of a retro rotary phone.

I miss his eyes on me as I reach for it on the nightstand and swipe the screen without looking at the caller ID. "Hello." I'm smiling at Kingsley again. He strokes his hand down my face, and his eyes fall to my mouth as he brushes his thumb over my bottom lip.

"Kitty Hamilton. Remember me?"

My heart jolts in my chest. I bolt upright and pull the sheet over my chest. "Hi, Hunter."

Kingsley stiffens next to me.

I tuck my hair behind my ear. My hands are shaking.

"I had a good time. You surprised me, Kitty. You have a certain innocence about you combined with a fire that's enough to bring any man to his knees."

I'm staring at my trembling hand in my lap. I need a manicure.

"I want to offer you the part."

Swallowing past the thick lump in my throat, I whisper a shaky, "Thank you." I don't know how I feel. Happy? Scared? Worried about Kingsley's reaction?

"Great, I'll have my receptionist email you the contract and all the details. If you have any further questions, give the office a call."

"Okay," I breathe. I really need a manicure…

"Good, I'll see you soon, Kitty."

The line goes dead.

I drop the phone in my lap, still staring at my hand.

The bed shifts. "I'm sorry. I know how much you wanted the job," Kingsley says, moving my hair aside to kiss my shoulder.

"I got the part."

He freezes with his lips on my skin, and for a moment, neither of us says a word. My pink nail polish is chipped. When did that happen?

Kingsley slides his hand down my arm. "You're going to turn it down, right?"

Am I?

A tear falls on my hand. I wipe my cheeks and meet his brown eyes. "Why do you want me to turn it down?"

*Just say it, Kingsley! Please, tell me you're in love with me, and I'll cancel it right now. I'll drop this opportunity—for you.* I think these things, but I don't voice them out loud.

Kingsley flicks his eyes between mine before standing up. He rubs the back of his neck. "It's up to you, Kitty. I just thought you didn't want to do it anymore?"

I search his face for what feels like an eternity as another tear escapes. It trails a slow path down my cheek and over my lips. I wipe it off. "Is that the only reason you want me to turn this job down? Nothing else?"

*Please say it, Kingsley. Please...*

Kingsley shrugs, grabbing his boxers off the floor. I watch in silence as he pulls them on. His movements are slow and controlled. He leans down for his jeans and puts them on too. "Take the job if you want. I don't want to be the reason you turn it down. You need to do what makes you happy." He puts his hands on the bed and leans forward, placing a soft kiss on my lips. "I'll see you tomorrow."

"Why do you always leave?" I ask, tears seeping past my lips into my mouth.

"Look,"—he pulls his t-shirt on—"I'm in your way. You wanted me to teach you, right? You don't need me anymore."

"That's not true," I whisper so quietly I know he can't hear, but on the inside, I'm screaming. I want to plead, beg and crawl on my knees if I have to.

I stare down at my lap as he walks out.

Again.

*"Have you ever been in love, Kingsley?"*

*"No, I haven't. Have you?"*

*"No. I don't think I would know what love feels like..."*

# TWELVE

I turn another page in the photo album and wipe a stray tear from my cheek. I'm crying a lot these days. As if the past has caught up with me, and now I have no choice but to *feel*.

I startle when a warm hand squeezes my shoulder and look up to find Geoffrey behind me. He's smiling at the photograph of my father and me at the local science museum.

"I remember that day, miss. Your father was particularly fond of the Second world war exhibition."

Smiling, I turn another page as Geoffrey rounds the couch. I'm sitting in the living room. The lit fire was unnecessary, but I've missed the crackling sound, so I lit it earlier, and now it's too hot in here. "If I remember correctly, I was bored."

"Correct, miss," Geoffrey says, pinching his trousers above the knees as he takes a seat next to me. "You were eight years old and complained the whole time. There was too much information to read and too little to do. Your father enjoyed staring at old items from the war, but you certainly didn't. If it didn't sparkle, make a noise, or taste good, you weren't interested."

I trace my fingers over my father's big smile. "You've been like a father to me too, Geoffrey."

His mustache twitches. "Your father certainly couldn't handle such a confident young lady by himself."

I laugh, turning the page. The next photograph is one of us planting strawberry seeds. "I wasn't confident."

"But you certainly knew your own mind from a young age. You still do, miss. When you want something, you go after it, and you don't give up."

I contemplate his words. The fire continues crackling. "Even if I sometimes go after the wrong things?"

Geoffrey rubs his mustache. "I don't think it's that black and white, miss. They say all roads lead to Rome. In that case, even the wrong roads guide you home."

I lift my eyes. "Were you always this wise?"

He smiles softly, then points to another picture. "We tried to warn you not to jump down from that branch. Did you listen?"

I shake my head with a laugh. "You told me I couldn't climb up the tree. I had to prove you wrong."

"Aye, miss, and you ended up with a broken ankle." He tuts. "Most unfortunate."

I turn the page and smile when I spot a photograph of Geoffrey covered in flour after eight-year-old me decided he had to help me bake a cake. "Was that the time I decided to decorate you in icing sugar instead of the cake?"

Geoffrey chuckles. "That would be correct, miss."

I close the photo album and shift on the couch, so I'm facing Geoffrey. "I have to make a choice Geoffrey. And I don't want to make the wrong one."

"Then you have to listen to your heart."

I look over at the fire, watching the flames dance. "The heart is a fickle thing, Geoff."

He stares at the fire, too, humming under his breath. His eyes are warm and kind when he looks back at me. "Even so, I think you should listen to it. You'll regret it if you don't." He stands back up and squeezes my shoulder before taking his leave.

∼

The wind is howling outside, and rain is hammering on the bedroom window. I roll over on my side and pull the quilt up to my chin. It's still early, but I feel mentally and physically exhausted.

*"You're going to turn it down, right?"*

*"Why do you want me to turn it down?"*

*"It's up to you, Kitty. I just thought you didn't want to do it anymore?"*

*"Is that the only reason why you want me to turn this job down? Nothing else?"*

*"Take the job if you want. I don't want to be the reason you turn it down. You need to do what makes you happy. Look, I'm in your way. You wanted me to teach you, right? You don't need me anymore."*

Kingsley wants me to turn down the job and choose him. He didn't say so outright but in a roundabout way. He wants me to pick him because I truly want to be with him and not out of pity. He's so confusing. He doesn't want a girlfriend, but he expected me to turn down the job. Why?

Right now, I'm struggling to remember why I ever thought Hunter seemed like such a good idea. He's handsome and successful, but what kind of person decides they want to marry someone they spill coffee on in a coffee shop because they're attractive? Me. That's who. I'm that person. Kingsley was right all along. I am shallow.

I bury my head in the pillow and groan. I do want Kingsley. So what am I doing? Why didn't I tell him that I didn't want to accept the part?

"Fuck it," I breathe and reach for my phone on the bedside table. I pull open the drawer and grab the papers I printed from Hunter's email. I dial the number at the top of the page. It connects on the third ring.

"Hunter," his deep voice sounds in my ear.

I freeze, my breath catching. "Hunter? This is Kath—err, Kitty. I thought you gave me your secretary's number? I was going to leave a message."

His chuckle is deep and raspy. "No, I gave you my personal number."

*Obviously!*

"Oh, okay," I whisper, my heart racing in my chest.

"So, Kitty," he purrs. "What can I do for you?"

I swallow thickly and close my eyes. His deep voice makes my skin erupt in goosebumps. "I... something came up."

Hunter hums, and I feel it all the way down to my toes. "Something came up," he echoes. I can hear him uncap a decanter and pour whisky into a glass tumbler in the background.

If I close my eyes, I can still taste it on his tongue. "Yes," I whisper shakily.

He swallows down the amber liquid, and the sound sends shivers down my back. "Such a shame, Kitty. I was looking forward to working with you."

*Fucking.* Hunter means fucking. He was looking forward to fucking me.

*Throb. Throb.*

"Definitely a shame," I concur breathily, squeezing my thighs together. Outside, the wind continues howling.

"There's something about you, Kitty. You could've brought something very special to the business."

I watch the branches of a tree beat against my window. "I'm sorry to disappoint you, Mr. Wood."

He takes another sip. I listen to his breathing.

*Throb. Throb.*

"You take care now, Kitty."

I nod even though he can't see it and whisper, "You too, Mr. Wood."

The line goes dead. I'm still staring at the window. The wind is picking up, and the rain is coming down heavier. The branch continues beating on my window like a scorned lover demanding the truth. In weeks, its yellowed leaves will be a carpet on the lawn.

I'm feeling a mixture of emotions. I don't know why this idea of porn has come to mean so much to me, but it has. It's more than just some silly notion.

I'm also relieved. Now I can tell Kingsley that I choose him.

I'm following Geoffrey's advice. I'm listening to my heart.

∽

"Is here good, miss?" Geoffrey grunts and puffs as he drags the small airbox ramp into place outside the classroom. Classes have not started yet, but we are running short of time. If we don't hurry up, we'll get caught.

"That's great, Geoff. And now the launch ramp. Place it over there."

Geoffrey gives me a droll lock. "You could always carry it over yourself, miss."

"Nonsense, Geoff. I'm on lookout duty. Besides,"—I hold my nails up—"look at these babies. They're new."

Geoffrey's face turns red as he drags the launch ramp over. "And I'm old, miss. My body squeaks. I might not be able to stand up straight ever again after this. I might become a modern Hunchback of Notre Dame. I'll have no choice but to sue you for a work-related injury."

I huff a laugh. "You'll be fine, Geoff. You're a spring chicken."

Geoffrey grumbles under his breath as he drags it in to place before straightening back up and performing a number of stretches that have me in stitches.

I dig around in my bag and pull out a pair of bolt cutters, then grin widely as I hold them up in the air. "Are you ready to get your criminal side on?"

Geoffrey's eyes bug out. "Miss, mind explaining why you have brought a pair of bolt cutters to school?"

I wink. "I'm going to need a bike."

Geoffrey looks dumbfounded as he scans the bike shed. "What's wrong with your bike, miss?"

I pull him along by his elbow. "Geoffrey, my bike is at home."

"Are you telling me I nearly died dragging ramps into the school grounds undetected, and you didn't bother to bring your own bike, young lady?"

"I don't want my bike. I want *that* bike!" I reply with a grin, pointing to Kingsley's shiny BMX.

*"Are you offering to let me ride your bike?"*

*"Not a chance. No one rides her but me."*

"Well, today I'm riding your bike, Kingsley," I whisper

to myself, fighting the urge to rub my hands together and cackle like the wicked witch.

*"One call, Kingsley. One call, and Geoffrey will cut your lock, buddy. Watch me ride your bike outside these windows."*

*"You wouldn't."*

*"Oh, but I would!"*

"Are you okay, miss? You're talking to yourself?"

I hand the bolt cutters to Geoffrey, who stares at them like they're an alien life form.

"Why am I holding bolt cutters at a school in broad daylight?"

"Would you be more comfortable if it was dark?" I tease, then laugh at the dry look he gives me. "You're going to cut Kingsley's lock for me."

Now it's his turn to laugh. Oh, how he laughs! "Miss, did I ever tell you that you inherited your father's terrible sense of humor."

I tug on his mustache. "I've never been more serious, old man."

His laughter dies in his throat. He crosses his arms, nearly poking me with the bolt cutters in the process. "Why should I involve myself in your criminal activities? Cut the lock yourself."

I hold my nails up and batter my eyelids. "I would but look at these babies. Aren't they beautiful? Besides, look at my arms"—I squeeze my skinny bicep—"I'm weak. That's not a cheap lock, and cutting it requires a certain level of strength." I poke his bicep. "You're stronger than me."

"And when you're done with your little joyride, miss. What then? How is he going to lock his bike up?"

I wink as I unzip my bag and pull out another lock. "I'm already one step ahead of you." I hold it up for him to see.

"It's an even better lock. Think about it, Geoff. You'll be doing him a favor by cutting his very average midrange lock. His bike will have even better protection with this one."

"You are positively evil, miss," Geoffrey grumbles as he crouches down. "With your kind of persuasion powers, you'll soon be recruited by the Russian mafia. Just you wait—it's bike locks today and waterboarding enemy drug lords tomorrow."

The bell rings.

"Oh my god, Geoff!" I laugh. "Hurry up before someone spots us." I can already see students entering the classroom.

"Alright, alright, miss, don't stress your old man. My blood pressure can't handle it." With a squeeze and a grunt, he manages to cut the lock, and I have to fight very hard not to squeal and jump up and down like a twelve-year-old girl.

I pull the beauty out of the stand and run my hands over her beautiful handlebars. The bike Kingsley lent me is a granny compared to his shiny baby.

"Now what, miss?"

"Now you watch." I mount the bike and spin the pedals with my feet. Yes, perfect tension in the chain. I can easily perform an entire rotation with the cranks. What did I expect? This is Kingsley. Everything about his bike is perfection.

I feel like a kid at Christmas as I ride circles around Geoffrey. "I think the criminal life looks good on me, don't you, Geoff?"

"I think I am quite going to enjoy your trip to detention today, miss."

"Detention today, juvie tomorrow. I'm living on the wild side." I perform a Bunny Hop and grin so big that my cheeks hurt. I spot Kingsley in the window. He sits hunched over his desk.

I plant my feet on the ground and put my helmet on before sending him a text.

Me: Full Cab. Exit from Fakie by performing a
360° rotation backed on rear wheel. In order to spin
harder, end the arch with a bitch crank.

I pocket my phone, grab the handlebars, and kick off the ground.

~

KINGSLEY.

Why is it that teachers know how to bore you to death? An hour's lesson with Mr. Wilbur can feel like a fucking century.

A text from Katherine pops up on my screen, so I grab the phone off my desk and swipe the screen. I can't stop my smile when I see another description of a trick. I begin to type out another text, but Olivia taps my shoulder.

"Isn't that your bike, Kingsley?"

I furrow my brows as I follow her line of sight. It takes me a moment to process what I'm looking at. Other students are starting to notice now too. Katherine is riding my bike and landing trick after trick. Sure, they are beginner's tricks, but still. The last time I saw her on a bike, she squealed every time she thought she would fall off, and now she can perform a full 360° rotation jump.

*"Watch me ride your bike outside these windows."*

Anyone else, and I would be angry, but I can't find it within myself to be anything but amused. I'm fucking proud as I watch her mount the airbox, hop, and spin. Those are tricks you don't learn overnight. She has spent hours and hours practicing.

*And her smile...*

My heart hurts when I think about the phone call from Hunter. She accepted the part... She's going to act in a porn movie and let that Hunter guy fuck her on camera for everyone to see.

"What the fuck is she doing?" Olivia asks behind me as I stand up and walk over to the window. I'm not the only student pressed up against the glass.

Katherine pauses on top of the airbox, and our eyes collide before she winks and rides back down. Her long hair flies in the breeze. I stand frozen, watching as she performs a series of hops, barspins, and rotations.

She fucking terrifies me! Katherine puts her heart into everything she does and jumps right in at the deep end without a second thought. She's a force to be reckoned with.

In the last couple of weeks, she's dug her way deeper under my skin than I ever intended... I have to let her go! I can't let myself feel any more than I already do. She has the power to shred me to fucking pieces and she's leaving to join Hunter soon. She got what she wanted.

What can I offer someone like her? I'm a homeless eighteen-year-old little shit with nothing but a useless fucking bike. Hunter is a renowned pornstar and has his own production company.

Olivia's hand on my back interrupts my self-deprecating thoughts.

I look back out the window and watch Katherine get escorted away by security. She's laughing like this is the funniest thing to happen all year. Poor Geoffrey is forced to follow behind like an embarrassed parent. It makes me smile despite the pain in my chest.

"Come on, Kingsley. I want to show you something!" Olivia says when the bell rings, and because Katherine accepted the part in Hunter's movie, I let Olivia lead me away from the window. Away from the only girl my heart aches for.

∞

*Katherine*

"Gazelle, I heard you're joining us in detention later?"

I close my locker and turn to Josh, the detention guy. It's the end of the lunch break. I spent an hour in the principal's office earlier getting a very stern telling off. Apparently, it's not acceptable to bring skate ramps to school and steal students' bikes. *Who knew?* They soon let me go when it became apparent that Kingsley isn't pressing charges.

How very generous of him.

"I am, indeed. How did you find out?"

Josh grins and puts his arm around my shoulder as we join the river of students heading for class. "It's all over school, juicy meat. And YouTube."

I pause in my step, then glare at the poor guy behind me when he bumps into my back. He scurries past. I bring my attention back to Josh. "YouTube?"

"You're going viral."

We start walking.

"I guess I should have seen that coming."

Josh hums. His blonde-haired friend Matt sidles up next to him, and they do some weird fist bump.

"Gazelle, right?"

I roll my eyes.

"I saw you riding Kinsgley's bike earlier. That was awesome! You should join us at skatepark one day." Matt winks.

"Never going to happen."

Matt shrugs, unperturbed. "I'd love to see some of your tricks up close and personal."

"Do you know what this is?" I ask, holding my middle finger up.

Matt grins, and Josh laughs next to him.

"It's my middle finger, and it is kindly telling you to fuck off."

"She's feisty," Matt says to Josh.

Josh nods. "Tell me about it. She's awesome!"

"I'm right here, guys."

They blink.

Josh flashes another grin. "Hi, Gazelle."

I extract his arm from around my shoulder. "This is me. I need the toilet before class."

"Want me to join you?" Matt winks.

I can't help it this time; I laugh as I push open the bathroom door with my back. "Tempting,"—I flip him off again—"but no, thank you."

"See you in detention, gazelle," Josh shouts, grinning as they set off down the corridor.

I turn, smiling, only to be frozen in my tracks.

"Fuck, Kingsley! Harder!"

*Thrust.*

"Ahhh... Yes!"

Olivia's eyes flick up, and she looks at me as if she knew

I was here all along. The taunting smirk on her lips feels like a thousand knives to the heart as Kingsley fucks her on the counter.

Kingsley's face is buried in her neck. It's funny what you notice in those few moments in life when your heart shatters. Right now, all I can seem to focus on are Olivia's blood-red heels on Kingsley's naked ass and his tanned hands on her pale thighs.

He grunts, fisting her long hair, and it reminds me of the many times I've heard those sounds of pleasure in my own ear.

Olivia moans theatrically as she throws her head back.

"Kingsley?" I whisper shakily before I can stop myself, and he freezes with his lips on her neck, but I don't stay.

I run!

Students turn and stare at me as I escape through the corridors, tears streaming down my cheeks.

How far can the human body run before it collapses? I don't know, but I'm intent on finding out. Right now, running seems to be the only thing that holds me together and stops me from shattering into a million tiny pieces. The burning pain in my thighs is a relief.

I burst through the doors. It's now raining heavily as if the universe itself knows how I'm feeling. Not even that can stop me.

"Katherine!" Kingsley's voice filters through my soul-wrecking sobs.

I don't stop.

"Katherine! Stop! Fuck, just stop!"

I don't.

I will never stop running. I'll run until I physically can't anymore. The rain keeps falling in heavy sheets, obscuring my vision.

Kingsley's grabs me around my waist and lifts me off the ground. "Stop running!"

I kick and scream, clawing at his hands. *Hands that squeezed Olivia's thighs in pleasure earlier.* I don't want them anywhere near me right now. Or ever again!

Kingsley carries me over to an alleyway and pushes me up against the brick wall. He cages me in with his hands. "Stop running!"

I sink back against the rough brick and turn my face to the side. I can't look at him right now.

"I'm sorry, okay? Is that what you want to hear?"

I don't answer.

Rain keeps falling.

"You weren't meant to see that."

The rain comes down so hard, it bounces on the slabs. "You told me you weren't fucking her."

"Did I?"

I meet his gaze. He's trying to hurt me. I know he is. He doesn't mean what he's saying right now.

"Did I?" he presses, and another sob rips past my lips.

"You told me it was a hug."

"It was. That time."

I shake my head in denial. "You're trying to hurt me."

"You don't get to be hurt, *Kitty!* You sucked Hunter's dick, remember? What was it you said again? It meant nothing? Well, Katherine. It meant nothing."

I flick my eyes between his. "So you fucked her to get even?!"

Rain drips from his nose as he laughs bitterly. "Is that what you think of me? That I would fuck a girl for revenge?"

I push off the wall. The pain is turning to anger. "I don't

know what to believe, Kingsley? You bring up Hunter after I walked in on you fucking Olivia."

"No, I said you don't get to be hurt when you did the exact same thing!"

I turn my face away again, staring at nothing. My heart is an open bleeding wound.

Kingsley presses his forehead to my temple, breathing harshly through his nose like he's in pain too. "We're not in a relationship, Kath. You don't belong to me, and I don't belong to you. You're going away in a matter of days to film Hunter's movie. Do you think I want to be with someone who fucks other men for a living?"

I meet his gaze and say in a broken, trembling voice, "I turned it down..." Kingsley stares at me as if he can't comprehend my words, so I continue, "I turned it down *for you.*"

His face collapses in pain, and he shakes his head. "No..." His voice is as weak as mine.

"Yes, Kingsley," I whisper. "I was going to tell you today. That's why I rode your bike... I wanted to surprise you."

This is the end of the road for us. We both know it.

"FUCK!" he yells, punching the brick wall by my face, and causing me to cry out in fear. When he steps back, there's blood on his knuckles, but he doesn't seem to notice. He stares at me with such undisguised pain, I almost reach for him. *Almost.* Neither of us speaks a word. We simply stare at each other while the rain keeps pouring.

"Ask me if I have been in love, Kingsley."

He squeezes his eyes shut and shakes his head.

"Ask me!" I press. Fuck him! He can give me this much!

His pained eyes meet mine. "Have you ever been in love, Kitty Hamilton?"

I break, and a pitiful sob slips past my lips as I nod. "Yes, Kingsley. I have."

He looks up at the sky and fists his dark hair, releasing a gut-wrenching sob. His cap lies discarded in a wet puddle.

"Goodbye, Kingsley." As I walk away without another backward glance, I know I have left a piece of my heart in his hands. I hope he takes good care of it because I will never be able to get it back.

I hug my arms around myself as I walk through the heavy sheets of rain. My broken heels click on the sidewalk, and my hair lies plastered to my face. Cars drive past, oblivious to my inner torment. It's only past noon, but it's a dull day, and most drivers have their lights on.

*"You're cute when you concentrate."*

*"Oh please, stop that."*

*"Stop what?"*

*"The flirting. I'm not one of the bimbos at this school. I'm not going to fall to my*

*knees because of some smooth pick-up line."*

*"Can't blame a guy for trying."*

Another pathetic sob rips through me.

*"Now you know why I don't do the girlfriend thing. I have nothing to offer."*

*"You have plenty to offer."*

*"No, I don't, Katherine Hamilton."*

I open the glass door to the building and ignore the receptionist shouting for me to stop. I don't even realize I'm in the lift until it dings and the door opens to Hunter's floor. I knock on his door and then stare at my own hand, wondering who's pulling the strings right now because I feel like I'm moving on autopilot.

The door swings open, and there he is, leaning against the door frame with a predator's smile and a glint in his eye that can only spell trouble. "Well, well. Kitty Hamilton. I had a feeling I would see you again," he says in a deep voice, reaching forward to cup my chin. He presses down on my bottom lip with his thumb. His touch is possessive. "You made the right choice." He moves back and lets me pass.

I step through, and the sound of the door clicking shut behind me propels me into a whole new world.

"Welcome to Hunter Wood Productions, *Kitty*," Hunter purrs as he steps up behind me and buries his nose in the crook of my neck. "We're going to achieve some amazing things together." He slides the straps off my shoulders before pressing himself up against me. My soaked-through dress soon lies pooled around my feet as his shadow looms over me. I welcome it—the darkness. I let it numb the pain and shelter my fractured heart.

# THIRTEEN

*1 year later.*

"I just need to apply the hairspray, and then you're done," Gerard, my hairstylist grins. "You're going to wow everyone at the award show tonight, darling."

I adjust the strap on my gold sequin dress. It glitters every time I move. Beneath tonight's spotlights, it will be an eye stopper. Hunter purchased it for me specifically for tonight, and I couldn't stop myself from smiling when I opened the gift box on our bed.

"I can't believe it, girl. Not just one but three nominations!" He claps his hands excitedly. "You make me proud!"

I laugh just as Hunter joins us in the dressing room.

"She's made us all proud this year." He leans down for a lingering kiss. "You look beautiful."

I pull back. "You'll ruin my lipstick."

"Oh, trust me, babe. We will ruin it plenty later." He winks and starts talking to our assistant, Alison.

"So, how does it feel?" Gerard asks, spraying a mist of hairspray.

How does it feel? I don't feel much of anything, to be honest. I've done what I set out to do. I've made a name for myself this year, but has it brought me happiness? No. "It feels great!" I smile, praying it looks genuine.

Gerard leans down and looks back at me through the mirror, his head next to mine. "Repeat after me. I'm Kitty Hamilton. I'm fucking amazing!"

I laugh.

"Go on," he says, grinning even wider.

"Fine. I'm Kitty Hamilton, and I'm fucking amazing!"

"Good girl!" He straightens and begins packing away his things. "Come on, Alison, let's leave these lovebirds alone."

I smile at Gerard as he blows me a kiss.

They walk out.

Hunter watches me for a minute, sweeping his eyes down my body. "Perfection."

I duck my head as a blush creeps up my neck.

He walks up to me and lifts my chin with a finger. "You deserve tonight!" He takes my hand, placing a small white pill on my palm. "A little something to take the edge off." When he's swallowed his own pill, he hands me the water bottle and watches me place mine on my tongue. I swallow it down.

"Good girl!" he whispers against my lips, cupping my pussy through the slit in my dress.

I whimper as he moves my panties aside and slides a finger inside me.

"Tonight is going to be great. We've accomplished a lot this year." He pumps his finger, his eyes on my mouth.

My lips part. I grip the dresser behind me, meeting his finger thrust for thrust.

"It's only the beginning, Kitty." He pulls out and sucks it clean before winking knowingly and walking out.

I'm throbbing. "Dick!" I shout after him, making him laugh.

He pops his head back in, "You love my dick!"

Laughing, I throw my bottle of water at him, and he only just manages to duck in time. When the door is closed, I sink back in the chair and stare at my reflection. The pill is starting to take effect, loosening my muscles and dimming the ache in my chest.

"I am Katherine Hamilton, and I am amazing," I whisper, my eyes pricking with tears that I will not allow to fall right now. I've had my make-up professionally applied after all.

A soft knock on the door startles me. "Come in."

Geoffrey smiles at me as he steps inside and closes the door behind him. "You look beautiful."

"Thank you," I whisper, looking back at my reflection in the mirror. My make-up might have been applied by a professional, but no amount of highlighter or mascara can hide the haunted look in my eyes. "Will you be honest with me if I ask you a question, Geoffrey?"

He comes to stand behind me, meeting my gaze in the mirror. He looks handsome in his tux. "I will always be truthful with you, miss."

I wring my hands. "Do you think less of me?"

His eyes soften. "I could never think less of you, miss."

I tip my head back and blink rapidly to stop the tears from falling.

"I may not understand your choices, miss, but like always, you have succeeded and then some."

I smile weakly. "But?"

Geoffrey places his hand on my bare shoulder. He squeezes gently. "I think the fire in you has dimmed."

We stare at each other in the mirror before I lower my gaze, nodding. "Thank you for being honest with me, Geoff."

"It's no problem, miss." He starts coughing, and I furrow my brows, turning in my seat before remembering the water bottle I threw at the door. I retrieve it and hand it to him. He accepts it with a smile, unscrews the lid, and takes a large gulp.

"Are you okay?"

He lowers the bottle, wiping water droplets off his bottom lip. "I'm okay, miss. Just a cold."

"Are you ready, Kitty?" Hunter asks as he walks into the room.

My eyes linger on Geoffrey a while longer before I nod and grab my purse.

"Come on, miss. You don't want to be late for your big evening." Geoffrey smiles as he holds the door open for us.

Hunter leads me to the waiting car with a possessive hand on my back. The drugs floating through my system make the world a hazy, beautiful blur.

∽

Cameras flash as we exit the limousine and make our way up the rolled-out red carpet. I've never been to Las Vegas before. The desert heat is more pressing than I could have anticipated.

"Smile, babe. The world is watching," Hunter whispers in my ear, his hand on my hip as we grin for the cameras. I try, I really do, but the lights are blinding, and the voices from the shouting crowds blur into one buzzing sound. We stop to pose for some photographs before we're ushered to where the interviews are in full swing. Hunter doesn't leave my side. He's smirking and working the place like he was born for the spotlight. I smile as if I'm the happiest woman in the world, but I'm slowly dying on the inside.

"Kitty Hamilton. You're up for three awards tonight. Best New Starlet, Breakthrough Award, and Best Actress. That's a phenomenal achievement. How does it feel?"

When Hunter tightens his grip on my hip, I plaster on a smile.

"It feels fantastic." I gesture around me. "I can't believe I'm here tonight surrounded by all these huge stars. It's an honor."

"Yours and Hunter Wood's love story is the talk of the industry. How does it feel to be part of such a power couple?"

Hunter leans down, kissing me on the cheek. "I'm a very lucky man indeed."

I smile, but it feels plasticky. "I don't think of us as a power couple. We're just a couple like any other."

"Beautiful and humble. I like that. So, Kitty, how will you celebrate tonight if you win all three awards?"

I laugh. "Hunter has kept a very old bottle of whisky which will finally see daylight should I be so lucky."

"And you, Hunter. You're up for awards too. Best Director of the year and Male performer of the year. It will be the fourth year running for you. Your production company is also up for Best Film. Not to forget you and Kitty are nominated for Best Boy/Girl scene. How do you feel to be here again?"

I tune out as Hunter swoons the reporter with his success stories. I've heard them all before. I can't believe I'm here. I don't feel like the same girl who spilled coffee on Hunter back in the local coffee shop. I'm a much more unrefined version of that girl. She was innocent, naïve, and impulsive. All the things I'm not anymore.

We're moving again. I focus on placing one foot in front of the other as we enter the building.

We spend time mingling with performers, directors, and other important people in the industry. This is where Hunter shines. I can't help but admire his skill at working a room. I'm a trophy on his arm as he introduces me to people and squeezes my hip when he wants me to smile or laugh.

Before I know it, we're seated in the theatre, and the award show is underway. Giggling girls take to the podium, thanking everyone, from their best friends to directors and everything in between.

"She came into the business and took everyone by surprise with her heady mix of innocence and fire, which she brings to every performance. Let's welcome to the stage, this year's Best New Starlet, Kitty Hamilton."

Lights blind me as Hunter stands up and guides me up by my hand, whispering in my ear, "You did it, babe."

I walk on wobbly feet, not sure if it's nerves or the drugs, but next thing I know, I'm gripping the podium, smiling out at the sea of people. My heart pounds in my chest as I lean close to the microphone. "There are a lot of people I want to thank tonight, but no one more than Mrs. Ackland, my career advisor." The audience laughs.

My smile is genuine this time. "I'm serious! I told Mrs. Ackland not to underestimate me. I'm a Hamilton. Every time someone tells me that I can't do something, I try that much harder! Failure is not in my book. Guess what Mrs. Ackland replied?" I pause for effect. "She said I couldn't become an adult entertainer. She told me I would fail." I lift the trophy and hold it up in the air. "Well, who's laughing now? Thank you!"

I rejoin Hunter, who places a kiss on the side of my head.

"You did fucking fantastic!"

I win the other two awards too, but it's not until Hunter drags me up to stage for the Best Boy/Girl performance that the significance of the night truly dawns on me. I honestly didn't expect I would win anything tonight.

"I'll let this fantastic woman go first," Hunter grins, and I step up to the podium once again, gripping the sides firmly. I take a deep breath as I think back to when I first met Hunter.

*"What the fuck?!" a deep and gravelly voice says.*

*I look up, up, and up again until I met the stormy cobalt blue eyes of the most handsome man I have ever seen.*

*"You need to fucking watch where you're going!" he growls, shaking his wet hands. Drops of coffee fly everywhere.*

*I finally snap into action and grab a handful of paper napkins from the dispenser on the desk and begin patting him down, secretly admiring his hard chest.* "Oh god, I'm so sorry!"

"I first met Hunter in a local coffee shop in my hometown. I spilled my coffee on his white t-shirt, which he didn't take kindly to." The audience laughs on cue again, and I smile a soft smile, remembering how naïve I was. "I thought he was the most handsome man I had ever seen. I told my girlfriends there and then that I would do anything to make him fall in love with me. Even auditioning for a part in one of his movies. And here we are." I lift the trophy and look at it. Our names are inscribed on the bottom.

When the audience makes a swoony noise, I look up to

find Hunter on one knee. In his hand is a ring box with a sparkling diamond in it.

"Oh my god," I whisper, pressing a hand over my lips.

"The day you spilled your coffee on me... well, when I look back at that day, I realize how fortunate I was. I don't know if you believe in fate, baby? But I do. You asked me at your audition when was the last time I was surprised by a woman. I've seen a lot of things, Kitty, but no one has surprised me more than you. Not a day goes by where you don't manage to take me by surprise in some weird and wonderful way. You don't just complement me. You make me better. Together, we can accomplish amazing things. What do you say, Kitty? Will you make me the luckiest man on earth? Will you be my wife?"

I know I should feel nothing but overwhelming happiness right now. Isn't that what they say? But it feels staged. It seems to be the theme of my life lately. Everything is one big performance. Still, I nod, watching as he slips the ring on my finger before slamming his lips to mine.

"Welcome, Kitty, to Wood & Hamilton Productions," he whispers in my ear.

～

*2 years later.*

Twisting the diamond ring on my finger, I throw my head back with a groan. "No, no! You're doing it all wrong."

The new girl, Ashley, stops sucking on Tyler's dick and looks at me over her shoulder. We're filming in the studio today, and the set has been made to look like a hospital room. Ashley is the patient, and Tyler is the male doctor. Cliché shit that sells well. The only problem is that Ashley sucks Tyler's dick like she would rather be at home doing gardening or crocheting.

I stand up from my director's chair and walk over to where she kneels between Tyler's spread legs. "It's all about eye contact, Ashley. See that?" I point to the camera. "That's the camera. Stare at it when you suck on Tyler's dick like it's the best fucking lollypop you have ever tasted." I point to her lips and tits next. "You need your nipples to show at all times and to really fucking purse your lips around the head. You want the guy jerking off on the other side of the screen to imagine it's his cock in your mouth and your nipples he's tweaking. He can't do that if he can't see them, so stop hunching."

Hunter laughs loudly behind me where he's got a fluffer on her knees who's stroking his dick.

"Look," I say as I walk over to my bag. I root through it and pull out the circular rock-candy lollypop Becky got me as a gift for my birthday to remind me of the good old days. "I'm not going to demonstrate on Tyler's dick because he'll end up ejaculating too soon, and I spent an hour doing my make-up this morning." I unwrap the lolly and sink to my knees next to Ashley, who stares at me with her big doe eyes. I point to the camera, where James holds it above Tyler's shoulder. "You don't look away from that camera. Now watch me."

This is what my life has come to—me on my knees, demonstrating on a rock-candy lollypop how to suck dick so that it looks great on camera. As if that's not bad enough, my husband has his cock stroked by a hired fluffer in my periphery.

Tyler stares wide-eyed as I give the lolly one last lick and get to my feet.

"Think you can manage that, Ashley? Remember, you want the audience to think that the cock you're sucking on is the holy fucking grail. Make it believable."

"Can you not suck my dick instead?" Tyler groans, staring after me longingly as I walk over to my chair.

I snort a laugh as I take a seat. "Come see me when you're an established name in the business."

Hunter is laughing like this is the funniest shit ever. "You want to fuck my wife, Tyler?"

Tyler nods eagerly. "I really fucking do!"

I can't help but laugh too. Newbies are funny. "We don't have all day. Are you ready to make it believable this time, Ashley?"

Half an hour later, I'm scrolling through the news on my phone while my husband is balls deep in Ashley's ass, and Tyler pounds her pussy. Just another normal day in the office.

"Fuck! Shit!" Hunter groans as he grabs her auburn hair in a ponytail and twists it around his wrist.

I stop scrolling, my eyes on the screen, seeing but unseeing.

*"Kingsley Delanoy, 21, wins gold again."*

"You like both holes filled, huh?"

I click on the article and zoom in on the picture of Kingsley performing a trick in the air. There's another photograph further down the page of Kingsley smiling and holding his trophy in the air. I'm back in the rain, my heart breaking into pieces as I tell him goodbye for the last time.

Isn't it funny...? I was heartbroken when I walked in on him and Olivia, yet here I am, watching my husband fuck a girl in the ass, and I feel nothing. In fact, emotions would take effort.

I stand up and walk out, leaving them to finish the scene without me there pretending to direct it. Who the fuck cares about the perfect angle anyway?

I lock myself in the dressing room, sink back against the door, and close my eyes.

*"Ask me if I've been in love, Kingsley."*

*He squeezes his eyes shut and shakes his head.*

*"Ask me!" I press. Fuck him! He can give me this much.*

*His pained eyes meet mine. "Have you ever been in love, Kitty Hamilton?"*

*I break, and a pitiful sob slips past my lips as I nod. "Yes, Kingsley. I have."*

I push off the door. Tears blur my vision as I stumble over to the dressing table and tip out the contents of my bag on the table, rummaging through the mess for what I need. I pick up my credit card with trembling hands and use it to line up the white powder, but I hesitate. I lift my head. My own reflection is staring back at me. Who am I now? I don't recognize the woman in the mirror with her haunted eyes.

I lean over the counter, snort a line, and tip my head back, wiping under my nose. It started with the occasional pill, and then Hunter introduced me to more potent stuff to take the edge off. My father would turn in his grave.

My phone on the dresser draws my attention, so I pick it up and unlock the screen. *Kingsley's smile...* He looks happy.

A knock on the door startles me, and I scramble to put my supplies back in the bag. "Jesus, fuck!" I whisper, my hands trembling. I'm wiping down the counter just as Geoffrey steps inside.

He saw the white powder inside the plastic pouch. *I know he did.*

"Are you okay, miss?" he asks as he takes a seat on the plush cream couch. In his hands is the paperwork I asked him to bring. He puts it down next to him.

I lean back against the counter. The drugs are taking effect. I'm numb, and everything feels pleasant. "Never been better, Geoff."

He stares at my bag until I want to fidget. "You need to seek help, miss."

I sniff and avert my gaze. I know he's right, but I'm not ready to admit it. "Did you need something?"

Geoffrey starts coughing. He shakes his head. "I wanted to check on you."

I look back at Geoffrey. There's an uneasiness in my stomach. "Have you been back to the doctors, Geoffrey?"

He waves me off as he gets to his feet. "It's nothing to worry about, miss." His eyes flick between mine. "I am worried about *you*, Katherine. It's like I don't know you anymore."

My face crumbles. "Geoff..."

"No, you listen to me, young lady. I promised your father I would always look out for you. This is me keeping that promise. I will not stop pestering you!"

"You're the *only* person who knows me, Geoffrey," I whisper, my lip trembling. It hurts that he would say otherwise.

He squeezes my arm soothingly. "I *did* know you. I don't know this self-destructive version of you standing in front of me. You got lost somewhere, miss."

I wipe my cheeks, glancing at my phone on the dresser behind him. It's still lit up with a picture of Kingsley.

Geoffrey lifts my chin. "It's not too late to rekindle the fire in your eyes."

"Have you ever lost your way?"

A shadow flicks across his eyes. "I've been very lost, miss."

I grow still, searching his face. There's something he's not telling me. "Geoff?"

He squeezes both of my arms this time, placing a kiss on my forehead. His mustache tickles my skin. "It's not too late, miss."

I stare after him as he walks out and shuts the door behind him. Why do I feel like there's a storm on the horizon?

# FOURTEEN

"Fuck, Kitty!"

I continue stroking Hunter's dick as I swallow down his salty cum. His hand in my hair falls away, and I wipe my mouth before sitting back up and reaching for the glass of whisky on the coffee table. I take a large gulp.

Hunter tucks himself away and rests his arm behind his head on the couch. The credits run on the large TV screen. "Fuck, I have the best wife in the world!"

I roll my eyes and light up the joint he got for us. Smoke swirls in the air as I watch him. "Did you ever do anything besides fuck?"

Hunter laughs. "You do come out with some random shit."

"I'm serious! I feel like I know nothing about you. We fuck, but we don't talk, Hunter. What did you do before porn?"

He shrugs. "Same as everyone else."

"Same as everyone else?" This joint tastes like shit.

"What do you want me to say, Kitty?"

I remove the tobacco off my tongue before taking another hit. "I don't know. Did you have any hobbies?"

"Oh yeah, I did crochet with my grandmother before church on Sundays." He takes the joint from my fingers and places it between his lips. The tip glows orange.

"I did BMX."

He chokes on the smoke. "What's in that joint?"

Rolling my eyes, I rest my head back on the couch and stare at the patterns on the ceiling. We live in a luxury condo decorated in grays and blacks because that's what Hunter wanted. I couldn't be bothered to argue. "I shouldn't have stopped."

"What are you saying, babe? You want to ride a bike?"

I roll my head and watch him take a hit. His blonde hair is a tousled mess, and he needs a shave, but we don't have a shoot until next week. "Have you ever been in love, Hunter?"

He looks at me like I have three heads as he blows smoke through his nostrils. "What kind of a question is that?" He points to my wedding ring. "Would you wear that if I hadn't?"

I shrug. "You tell me, Hunter?"

He ignores me as he leans forward and prepares another line of white powder. I watch him snort one before he hands me the rolled-up paper.

I shake my head. "No, thank you."

"No, thank you?" He laughs. "What's gotten into you?"

I reach for the joint and take a drag, watching him through the swirling cloud of smoke. "I don't know."

Hunter gets up, switches off the tv, and leaves me in the dark living room by myself. I feel like I'm slowly fading away. As if I'm flickering out—disappearing into nothingness.

The spotlight shines in my face. I did tell Hunter it needed to be dimmed, but he didn't listen.

When he shouts action, I readjust my glasses and pretend to grade papers behind my desk. The door opens, and in walks Callum, my co-worker. I lift my head and remove my glasses. "What are you doing here? Lessons ended half an hour ago."

He locks the door and smirks at me. "I think you know what I'm doing here, miss." It's impossible not to notice the innuendo.

I sweep my gaze down his body and ignore James, the cameraman, behind him. "I told you, we can't see each other anymore. What happened between us must never happen again."

I scoot my chair back and round the desk, dragging my long nails over the surface as Callum walks toward me, past the students' desks.

"I can't stop thinking about you, miss, he says as he comes to a stop in front of me and palms my tit through my white blouse. He tweaks my hardened nipple.

"This is a bad idea!"

Like a scene out of a terrible B movie, he rips my blouse open. Buttons scatter everywhere. "Just admit that you think of my cock when you touch yourself at night."

"Cut!" Hunter shouts and jogs over. "That was great, Callum, but I need you to be rougher with her. The audience responds best to Kitty in movies with rougher sex."

"Just what every woman wants, Hunter. A husband who tells another man to be less gentle with his wife." I mimic Hunter's deep voice as I continue, "You need to be rougher, Callum. Fuck my wife harder!"

"Ha! Ha!" Hunter says drily.

I grin, amused to have annoyed him.

"Just be rougher, okay?" Hunter says as he jogs back to his spot on the director's chair behind the screen. "And action."

Callum grips my jaw tightly and presses me back against the desk. "Just admit that you think of my cock when you touch yourself at night."

I shake my head or try to, but his grip is too firm to allow much movement. "You're my student."

He flips me over, hikes my skirt up over my waist, and slaps my ass. Hard. "I bet your pussy is soaking for me."

James moves around the desk with his big camera and comes to a stop in front of me as Callum sinks two fingers inside my tight heat, meeting no resistance. *Jesus.*

Callum slaps my ass again, pumping his fingers with such force my tits bob. I've been in this business long enough to know this is a golden shot. I trap my lip between my teeth and roll my eyes to the back of my head for effect, whimpering low in my throat.

"Do you want my cock?"

"God, yes!" I moan, arching my ass in the air.

"Cut!"

*Fuck!* I drop my forehead to the table, and my poor clit throbs as Hunter jogs over.

"James, come here. I want a zoomed-in angle on his fingers in her pussy. It will go great with the face shot you just filmed."

I bang my head, clamping around Callum's fingers still inside me.

"Are you okay, babe?" Hunter asks, and I fight the urge to get up off this desk and punch him in the face.

"Never been better."

"Great," he replies, amused, as he jogs back and shouts action once more.

Callum starts fingering me again. "Are you getting this shot, James?"

"Yeah, got it!"

"Great."

"Just get me off already!" I growl, making them both laugh.

"Easy tiger," Callum chuckles, stroking his thumb over my puckered hole. It wasn't in the script. *Dickhead!* I can't deny how good it feels, though.

"Are you going to be a good girl for me?"

*"Name a trick I can't do."*

*"Show it to me sometime?"*

*"If you're a good girl."*

"We shouldn't do this! You're my student! We'll get caught." I sound ridiculous. I can suck cock, but I'll never win an Oscar for dialogue.

*Smack!*

"Spread your legs nice and wide for me."

James moves around the desk again, and I stare at the camera as Callum frees his dick and slams into me from behind, stretching me with his impressive girth.

*"Got you!" he whispers in a tone that makes my heart race.*

*Water bobs around my chest as the sun beats down on us. "I can't be caught, Kingsley."*

*His eyes fall to my mouth. He lowers himself down in the water until it's up to his chin. "Maybe not."*

"Kingsley," I moan under my breath as I squeeze my eyes shut against the memories flooding in.

"Shit, you're so tight!"

Tears sting my eyes.

*"You have to find the sweet spot."*

*"Sweet spot, huh?"* I grin, winking.

He chuckles deeply. *"You have a filthy mind for a virgin."*

*"What can I say? You're corrupting me, Kingsley."*

Callum stops thrusting as the door slams open, and my personal assistant runs into the room. The moment her eyes collide with mine, I know something is terribly wrong.

"What are you doing here? Can't you see we're in the middle of shooting!" Hunter says, exasperated.

I pull my skirt down and hold my ruined blouse closed as I go to meet her halfway.

"It's Geoffrey," she says. "He's collapsed."

My blood turns to ice. I search her eyes. "No..."

"The paramedics are here. They're taking him to the hos—"

I don't stay to hear the rest of her sentence. I run. The hallways blur as my world crashes down like a house of cards. I trip and hit my knees hard on the floor in my haste to get to Geoffrey, but the pain is nothing compared to the fear I feel coursing through me.

"Geoffrey?" I scream as I burst through the front door and push past the paramedics in my rush to get to him. He's on a gurney, being lifted into an ambulance. His mouth is covered by an oxygen mask.

He's pale—so pale.

"Miss, you can't be here. We need to transport him to the hospital."

I drag my eyes away from the gurney and look at the paramedic, but I can't see her. Not really. "I need to see him! Please let me see him!"

As if she can sense how desperate I am, she nods and guides me over to where Geoffrey lies.

Tears stream freely down my cheeks as I press a palm over my lips. "Geoffrey, wake up! Oh, my god! Geoffrey..."

"Time is of the essence, miss."

I somehow manage to nod and step back, watching them close the ambulance doors. I'm wrapped up in a strong set of arms, but I'm too hysterical to notice. Someone is screaming, and I realize it's me.

"Come on, babe. I'll drive you to the hospital." Hunter leads me to our car and helps me inside.

"He can't leave me," I whisper as Hunter pulls out of the driveway. "I lost my dad. I can't lose him too."

Hunter squeezes my hand.

I look down at his calloused fingers. "He's the only one who knows me..."

"We don't know anything yet."

I stare out the passenger window at the passing houses. "He's been coughing for the last two years. He told me it was nothing to worry about."

"It could be unrelated to that."

We drive past a man who's teaching a young boy how to ride a bicycle. They're laughing as they run down the sidewalk.

"Breathe, Kitty. We don't know anything yet."

I rip my hand away. "People don't just collapse, Hunter."

He nods, wringing the steering wheel. "I know."

∼

The wall is painted off-white with an orange partition stripe in the middle, running down the length of the corridor. Who thinks to decorate hospitals such depressing colors? How many people have sat in this same seat with their knees bouncing restlessly, waiting for news? Nurses walk past with clipboards, barely acknowledging me as I sit, bleary-eyed, staring at the ugly wall. Hunter is talking on the phone. Every now and then, he squeezes my thigh as if to reassure me. Of what, I'm not sure.

"Here, drink this before it goes cold," Hunter says, bringing my paper cup of lukewarm coffee to my lips. I shake my head, still staring at the wall, and push the cup away from my face. I can't stomach anything right now.

Hunter sighs as he puts it back down.

He's back on his phone.

"You can leave," I whisper.

Hunter looks up. "Excuse me?"

I drag my eyes away from the ugly orange stripe. "Your phone is obviously more important."

His jaw ticks. He waits for the nurse to walk past, following her with his eyes before leaning in close. "We have a lot riding on this project, Kitty."

My jaw drops. I fist my trembling hands so I don't punch him in the face. "Geoffrey could be dying for all we know, and all you care about is work. It's porn, Hunter. Fucking porn!"

His chuckle is bitter. "Do you hear yourself right now? I know you're angry and scared, Kitty—"

I shoot out of my seat as a doctor approaches. His clothing is wrinkled, and he looks tired. His nametag reads Dr. Weatherford.

"I'm afraid it's not good news."

I flick my eyes between his. Then look over at Hunter, who presses his lips together and lowers his head. I turn back to Dr. Weatherford, shaking my head in denial. "He was fine this morning…"

"Mr. Nicholl has stage four pancreatic cancer. It has spread to his lungs."

I continue to stare at him for a long minute, unable to process his words. I'm vaguely aware of a nurse dipping her head as she walks past. The world has ceased to spin. The loud clock on the wall has stopped ticking.

*"Daddy, daddy, throw me up in the air. I want to play airplanes."*

Dr. Weatherford squeezes my arm, his eyes shining with empathy. "I'm sorry."

My bottom lip trembles as I place a palm on the ugly wall to steady myself. "I lost my dad to cancer." My voice is barely audible in the loud emergency room.

"What's the prognosis?" Hunter asks. He's always level-headed.

Dr. Weatherford's eyes meet mine. "It's terminal. Mr. Nicholl's—"

"Geoffrey," I whisper shakily. "We never call him Mr. Nicholl."

Dr. Weatherford's hand on my arm falls away. "Geoffrey hasn't got long left."

"How long?" Hunter's voice is strong. Assured.

"A couple of weeks."

I press my hands over my lips as tears well in my eyes.

Hunter curses loudly next to me.

I feel his warm hand on my back as I say, "It doesn't make sense... There must be something we can do?"

Dr. Weatherford shakes his head. He looks exhausted, as if being the bearer of bad news has aged him a decade. "The best thing for him now is to keep him as comfortable as we can."

"Why didn't he tell me?" I whisper, wiping away tears from my eyes with my palms.

"I think you're best asking him that question yourself. You can see him now if you want?" He nods once before taking his leave. I watch him walk down the corridor with the weight of the world on his shoulders.

"Come on," Hunter says, steering me into Geoffrey's room.

The strong smell of antiseptic and the beeping sound from various monitors is what hits me first. Geoffrey looks frail in his hospital gown, surrounded by wires. Hunter goes to talk to him as I come to a stop just past the door. My heart is crumbling in my chest. Streaks of sunlight filtering through the gaps in the blind light up the bed where Geoffrey lies. It's such a contrast to the dark storm raging inside of me.

Geoffrey removes his oxygen mask and holds his hand out for me. "Come here."

My feet become unglued. I walk over to him, unable to look away from the sadness and regret in his kind brown eyes. I collapse into the chair next to his bed and grab his frail hand in a fierce hold. I refuse to let him go. "Geoffrey?"

He squeezes my hand.

I drop my gaze to his hand in mine as tears spill over and trail down my cheeks.

"I'm sorry," he whispers and smiles weakly beneath his wiry mustache.

My lips tremble. I feel Hunter's hand on my shoulder. "Why didn't you tell me?"

Geoffrey sniffs. His lashes are wet. "You lost your father to this terrible disease, miss. I didn't want you to have to go through it again."

"How long have you known?"

He strokes his thumb over the back of my hand. "Six

months. By then, it had already metastasized. It was too late."

I nod, lowering my gaze. My tears fall unhindered and drop onto his hand as I bring it up to my lips and press a kiss to the warm skin. "I'm sorry, Geoffrey."

He attempts to sit up straighter in the hospital bed, but he's too weak. "You have nothing to be sorry for, miss."

I swipe at my cheeks. "I've been too self-absorbed. I should have pushed you to seek help when I first noticed you were coughing."

Hunter squeezes my shoulder and leaves the room. The door clicks shut behind him. Particles of dust float in the air, visible where streaks of sunlight shine in through the vertical blinds. There's an orange stripe in here too, painted on the wall behind Geoffrey's head. I stare at it.

"None of this is your fault, miss."

I memorize his kind face. "I'm scared."

Geoffrey reaches up and strokes his fingers over my wet cheek. His hand smells of antiseptic where they inserted the drip. "I know."

I palm his hand on my cheek and smile through my tears. "What will I do without you, Geoffrey?"

"Who's going to cut bike locks for you, miss?" he jokes, making me laugh. He holds his arms out.

I climb onto the bed and curl up next to him, listening to his steady heartbeat. His wet breath rattles in his lungs.

I squeeze him tighter.

*Daddy, look, Geoff is my horse. Go horsey!" I shout, kicking him in the sides with my bare feet.*

*"Sir, I'm going to need that pay raise we discussed. Crawling on all fours with a toddler on my back is not in my contract."*

*My dad guffaws. "But you're doing such a fine job, Geoffrey."*

Geoffrey strokes my hair as we lie on the uncomfortable hospital bed, staring out of the window. After a while, his breathing evens out, and he falls asleep. I prop my chin on his chest and study his face. He's lost weight. How did I not notice?

I leave him sleeping as I carefully climb out of bed and grab my bag. I leave the room, keeping my head down. The corridor feels like it's closing in on me as I make my way to the nearest bathroom and shut myself inside.

My reflection looks as wrecked as I feel. My hair is a tangled mess, and my clothes are wrinkled. I'm still wearing the short skirt I had on while filming earlier, but Hunter gave me one of his spare shirts to put on. In other words, I look a mess!

I empty the contents of my bag and quickly make up a line, ignoring the deep sense of shame churning inside of me. I pinch the side of my nose and sniff the white powder. The relief I feel is almost instant. I sink to the floor, barely registering the cold tiles beneath my bare thighs. The world blurs in and out as I float in a cloud of bliss.

The pain is gone.

~

A big hand slaps my cheek hard enough to raise me from my slumber.

"Fuck, baby, you're a mess!"

I smile and mumble something incoherent before my eyes flutter shut again.

Hunter jostles my chin. "You've got to wake the fuck up!"

"Hunter?" I try to lift my arm, but it stays on the floor.

"What the fuck have I told you, Kitty? We can do that shit at home, but not out in public. Shit!"

"I'm losing everyone! My dad. Kingsley. Geoffrey..."

Hunter slaps me again, and I open my heavy eyes, watching him fade in and out.

"Have you ever been in love, Hunter? I have. It fucking hurts," I slur, pushing his hand away from my face, but he grabs my jaw again and shakes it.

"You're a fucking mess, Kitty!"

"He's dying..."

"Open your fucking eyes. Shit, how much did you take?"

"I don't want to feel anymore."

Hunter lowers his head, swearing up a storm. "Do you want this to be Geoffrey's last memory of you?"

I try to sit up straighter. "Geoffrey is here?"

"Fuck, Kitty!" Hunter gets up, grabs my bag of white powder, and holds it up in the air. "Geoffrey is dying. He needs you to be level-headed. No more, Kitty! Enough is enough!"

I watch him flush it down in the toilet. I'm too strung out to comprehend what's happening. He walks back over and sinks down next to me, elbows on his knees. "You can't leave this room in your state. If the media catches a whiff of this... I'll sit here with you."

"Why do fluorescent lights always flash in bathrooms?" I whisper, remembering the time I pulled Kingsley into a bathroom for the first time and tried to seduce him.

*"I'm locked in a bathroom with Katherine Hamilton. Did I hit my head this morning?" Kingsley mumbles under his breath.*

*I snap my fingers. "Attention, Kingsley." He looks*

*adorably confused.* "You're here because I need you to teach me sex."

*Kingsley chokes on air. His mouth opens and closes.* "Teach you sex?"

Hunter chuckles, leaning his head back against the tiled wall. "The lights aren't flashing, Kitty. It's in your head."

"Huh…" I roll my head, staring at his profile. His dirty blond hair is disheveled, and there are dark rings under his eyes. "He's dying…"

Hunter rolls his head too, searching my face. "I'm sorry."

"I need to get clean."

Hunter swallows thickly, his eyes flicking between mine. "Yeah, babe. You do."

~

I wake in the chair in Goeffrey's room with no recollection of how I got here. He's watching me with concerned eyes as I throw the blanket off and look around the room. The beeping machines bring me back to reality. Geoffrey is in hospital, and he's dying.

"You've been asleep all day."

I reluctantly meet Geoffrey's knowing eyes. I don't reply. There's nothing to say. I'm no longer the Katherine Hamilton I was back in high school. I'm a shadow of my former self.

When Geoffrey sighs tiredly, I clear my throat and whisper, "I'll make you proud of me, Geoffrey." I fidget with the blanket in my lap.

Geoffrey looks out the window, and his eyes follow a family walking past unbeknownst to the heartache in this room. "I know you will, miss. You have the heart of a lion."

I snort a sad laugh, swiping at my wet cheeks. It seems all I do is cry these days. "Are you in pain?"

Geoffrey waves me away. "Let's not talk about me, miss. There's something I want you to see in the box over by the wall behind you."

I turn in my chair. Sure enough, there's a box on the floor.

"I asked Hunter to retrieve it from my room."

I look at him questioningly before rising from my chair and walking over. It's a cardboard box, the kind used for larger gifts. I look over my shoulder.

Geoffrey nods, smiling softly. "Go ahead, open it."

I sink down to my knees. My fingers tremble as I slowly remove the lid and place it down beside me on the floor. I stare at the item inside.

"How?" I ask, tears blurring my vision as I tenderly lift it out and run my fingers over the countless band stickers decorating the black helmet. The same helmet Kingsley let me borrow when we were teenagers.

"Your eyes, miss. They burned bright back then. That boy brought you to life, miss." He nudges his head toward the helmet in my hands. "I would love to see you ride your bike again, miss. Even if I can't sit on the bench and watch you anymore."

I meet his gaze and hug the helmet to my chest, my throat clogged with emotion. "Thank you, Geoffrey."

A coughing fit hits him, and he doubles over, coughing into a tissue. It comes away red when he finally leans back and drags in a wet breath.

I drop the helmet to the floor, rush over, and throw my arms around him. I bury my nose in his neck as I hold him close. It hurts to be here again, watching someone I love fade away in front of my eyes.

He rubs my back. "It's okay, miss."

I shake my head, tightening my grip, staring at the stupid orange stripe on the wall. "It's not."

How do you let go of someone who's always been there, quietly cheering you on from the sidelines?

# FIFTEEN

The receptionist sighs like my request is unreasonable. She taps away on the screen. "Dr. Weatherford is busy."

I set my jaw and tap my manicured nail on the desk. I may look a mess, but I am still Katherine Hamilton. "I want to see him now. Time is of the essence, Miss."—I squint, reading her nametag—"Allen."

She stops typing. "And so is everyone else's time here. Take a seat, Mrs. Wood. Dr. Weatherford will see you when he can."

I tap my nails some more, but the lady has no heart apparently, or maybe she's just that used to victims of bad news.

I sit down a nearby seat and prop my cheek on my hand. This place is miserable. The walls need a lick of paint—any color other than the off-white and garish orange.

I watch a little boy with an oxygen tank roll a toy train over the seat next to him. His mother is watching him with a small, sad smile. The kind that says she's scared of the news she might receive here today.

"You're Kitty Hamilton."

I startle and look over at the middle-aged man next to me. His eyes sweep down my body like he's undressing me in the middle of a hospital waiting room. "Can I help you?"

"I've watched all your movies," he says to my boobs even though they're hidden underneath Hunter's shirt. I need to change my clothing. I'm starting to smell.

"Great," I reply, looking around the room for any sign of Mr. Weatherford.

"It's like that, is it?"

I give him a questioning look. "Excuse me?"

His beady eyes are anything but friendly. "You're a whore who fucks on camera for money, but you believe you're too good to acknowledge your fans?"

My mouth drops open. I scan my eyes across the busy room. Is he for real?

"You should suck my dick."

"I'm married." Stupid reply, but it's the first thing that comes to mind.

He guffaws, drawing attention to us. "That sham of a marriage. Your pornstar husband doesn't care who you fuck."

The worst part is that he's right. Hunter doesn't care as long as it furthers my career and our brand name. I've never felt dirtier than I do right now, sitting in a waiting room with a complete stranger calling me a whore. I live a sheltered life with Hunter.

"I like that thing you do with your tongue," he grins, his teeth stained from years of smoking.

"Shut up!" I say through gritted teeth, fisting my hands on the armrests to stop them from shaking.

He grins even wider and palms his cock with no regard for the families in the waiting room.

I shoot to my feet. "You're disgusting!" I don't wait

around to hear his reply. My heart thunders in my chest as I run down the corridor. I can't help but feel as if everyone here judges me for my life choices. I'm proud of what I have achieved as Kitty Hamilton in such a ruthless business. But it has also brought a host of complicated emotions, not all so black and white. Mainly shame. It presses on my soul like a heavy weight that I can't shift.

I'm brought back from my thoughts when I bump into a hard chest.

"Are you okay?"

I look up and meet the concerned eyes of Dr. Weatherford. His arms are on my shoulders, steadying me, and he smells of antiseptic.

I take a step back and tuck my hair behind my ear. I feel ridiculous all of a sudden. "I'm fine. I wanted to talk to you."

We're standing in the middle of the hallway, so he moves me aside to let a woman pass. "I've been in a meeting. I was on my way to see you now."

I still feel uneasy from earlier. "I don't want Geoffrey to die in hospital."

Dr. Weatherford waits for me to continue. I get the distinct feeling that nothing I say surprises him. He's seen it all. The thought comforts me.

"You said he only has a matter of weeks left? Let me take him away from here. He should spend his last weeks surrounded by nature. Money isn't an issue. I'll pay for a nurse to stay with us. Whatever he needs." I'm babbling.

Dr. Weatherford waits patiently for me to finish, then clears his throat and smiles softly. "I think it's a great idea, Mrs. Wood, but you must be prepared that the journey ahead will be rough. Geoffrey is going to deteriorate at a rapid pace."

I nod along eagerly, but his words are white noise by

now. My world is spinning out of control. All I know is that I want to take Geoffrey and escape somewhere far away from white walls, beeping machines, and orange stripes.

"...I'll sign off the paperwork." His voice drifts back in. He puts a folded-up piece of paper in my hand. "I'll sign him out, Mrs. Wood. If you complete this. It's Geoffrey's dying wish."

I sink back against the wall and watch him leave. The corridor seems to stretch into eternity as people enter and exit doors, all with their own worries and fears.

I look down at the folded piece of paper in my trembling hand.

*"It's okay to be sad, Katherine. You can't be strong all the time."*

*My eyes sting. "He would want me to be strong."*

*Kingsley's hand on mine feels like an anchor right now, like it's the only thing stopping me from sinking into the depths of this lake.*

*"You can be strong and feel sad. One doesn't have to cancel out the other."*

*"My dad was the strongest man I've ever met."*

*The sun warms my skin as it reappears from behind a cloud.*

*"You're strong too. Far stronger than you think."*

I unfold the note and quickly scan my eyes over the text. It's for a week's stay at a rehabilitation center. I swipe at my cheeks as I read Geoffrey's joined-up handwriting.

*Dear Katherine.*
*I am so proud of everything you have achieved, miss. Even if your choices sometimes set you down a path that would have your late father turn in his grave. You never give less than your all, and you*

*take the seemingly impossible and make it possible. You have been an inspiration in my life, miss. I have enjoyed watching you grow into the young woman you are today. That being said, you lost the spark in your eye somewhere along the journey. Please find it, miss. Do it for me. Leave no stone unturned until that fire in your eyes not only burn but lights forest fires. Dr. Weatherford recommended this rehabilitation center. Please, miss, go seek the spark to your fire.*
*/Geoffrey.*

~

"Where will you stay?" Hunter asks as I pack my suitcase on our unmade four-poster bed. The scatter pillows, usually organized neatly, lie on the floor by the bottom of the bed.

I shrug and throw in another top. I'm not even folding the clothes. My skin is clammy, my hands tremble, and my body aches from withdrawals.

"I'm renting a cottage."

"A cottage?" he asks, closing the lid to the suitcase when I go to put in a pair of jeans. "The fuck you are! What about production, Kitty? We start shooting next week."

"Is that all you care about, Hunter?"

He follows me into the lavish bathroom with its gold faucets and walk-in shower. I thought I liked the cream and gold design in the magazine, but it looks like a suite on a luxury ship. "We have a lot riding on this, and you know it! Contracts, Kitty. Fucking contracts!"

I whirl around and point my toothbrush at him. "I don't give a shit about contracts right now! Geoffrey is dying, Hunter. Dying! I'm taking him to live out his last days somewhere other than in the hospital. You will simply have to find someone to replace me."

I push past him and storm into the bedroom. I begin to zip up the suitcase, but Hunter rips it off me and throws it down on the wooden floor. "I can't just replace you, Kitty!"

Throwing my hands up, I laugh bitterly. "For fuck's sake, Hunter. Do you even care about me at all?"

"Of course, I care about you, but we have commitments."

I glance outside. The gray curtains rustle in the breeze from the open window. It's another sunny day. On the window ledge is a framed photo from our wedding day. I'm wrapped in his arms, smiling at the camera. "The only commitment that matters right now is Geoffrey." I meet Hunter's stormy eyes. "If you care about me at all, then please...help me carry my suitcase to the car, kiss me good-bye, and let me leave."

His jaw ticks before he drops his gaze and stares at the polished floor. He grabs the suitcase handle and walks out without another word, leaving the door open behind him.

I should follow him, but instead, I find myself by the window, holding our framed wedding photograph in my hands. I thought I was happy that day but look at me now. I trail my fingers over our smiling faces.

*"I'm going to make Hunter my husband."*

*"You are crazy! He's a thirty-year-old pornstar, and you're an eighteen-year-old high school student."*

I place the photograph back down on the window ledge and join my husband outside as he closes the trunk. He stares off into the distance and grinds his jaw before his eyes find mine. "I do care about you."

"I know." *In your own way, you do.*

Hunter strokes his fingers down my cheek in a tender

caress, eyes shining with regret. "I'm sorry for what I said earlier."

My throat clogs with emotion as I lean into his touch and kiss his palm. "I know you are."

Hunter pulls me in for a hug, and I hold him to me, breathing in his familiar smell. He presses a kiss on the top of my head, then steps back and opens the driver's door. He holds it open while I strap myself in and grip the steering wheel.

"I'll be seeing you, Kitty Hamilton."

"Take care of yourself, Hunter Wood."

He shuts my door with a small, sad smile and steps back, placing his hands in his pockets.

I start the engine and drive down the winding driveway, watching him fade in my rearview mirror. I need to take Geoffrey and escape far away from people and noise. I need space to say goodbye and mourn in peace, away from prying eyes and leering men in hospital waiting rooms. But first, I need to get clean.

*~*

*1 week later.*

I strap in Geoffrey's seatbelt, meeting his tired eyes before straightening back up. I close the passenger door and round the car. My hand is on the handle when Dr. Weatherford exits the revolving doors, carrying white envelopes.

"Good luck, Mrs. Wood," he says, handing them to me. "These were left behind in Geoffrey's room."

I can tell the letters inside have been read repeatedly by the creased and worn corners. I take them gingerly and scan my eyes over the cursive handwriting. It sparks a memory, but I don't know where from. "Thank you."

"It's quite alright," he says to me, then leans down with his hand on the car roof. "You look after Mrs. Wood now, Geoffrey."

Geoffrey laughs. "She's feisty, don't you worry about her. It's me you should worry about. She'll have me do all sorts of crazy things. Did you know she talked me into cutting a boy's bike lock once? I'm telling you, she's a bad influence on an old man like me."

Dr. Weatherford laughs. "Take care now, Geoffrey. Don't let her boss you around too much."

He straightens back up. "Drive safely."

I get in the car, close the door, and wave through the window. "Are you comfortable?" I ask Geoffrey as I shift in my seat and begin fiddling with the tubes to his oxygen tank. I want to scream at the top of my lungs until I lose my voice. Instead, I lock my emotions away and plaster on a weak smile.

"Stop fussing, miss," Geoffrey smiles. "Let's get out of here."

I turn the ignition, watching my hands shake and not from withdrawals this time. It was pure hell in the rehabilitation center. I wanted nothing more than to be by Geoffrey's side, but I knew I had to complete it for him. I puked, I shook, I thrashed in pain.

"I'm going to look after you, Geoff," I whisper as I drive us out of the parking lot.

His oxygen tank is a loud and painful reminder that time is slipping away, like sand in my hand.

∼

I help him into the wheelchair and close the passenger door behind him. The small beach house is a quaint little building with a wrap-around porch overlooking the sea. It has its own private little beach too. Privacy was the most crucial factor when I hunted for houses to rent short term.

"What do you think?" I ask Geoffrey as I open the trunk and smile at him over my shoulder.

He stares at the blue sea in front, dabbing his mouth with a piece of tissue. "It's beautiful!" No more words are needed. He's right; it's breathtaking.

I lift out our heavy suitcases and place them on the ground but pause as I go to close the trunk.

"I'm dying, so I get dibs on the biggest bedroom, miss."

His morbid humor barely registers as I lean down and touch my fingers to the cool metal frame of my old BMX bike. It's scratched and beaten up, proof of many hours of practice. I don't know why I brought it, but I knew I couldn't leave it behind.

"Miss, time is of the essence. I need a cup of tea."

His words startle me, and I hit my head on the trunk. I groan as I rub the tender spot. "I see you still have some humor in you, old man."

His mustache twitches.

I close the trunk and grab the handles of our suitcases.

"I see the tables have turned. Who's carrying whose bags now, miss?"

I stick my tongue out on my way past, making him laugh and cough at the same time. "Don't go anywhere, old man."

I place the bags in our bedrooms and go back outside to find him sitting with his head tilted toward the sun, a small smile on his lips. His skin is much paler than usual, and he's growing gaunt, but the sparkle is still there in his eyes when he blinks them open. "Did you put the kettle on, miss? I want my tea strong with a teaspoon of sugar and a dash of milk. But only a dash. If it's too milky, you will have to feed it to the cat."

"The cat?" I laugh, steering his wheelchair up the disabled access.

"Yes, miss. There's always a stray cat somewhere."

"I should have brought Mr. Boomer." I hold the door open. He uses his hands on the tires to wheel himself inside, but his strength quickly wanes, so I grab the handles and wheel him into the kitchen. It's scary how fast he's fading.

"Mr. Boomer. What a character that cat is. Just the other week, he turned his nose up at the catnip I gave him. It can't be any regular catnip. It has to be from that special store back in Hedgewood."

"He knows his mind." I boil water and prepare his tea the way I know he likes it. It's certainly not perfect. But with Geoffrey's guidance, it soon resembles something other than dirty dishwater.

I roll him out on the veranda, and we sit in silence, watching the sun set over the water. The warm breeze tousles my hair. I tuck it behind my ears. "Are you scared, Geoff?"

He shakes his head, blowing on his tea. "No, miss. Not anymore."

"What changed?"

Geoffrey watches the water crash against the beach for a long minute, then looks at me. "We left the hospital."

His words hang in the air. I take a shaky sip of my soda, watching him through blurry eyes. "I brought my bike."

His eyes light up. "Excellent news, miss. I can't wait to grow roots and have pigeons nest in my hair, although"—he looks out at the water—"I think it's more likely to be seagulls out here."

I laugh through my tears and rise from my seat. I walk over to him, wrapping my arms around him from behind and resting my chin on his shoulder. His wiry mustache tickles my cheek. "Have I ever told you I love you, old man?"

He pats my arm. "Now, now. Let's not get overly emotional. I'm not dead yet."

I smile, kissing his cheek.

We watch the sun slowly set over the sea and the silvery moon rise in the sky, sparkling on the waves.

## SIXTEEN

A week has passed. Two weeks since Geoffrey collapsed. He sleeps more and is growing weaker by the day. We have a lovely nurse who comes out to see him daily. She helps wash and change him and makes sure he's as comfortable as he can be pain-wise. I don't know how I would do this without her. Especially when she takes time out of her day to sit with me in the kitchen while Geoffrey sleeps. Some days we talk, and other days we sit in silence.

Today she's doing the dishes even though it's not part of her job. Her kind eyes watch me the way I suspect a concerned mother would.

She dries the plate in her hands, puts it back in the cupboard, and reaches for the next one. "How are you holding up?"

She asks me this every single day.

I shrug and take a sip of my coffee. It's still too hot. I can hardly sleep at night as I lie awake listening to Geoffrey's wheezing breaths.

"I have left a pie in the fridge."

"Thank you."

She puts down the dishtowel and turns, leaning back against the counter. "I saw the bike out front. Do you ride?"

"I used to." I blow on my coffee.

She watches me for a long moment, and I take a sip of the still too hot coffee to give me something to do.

"My nephew is a coach."

I pause with my lips on the mug, staring at her over the rim. I lower it slowly, careful not to spill it. "You're telling me this because?"

She pushes off the counter and takes a seat next to me at the table. "You brought it all this way for a reason."

My hands have started to tremble so much that I grab the edge of the table.

"He can help you get back into it."

I stare at her name tag. Mrs. Alvarez. "Do you know who I am Mrs. Alvarez?"

She places her hand atop of mine. "Yes, *Kitty*."

My face collapses, and my tears spill over. I wipe my cheeks with my sleeve, unable to meet her gaze. "I used to be proud of my achievements... Now I can't help but feel like I've achieved nothing."

Mrs. Alvarez takes my hand in both of hers. "Every experience in life is a lesson learned. Even if you feel like you have achieved nothing... Trust me, you have!"

"Why are you so kind to me?"

Mrs. Alvarez leans forward and tucks my hair behind my ear. "Because I know grief. I know how it tears your heart out and leaves you devastated in a world where you're expected to dust yourself off and move on."

"Have you ever been in love, Mrs. Alvarez?"

"A long time ago."

I nod, reaching for my cup again. She watches me take a hesitant sip.

"You'll find your way through this storm too."

∾

"I think this wheelchair is an improvement on that ghastly and uncomfortable bench back home," Goeffrey says as I perform a bunny hop—my first one in years. We're in a small local park, but we're the only ones here. Geoffrey looks deathly ill. His skin has taken on a yellow hue, and he now sleeps for such long periods that lucid moments like today are rare.

I perform a different trick, feeling my lips spread into a genuine smile. It's coming back to me much faster than I expected. "Admit it, Geoffrey. You loved that bench."

He tries to laugh but ends up coughing violently instead. I come to a stop, but he holds his hand up. "I want to watch your tricks. That's *all* I want, miss."

I hesitate for a moment before smiling weakly and kicking off the ground. I ride in circles around his wheelchair. "What do you want me to do?"

"Do that thing where you rotate the bars while in the air."

I laugh, and it's a carefree sound despite the circumstances. "We didn't bring a launchpad."

"You'll figure it out, miss. You always do."

I shrug, then stand up and pedal fast, whizzing through some trees. Dried leaves crunch beneath the wheels. Autumn is fast approaching.

We spend the afternoon like this. Geoffrey watches me for a bit but soon falls asleep. I don't stop riding, grabbing the handlebars in a death grip. The emotional pain will flood back in if I let go. My legs burn, and my lungs scream for air. I welcome the physical pain, and before I know it,

I'm spinning, hopping, twisting, and flying through the air. Geoffrey is still asleep when I finally come to a stop, breathing harshly, my cheeks wet with tears. The sun is setting behind the trees.

Another day closer to the end.

I crouch down in front of Geoffrey and stroke my fingers over his gaunt cheek, memorizing these last moments. He doesn't stir. "Let's go home."

∽

Geoffrey stirs as I tuck in his sheet. His nurse, Mrs. Alvarez, helped me move his bed into the living room. It now faces the big window overlooking the sea, and it's a breathtaking view, one I would love in my last moments.

I press the button on the side of the bed to raise it so he can breathe easier. The oxygen mask is back on his face.

He pulls it down, clears his throat, and points to the small stack of letters on the living room table. The same letters Dr. Weatherford handed me as he bid us farewell. "Read them."

I follow his line of sight.

His shaky hand lands on mine, drawing my attention back to his cracked lips and tired eyes. "I want you to be happy again."

I swallow thickly. "Don't worry about me, Geoff."

This moment right now is about him and his comfort. I'll worry about myself later.

He shakes his head, but it's an effort. "You never stopped loving him."

I move the recliner chair closer and clutch his hand in mine. I trace the protruding veins on the top of his hand with my fingers. "I'm with Hunter."

What does the past matter now? It's been years since I left Kingsley. I stand up and retrieve the letters, placing them down next to him on the bed.

Geoffrey taps the envelopes as I sit back down. "Read them when I'm gone."

I search his eyes, and he taps them again with his finger. His voice is firmer this time as he says, "Promise me, miss."

I tear my gaze away and stare at the choppy waves crashing against the beach. It's a windy day. A seagull dips to the side, riding the wind. "I promise."

He's asleep when I look back, so I place his oxygen mask over his mouth and stroke my fingers over his clammy forehead. "I'll do anything you ask, old man."

∽

I blink my eyes open and groan as I lift my head off the side of the bed where I fell asleep clutching Geoffrey's hand in mine. The morning sun casts a beam on the bed, warming my face. The waves are calm, lapping gently at the shore.

"It's a beautiful morning, Geoffrey. We should go down to the beach. I'm not sure how I'll get your wheelchair on the sand, but we'll manage somehow." I squeeze Geoffrey's cold hand—*his unnaturally cold hand*.

Silence. Absolute silence. No wheezing breaths, no phlegmy coughs.

"Geoffrey?" I ask, tearing my gaze away from the beach. "Oh my god, Geoffrey!" I jostle his cold hand as my tears spill over and trail down my cheeks. "Wake up, please..." But I know he won't. He looks peaceful as if he simply floated away on the morning breeze.

"Oh god, please no!" I plead. I jostle his hand more firmly this time and press my ear to his chest. I don't know why I do it; his skin is ashen, and he's not breathing. But I'm not ready to accept that he's gone. Maybe if I can just find a heartbeat...

Silence. I fist his shirt and bury my nose in the fabric. A sob rips through me as though I have been gutted by a knife. I'm right back to the moment I clutched my father's shirt as he passed away. One minute he was breathing. The next, he was gone, slipping away on a final exhale, leaving me behind with a piece of my heart missing. It feels like déjà vu to be here again, mourning the loss of someone I care deeply about. Life can be so cruel.

"It's such a fine day out there. I brought the oatmeal biscuits you love so much. I figured we could wheel Geoffrey down to the bea—"

The sound of bags falling to the floor echoes in the small room. I'm still clutching Geoffrey's shirt when I feel Mrs. Alvarez's trembling hand on my back.

"Oh, sweetie."

I shake my head and bury my nose further in his chest. I'm not ready to let go. I'm not sure I ever will be.

Mrs. Alvarez strokes my back soothingly. I both love and hate her touch. I love it because I need the anchor to keep me afloat above this sea of grief, but I also hate it because it means he's not coming back.

Geoffrey is gone.

*Gone...*

"Come on, sweetie," Mrs. Alvarez says, helping me to my feet, leading me over the tartan fabric couch with its too many cushions.

I sink down and stare at nothing while she hurries to pick up the groceries off the floor. Cupboards open and close. The cutlery drawer slams.

"Here," she says, crouching in front of me with a

steaming mug of hot chocolate. "Drink this. It will soothe the soul."

I would laugh if I wasn't so numb. I take a sip, and its chocolatey richness explodes on my tongue. To my right lies Geoffrey, seemingly asleep, but what's left is a shell. The Geoffrey who used to quip and make me laugh is no longer here.

Mrs. Alvarez's eyes shine with sympathy. She tucks my hair behind my ear. "I'm not leaving, okay? I'll take care of the arrangements."

The arrangements. Geoffrey's body.... More tears fall, but I don't have the strength to wipe them away as I stare out the window, seeing but unseeing. What was a sunny and beautiful day now feels gray and rainy. A clock ticks somewhere.

"Here, let me help," Mrs. Alvarez says, guiding the mug to my lips. "You're going to be fine, Katherine."

Nothing is ever going to be okay again, but I don't tell her that. What's the point?

I obediently drink the hot chocolate, and Mrs. Alvarez guides me back over to the chair next to Geoffrey as if she knows I need more time to say goodbye.

I sit and hold his hand. He's pale. So very pale. And cold.

"Say hi to dad from me," I whisper. "Tell him I miss him and his warm hugs. Tell him I wish that things could've been different..."

Mrs. Alvarez turned off Geoffrey's oxygen tank earlier. The house is quiet now except for the clock on the wall and the waves crashing on the beach. The occasional screech of a seagull.

"Tell him I'm going to make him proud. I'm going to make you both proud."

The icy waves lap at my bare feet in the sand. They retreat, only to come crashing back, splashing my shins and wetting the hem of my dress. In my hands are the letters Geoffrey wanted me to read. The edges are curled, and the envelopes are crinkled from usage. These letters have been read more than once.

I take a step back and then another until I'm met with dry sand that sticks to my wet feet. I lower myself down in the warm sand and tuck my hair behind my ears to stop it from blowing in my face. I lay the letters out in front of me and stare at them for a moment. There are three in total. I pick up the one on the top and run my fingers over the handwriting. I recognize it from somewhere.

I carefully open the flap and take the folded piece of paper out. A photograph lands in my lap. I swallow thickly as I pick it up with trembling fingers.

*"Why am I wearing a helmet, Kingsley?"*

*He grins, pocketing his phone. "Rather than show you my tricks, I should teach you some."*

The photograph in my hand is the one Kingsley took of me that day. I'm staring at the camera, looking adorably confused with the black helmet on my head.

I carefully unfold the letter in my hand. It's been folded and refolded numerous times before. It feels fragile in my trembling hands.

*Hi, Geoffrey.*
*How are you? I hope you're well. Thanks for*
*reaching out to me. I was immature and scared back*
*then. When I realized I had fucked up... It was one of*
*the hardest things I have ever gone through. She*

*made it clear from the beginning that she didn't want me, and I wasn't ready either. I kept pushing her away every time I began to feel too much. I don't think either of us were ready to admit our feelings at the time, and it was already too late when she told me she decided to turn the part down. She walked in on me with someone else that day, which I'm not proud of. I regret it every day, but I'm glad her dreams came true. She succeeded in the business, and Hunter proposed. It's what she always wanted and why she sought me out. I hope she's thriving. As for me, I'm taking life day by day. I'm entering more competitions, and it's going really well. You're a good man, Geoffrey. Look after her.*
*Kingsley.*

I drop the letter and rush to open the next one, almost ripping the fragile envelope in the process. This time I catch the contents—a letter and a folded up piece of notebook paper.

*Kitty's bucket list:*

- *Marry Hunter.*
- *Take on the porn industry (and be successful).*
- *Beat Kingsley in a BMX competition.*
- *Take on a more active role in my father's company.*

I press a palm over my mouth and laugh incredulously. When did he rip it out of my notebook?

*Hi, Geoffrey.*

*I came across this note over the weekend. I'm moving to a new house, and I found it inside one of my old notebooks while I was clearing out. I thought it might make you laugh. She's not done too badly with her bucket list. Point three is one she will never achieve, though. No one beats me. Ha!*
*How are things with you? And how's Katherine? I tried so hard not to, Geoffrey, but I looked up one of her movies the other day. Big mistake. I kept telling myself I would leave it alone but fuck it. I had a moment of weakness. I don't know if it would have been harder to watch her with a random man, but the fact that it was her husband... It hurt to watch! She's still as fucking beautiful as I remember.*
*Kingsley.*

I fold the letter and put it back inside the envelope.

He's seen one of my movies. *He watched me fuck Hunter.* I feel sick. I don't care that faceless strangers watch me have sex, but Kingsley... It doesn't feel right.

I unfold the last letter and scan my eyes over Kingsley's handwriting.

*Geoffrey,*
*Sorry that it's taken me this long to reply. I'm traveling all over the country competing. My schedule is jam-packed. I'm sorry about your diagnosis. You're a good man, Geoffrey. Life is fucking unfair. How are you holding up? How did Katherine take the news? Keep me updated, Geoffrey. It may take me some time to receive your letters, but I do read them.*
*Kingsley.*

I drop the last letter in the sand. Geoffrey and Kingsley kept in contact? I can only assume these three letters are a few of many.

Geoffrey told Kingsley about his diagnosis, but I didn't find out until the end. Would it have made a difference if I'd known he was dying?

Did he spare me months of heartache?

I dig a hole in the sand and bury the letters but keep the photograph and my bucket list. For some reason, I can't part with them. Looking at them brings me back to the old me. The young girl with hopes and dreams.

When I'm done, I pat the sand until it's compact and swallow down the sadness clogging my throat as I look out over the water. I may not see it from here, but there is land out there somewhere on the horizon, just like an island of refuge exists somewhere on the stormy waters inside of me.

～

The funeral turned out much bigger than I would have liked because Hunter was of the opinion that many people got to know Geoffrey throughout the years. I agree, and I don't. Many of the guests were familiar with Geoffrey through me and my work, but Geoffrey kept his close circle small.

I insisted on having the funeral back home in Hedgewood, where Geoffrey was born and raised. He loved this small town with its charming little church that may not be the flashiest but has a lot of character. We decorated the inside with lilies, and I may have gone a bit overboard judging by the strong smell of flowers and the poor priest barely visible amidst them all. Geoffrey's coffin is lined with my favorite photographs. I couldn't simply pick one, so I picked four. One is a picture my father took of me riding horsey on Geoffrey's shoulders. I can't have been any older than three.

Hunter wraps his arm around my shoulder and pulls me into his body on the pew. "You've done a great job here today, babe."

I rest my head on his shoulder and wipe away my tears with the crumpled tissue in my hand. "Thank you."

Hunter and I haven't seen much of each other since I came back. He's been away on a shoot, and I've been busy planning the funeral. I needed today to be perfect. Mrs. Alvarez has been there every step of the way, and I think I've made a friend for life in her. She hasn't told me her story, but I know she understands what I'm going through.

"You're up," Hunter whispers in my ear, removing his arm from around me. "You'll do great."

I rise from my seat and slowly walk to the altar, feeling the congregation's gaze on me as I ascend the steps. The last time I stood behind a podium was for an entirely different reason. This time there are no trophies to be won and no proposal. This time it's a sea of teary eyes staring back at me.

"Geoffrey started working for my father when I was a toddler, so he's been a part of my life for as long as I can remember." I grip the sides of the podium to help ground me. "He was my father's personal assistant, the head of our estate, and a father figure to me. I lost my dad as a late teen and without Geoff—" I drift off as more tears blur my vision. I scan the crowd of people. *So many people!* I have worked with a lot of them, which is fucked up. I blink, and my tears spill over, trailing down my cheeks. My bottom lip quivers. "Geoffrey was a good man. He was patient and kind. He never gave up on me, not even in his last moments when I was in a very bad pla—" I trail off as my eyes land on a head of dark hair in the back row. *Kingsley*. His brown eyes hold mine. I grip the podium until I feel like my knuckles might pop. He smiles softly and gestures for me to go on, but I can't take my eyes off him even when the mourners start to shift in their seats.

*He's here...*

A hand on my back startles me, and I tear my gaze away as Hunter says, "It's been a very challenging time for my wife. Geoffrey was like a father to her." He rubs my back, but my eyes are back on Kingsley. He's older, and it shows in his face and in the width of his shoulders. Gone is the boy.

My lips brush over the microphone, and my breath is shaky as I continue, "I used to say to Geoffrey that I wouldn't know how to sail my ship without him. He was the first one I turned to for advice. Even in such a controversial business"—my co-workers laugh—"he took his time to listen and tell me his thoughts. Sometimes he would joke that he needed a pay raise but he never made me feel like I should have made different choices. He was a funny man, always at the ready with one of his famous quips." My co-workers laugh again, and Hunter places a kiss on the side of my head.

"Well, Geoffrey, I know you and dad will watch me sail my ship from your seats in heaven and probably laugh at my stumbles. We all know I make some questionable choices, but I hope I will make you both proud."

Hunter guides me back to my seat. No sooner has my butt hit the pew before I'm looking over my shoulder and searching the crowd for the only pair of brown eyes with the power to knock my world off its axis. Kingsley is watching me as if he, too, needs to memorize the changes that time has carved. I wonder what he thinks, seeing me after all this time?

"Are you okay?" Hunter asks, startling me.

"Huh?" I tear my gaze away and face forward in my seat.

Hunter squeezes my thigh, and for the first time since we met, I want to slap his hand away. But I don't.

As the funeral carries on, I stare at his profile, wondering how many women he fucked this week at work. It has never bothered me before, but something feels so wrong about it now. I have spent weeks watching someone I love fade away before my eyes, and my husband refused to drop his commitments to support me through it. I'm not sure what's worse? That he showed me where his priorities lie or that I felt relieved and welcomed his absence?

"I need air." I don't wait for him to reply as I stand up and speed walk down the aisle. My lungs constrict. I can't fucking breathe!

The guests watch me go. The curiosity in their eyes is too much. I feel like everyone can see right through me—as if my grief belongs in Barnum's circus. An oddity to gawk at.

I burst through the doors and drag in lungfuls of air as the autumn sun warms my skin and birds sing in the nearby trees, oblivious to my inner turmoil.

When the door opens behind me, I don't need to turn around to know it's Kingsley. I can feel him, even after all this time.

"Are you okay?" he asks. His voice is deeper than it used to be. "I'm sorry that was a stupid question!" He rubs the back of his neck as I straighten and meet his gaze.

"You're here..."

He rocks back on his heels, looking uncomfortable. "I am."

I don't know what is wrong with me, but I walk off and leave him there. I'm by the small stream running alongside the church when he catches up and pulls me to a stop with his hand on my elbow.

"I'm sorry."

I stare at his tanned fingers on my arm. It burns my skin in a way I haven't felt since I left him three years ago. "Thank you," I whisper as his hand falls away.

He lowers himself down on the grass, and I do the same, watching the water flow downstream. "I'm sorry for what I did with Olivia."

I nod but don't reply. Kingsley's apology means a lot more than I want to admit. "Geoffrey gave me some of your letters."

Kingsley throws a rock into the stream before resting his arms on his knees. "That doesn't surprise me."

I smile despite myself. "He liked you."

Kingsley chuckles. God, how I have missed that sound. I turn my head and watch him. His smile still takes my breath away. This is the first time I have seen him in a suit.

"Geoffrey was a rebel at heart."

I laugh, and his eyes land on my mouth as he smiles too.

"You can say that again. When I asked him to cut your lock, he only gave me a small amount of grief. I think he secretly loved it!"

Kingsley throws his head back with a laugh, exposing his long tanned neck. My skin erupts in goosebumps. "I almost forgot about that. You took me by surprise."

I lift my chin. My smile is smug. "I told you I would take you by surprise."

He watches me for a long minute, his eyes roaming over my every feature. "That you did!"

"So, what do you do these days?"

He shrugs. "I compete a lot."

His eyes warm my skin despite the slight nip in the autumn air. "I've read about it in the newspaper a couple of times," I admit, tucking a wayward strand of hair behind my ear. "You should be proud."

"So should you. You got your dream."

I look down at a yellow leaf in the grass. I don't know how to reply, so I simply nod as I pick it up and begin shredding it to pieces.

"What is it now? Two years running that you've won Best Actress?"

I cringe, throwing the shredded pieces of leaf back down on the grass. I can't believe that he's kept track of my career.

"And Hunter... Remember how I laughed that day when you dragged me into the bathroom and told me you would make him your husband?"

I throw a piece of grass at him and smile even though I feel like an open, bleeding wound inside. "I always told you not to underestimate me, Kingsley Delanoy."

"Lesson learned." We fall silent. The only sound is the breeze in the trees overhead and the bubbling stream.

"What about you? Girlfriend? Wife? Or do you still not have anything to offer?" The question slips out before I can stop it. I dread his answer.

"I've dated here and there," he replies as he leans back on his elbows and spreads his long legs out. "But no, no one who stuck."

The thought of Kingsley with other women turns my stomach. I'm the biggest hypocrite of all.

I lie back on the grass and stare up at the cloudless sky overhead. My hair is ruined, but I can't find it inside me to care. I know I should be in the church right now, saying my goodbyes to Geoffrey, but I think he would have rather seen me lie out here by the stream with Kingsley.

Speaking of Kingsley, his fingers brush up against mine, and at first, I think it's accidental until it happens again. It's a barely-there touch that burns my skin. I know I shouldn't, but I find myself interlacing our fingers as my heart begins racing in my chest.

I'm staring up at the blue sky, and he is lying on his side, running his eyes over my face. We're not too close to each other, but it feels intimate. Maybe because his thumb is stroking the back of my hand.

I roll my head and search his brown eyes. "What are we doing, Kingsley?"

"I don't know."

I resist the urge to reach up and stroke his cheek. He had a shave this morning and now has a very tempting five o'clock shadow. "Do you ever think of me?" My voice is almost lost in the breeze. I shouldn't ask him such a forbidden question. The diamond ring on my finger feels like a heavy weight that's sinking me further down into the dark depths of the stormy seas inside of me.

He swallows thickly like the question pains him as much as it does me. "Every day."

His words hang in the air. I search his eyes, and he searches mine.

I go to open my mouth, but a voice from behind startles me.

"You okay, babe?"

I bolt upright, brushing pieces of grass off my dress. "I'm fine, Hunter. This is Kingsley. He's a childhood friend." I turn to Kingsley and gesture to my husband by my side. Hunter's arm around my waist makes my skin crawl. "This is my husband, Hunter Wood." I feel like I slapped Kingsley with those words.

He stands back up and extends his hand. They're matched in height. Kingsley is more sculpted and rugged than Hunter, thanks to hours of exercise on his bike. Whereas Hunter, with his dirty blonde hair and perfect tan, is the kind of guy your mother would love at first glance. Hunter looks good on screen. He's handsome and charming with a dimpled smile that melts panties. Kingsley is a wild card but no less attractive with his tousled dark brown hair and chocolate eyes. "It's good to meet you, man."

Hunter shakes his hand. I can tell by the crease between Hunter's eyebrows that he's suspicious. "You too. You staying for the wake after?"

Kingsley shakes his head. "No, I have to set off to the airport. I have another competition tomorrow."

"You compete?"

Kingsley nods and glances at me as he puts his hands in his pockets. "Yeah, I compete in BMX."

"He's modest," I say to Hunter without looking away from Kingsley's dark eyes. I feel his intensity down to my toes. "He's one of the best BMX riders in the country."

Hunter lifts his eyebrows and tightens his grip on my waist. "Is that so?" His voice is not hostile, but there's an edge to it.

Kingsley breaks eye contact. "It was nice to finally meet you," he says to Hunter, and to me, he says, "Take care, Katherine."

I watch him leave, knowing I might never see him again, and like the first time, it hurts, but it's not an explosive rush of emotional pain. It's an ache. I won't find myself running blindly in the pouring rain.

The sadness inside my chest is one I know I will always

carry with me. It's the price I paid for falling for Kingsley. When I dragged him into the bathroom, I should have known that he would steal a piece of my heart for himself.

I'm pulled from my thoughts and my first and possibly only love when Hunter says, "We need to go back inside."

I look over my shoulder the entire way, even when Kingsley is long gone. If Geoffrey was here, he would nudge his head and tell me to chase after him, but he's not here, and I don't. I let the church doors click shut behind me.

## SEVENTEEN

I plop down on the chair and smile at my friends. It's been so long since I last saw Becky and Hazel. They flew in to attend Geoffrey's funeral, and we decided to meet up the next day at our favorite café downtown. The same one where I spilled coffee on Hunter.

Becky pulls the chair out and carefully lowers herself down. It's not easy with her huge, pregnant belly.

Hazel smirks and bites into her brownie, saying around a mouthful, "You look like you're about to give birth right here."

"That's because I am." Becky takes a sip of her sparkling water. Her eyes meet mine. "How are you holding up?"

"I don't know," I answer honestly. I'm still numb.

Hazel extends her hand and interlaces our fingers. "Geoffrey was such a good man!"

I smile weakly. "How about you two? Any news?"

"I broke up with Jamie," Hazel says, taking another bite of her brownie.

"Oh, no, I'm sorry!" I reply as Becky rubs Hazel's back.

Hazel and Jamie met at a local farmers' market and dated for a year.

Hazel shrugs, avoiding our eyes. "It's for the best. We're too different."

"What dickish thing did he do now?"

Hazel laughs, but her eyes betray her. She's hurting. "He didn't do anything. I care about him, and I am sad about the breakup, but I want more. I don't know what exactly, but I want a consuming fire. I want to feel like I can't live without him, and with Jamie, it felt 'meh.'"

I drop my eyes to the table and trace the carving of someone's name in the wood with my fingernail. Her words hit a little too close to home.

Becky smiles softly. "You'll find it, Hazel. Whatever you're searching for. It's out there, searching for you too."

I swallow thickly. Do I want more too? Do I want fire? With fire comes burns, but the reward is all the greater. "How long have you got left now?" I ask Becky before taking a sip of my coffee.

She rubs her stomach affectionately. "Two weeks. Thomas is more stressed than me. I think he's checked the bolts on the crib at least three times in the last couple of days."

Hazel brushes brownie off her fingers. "Did you decide on a name?"

"Summer or Lily. We'll decide when she's born." She turns her eyes on me. "When are you going back to work?"

I press my lips together and twist my coffee cup on the table. "I'm not."

They stare at me. Becky with her glass of orange juice pressed to her lips and Hazel with her wide green eyes.

"Why not?" Hazel asks, leaning her elbows on the table.

I look out the window to my right, watching leaves blow

along the sidewalk. The trees are almost bare. "It doesn't feel right anymore." I drop my gaze and stir my coffee with my teaspoon. "I'm going through some things right now. I need time to figure them out."

Becky's eyes brim with hormone-induced sympathy. She's usually the hardened one of our trio. "It's a good idea, Kath. What did Hunter say when you told him?"

I furrow my brows as I continue stirring my coffee. It's going cold. "I haven't told him yet." He won't take the news well at all. I glance at my wedding ring and the diamond ring next to it. I have the sudden urge to rip them off. When I look up, Hazel and Becky are watching me.

"You need to do what is right for you," Becky says, stroking her stomach. I nod. She's right. I need time to find out where my priorities lie and what I need to do to be happy again.

"I missed you both!" I'm growing emotional again. They lean forward, and we all grab hands on the table.

"We don't see each other enough," Becky whispers, and Hazel nods in agreement.

"We don't."

I feel a tear trail a path down my cheek. All I seem to do is cry these days. "Let's make a promise to change that."

Becky smiles through tears of her own. "Pinky promise?"

"Pinky promise," Hazel grins, holding her little finger up, and I hook mine in hers. "Pinky promise."

Becky joins in. "The crazy trio is back!"

∽

Hunter didn't take the news well that I won't be returning to work anytime soon, if ever. I'm staring at the broken coffee table in our living room as a glass vase goes flying, smashing against the wall. I feel strangely detached. Next up are my award trophies. He throws them as well, and all I can think is what a weird achievement it is to win trophies for fucking your husband on-screen or sucking your co-worker's dick.

"You can't fucking quit!" he growls, holding my trophy for 'Breakthrough Starlet of the Year' up in the air. "I made you, Kitty Hamilton!"

There goes that trophy too.

I cross my arms and wait it out as he continues to rage. I know he's been using, or he wouldn't be this irate.

"You wouldn't have gotten anywhere in this industry if it wasn't for me!"

I raise an eyebrow. We both know that he's lying! Our on-screen romance helped, but I was never a three-month wonder. In fact, I did as much to make his company what it is today, three years later, as he did. We both worked equally fucking hard!

With no more trophies left to throw, he storms up to me. His bloodshot eyes are the only warning I get before he grabs my jaw so hard that I cry out. "You think you can just walk out on our business because you've had enough? You're my wife!"

"You're hurting me!" I say as calmly as I can despite the fear coursing through me.

Hunter stares at his hand as if he can't understand why his grip on me is so tight—like his actions aren't his own. He lets go of me just as quickly and staggers back.

"You need help!" I whisper. He agreed that I once needed help. Now it's my turn to remind him that he's equally messed up.

Hunter drops down on the plush couch and rubs his

hands through his sweaty hair. "How the fuck am I going to explain this? My wife quitting the business... We're a brand, Kitty. You can't quit the brand!"

"You managed without me once. You'll do it again."

He chuckles bitterly, then picks up the scatter cushion next to him and throws that too. It lands with a soft thud, hardly anywhere near as satisfying as smashing glass.

"Are you done trashing our home?"

He lowers his hands from his face and stares at me for a long moment as if something occurred to him. "This is because of *him!*"

"Him?"

"The guy at the funeral. Don't think that I'm fucking stupid, Kitty! The way you looked at him..."

I push off the wall and pick up the cushion off the floor. "You think I want to quit porn over a guy?"

*I don't, do I?*

"Does he fuck you better than I do, is that it? Did he ask you to quit?"

"Excuse me?" I stare at him in disbelief. What the fuck is he insinuating?

"You heard me!" He rises from the couch and walks over.

"Since when do you care? You've watched me fuck other men for three years and not given a shit. Why start now?"

Hunter toys with a strand of my hair. He's a sweaty mess. "Until now, no man has threatened the brand we have created."

I swallow past the lump in my throat. My hands are trembling by my sides. "I've had men leer at me for three years! One even asked me to suck his cock in the waiting room in the hospital. But no man has ever made me feel dirtier than you did just now! Our marriage is not a business transaction, Hunter!"

"Is it not?" he asks, raising an eyebrow. "Look at me the way you looked at that guy." He drops my hair and strokes his clammy fingers down my cheek. His touch is tender, but there is an edge to his voice. "Go on, do it. Right now!"

"Hunter," I whisper, pleading with him to stop.

He grasps my jaw again and leans in to brush his lips over mine. He smiles cruelly. "Do it!"

"I can't..."

He plunges his tongue past my lips and steals a violent kiss that makes tears well in my eyes. His grip on my jaw is rough. He cuts me open inside. His lips are smeared with pink lipstick when he pulls away and stares at me like I have betrayed him when all I want is to take time off work to seek happiness again.

"Exactly," he whispers before walking out and slamming the front door behind him.

I don't know how long I stand in our trashed living room. The silence is deathly, as if even the birds outside know not to sing right now.

I can't do it anymore. The ring on my finger weighs me down beneath the waves. I can see the sunlight sparkle on the surface above, but I can't swim up. This heavy rock keeps me tethered to the sandy bottom where the sun's healing rays don't reach.

I walk into our bedroom and look over at one of the wedding photographs mounted on the wall above our bed. "I think you will agree with what I'm about to do, Geoffrey," I whisper as I remove my wedding ring and place it down on Hunter's pillow. He'll be fine without me. I know he will. His company will bounce back once the news settles. Hunter is a successful businessman in his own right. He was Hunter Wood before I met him, and he will still be Hunter Wood when I'm gone.

As I walk out of the front door for the last time with only a suitcase and Mr. Boomer in his travel carrier, I know that I'm making the right decision. I promised Geoffrey that I would find my spark again. It's time for me to set sail on that journey.

~

I rent a small apartment in a nearby town. It's nothing fancy. I could afford a house in the most expensive part of town if I wanted to. I don't. There's something humbling about my current situation as I sit here on a cheap couch with Mr. Boomer purring in my lap. I don't know how long I've stared at the peeling wallpaper, but my legs are starting to ache.

The news broke about our separation the other day. The first thing I did was to flush my phone down the toilet. Well, I tried. Turns out it's not so easy to flush a phone away… I managed in my mission to destroy it though, and now there's nothing but blessed bliss. No one knows where I am. It's just me, my thoughts, and my purring cat.

My crumpled bucket list lies on the stained coffee table, and next to it is the phone number Mrs. Alvarez left me for her nephew. I've been debating if I should give him a ring.

"I'm sorry, Boomer," I say as I lean forward and reach for the list, jostling Boomer in the process.

*Kitty's bucket list:*

- ~~Marry Hunter.~~
- ~~Take on the porn industry (and be successful).~~

- *Beat Kingsley in a BMX competition!!!!!!!*
- *Take on a more active role in my father's company.*

Fuck it. I need a challenge—something to take my mind off this emptiness inside. There's only one problem. I flushed my phone down the toilet, and now I can't make a phone call.

"Well shit. That's an inconvenience," I whisper, scratching Mr. Boomer behind his ear. I press a kiss to his furry head and move him aside so I can put my shoes on. My hair is a rat's nest, and there's a stain or two of tomato soup on my t-shirt, but shit, I can't find it in me to care.

And that's how I find myself inside this Apple store with a pimply young sales assistant staring at me like I need psychiatric help.

*Fuck, maybe I do?*

"Let me get this straight. You don't want to buy a cellphone because"—he makes quotation marks—"you're a pornstar who broke up with your pornstar husband and then flushed your phone down the toilet. And you came in here because you want to *borrow* a phone to make a phone call?"

"Exactly," I reply, snapping my fingers.

"Oookay," he says, looking around for help. Possibly someone carrying a straight jacket.

"Do you live under a rock?"

He opens and closes his mouth, still looking around for help. "I don't watch porn," he says distractedly.

I throw my head back, laughing. "Good one!"

He meets my gaze. The look on his face is comical. "I don't!"

"Right, and I'm an eighty-year-old lady. Come on, there's no shame in it. All young men watch porn."

"They really don't!" he says, pushing the phone on the counter toward me while staying a safe distance away from my crazy.

"Thanks." I dig inside the pockets of my jogging bottoms for the note with the phone number on it.

"Yeah... just make the phone call and then don't come back. Like ever."

Typing in the number, I glance at his name badge. "I like you, Danny. You're funny!"

"Sure. Can you dial any faster?"

"Danny, Danny, Danny. Turn that frown upside down."

"Hello?" a deep voice answers.

I wink at Danny and press the phone closer to my ear. "Hi, my name is Katherine Wood. Your auntie gave me your number. She said you're looking for a client to coach BMX?"

"Yeah, that's right. She mentioned you. Do you have much previous experience?"

I poke pimple boy's cheek because why the fuck not? "Well, that's debatable. I can do basic tricks, and I learned some intermediate tricks."

He hums. "What's your goal? Are you looking to compete?"

I smile, feeling a part of the old me resurface. "Mr. Alvarez, I'm going all the way. I'm going to beat Kingsley Delanoy!"

I pull the phone away from my ear while Mr. Alvarez spends the next couple of minutes laughing. "He's cuckoo," I whisper to Danny, rolling my finger against my temple.

Why do people always laugh at me when I tell them my plans?

"You're serious?" he asks when he's finally composed himself enough to wheeze out a reply.

"Trust me, Mr. Alvarez. I have never been more serious!"

I can hear the smile in his voice as he says, "Call me Marcos. We better get started then."

∽

*18 months later.*

Becky taps her teaspoon against the glass, balancing her squirming toddler on her hip. We're in my sunny back garden celebrating my birthday and what has been a grueling eighteen months since I first phoned Marcos. It was the best decision of my life. Amidst the sweat, tears, and hard work, I slowly pieced together my broken heart and found my way back to myself.

Everyone gathered around the garden table falls silent as Becky lifts her champagne glass. "Thank you for inviting us to celebrate your birthday at your new house. I can't believe you're twenty-three today. We've come a long way since we were silly teenagers with even more ridiculous ideas. None less than you. I remember when you spilled your coffee on Hunter Wood and got it into your head that you would become a porn actress and marry the biggest name in the industry. And now you are only days away from competing in your first BMX competition.

I'm blown away by the effort and dedication you put into everything you set your mind to. Regardless of whether you beat Kingsley or not, you will go far. The world better hold its breath because it won't know what hit it. I love how brightly you shine, Kath. It's an honor to get to call myself your friend, and if your dad and Geoff were here today, they would be so proud of you!"

We all raise our glasses.

I take a sip. The cool champagne bursts on my tongue. I mouth thank you to Becky just as Marcos scoots his chair back from across the table and raises his glass for another toast.

Next to me, Hazel squeezes my hand in support.

"For those of you who don't know me. I'm Marcos Alvarez, and this is my aunt, Euletta Alvarez. She was Geoffrey's nurse. That's how my family first got introduced to Kath Hamilton. I've had the honor of coaching Kath for the last year and a half. It's been a challenging time for her with the sudden death of Geoffrey and the subsequent divorce proceedings. Even so, she jumped right in at the deep end and never gave up. Not even on the most difficult days when she wasn't just hurting emotionally but physically too.

If she couldn't land a trick, she kept at it, come rain or shine until she nailed it. She has been a true inspiration to my family and me. When she first rang me, I asked her about her ambitions, and her exact words were 'Mr. Alvarez, I'm going all the way. I'm going to beat Kingsley Delanoy.' It wasn't my finest hour—I laughed so hard I couldn't talk, but I've had to eat my words since I started training her. She may or may not beat Kingsley, but she will sure as hell give him a run for his money, and regardless of the results, I want Kath to be proud of herself.

This has been about so much more than simply a goal to beat the champion. It's been a journey of self-exploration. Kath had to rediscover those parts of herself that were lost along the way. I think she's come out a much stronger woman as a result. I'm proud of you!" he says, smiling at me as he lifts his glass.

I raise mine too. Tears well in my eyes, but for once, they're happy tears.

# EIGHTEEN

"Look at me, Kath!" Marcos says. "I don't want you to doubt yourself. You're ready! You've got this!!"

I tear my gaze away from the crowd. I can't see the ramp because of the sheer number of people, but I can hear the commentator through the big speakers. I lower my bottle of water. "I don't think I will ever feel ready. This is insane!"

Marcos puts his hand on my arm. His brown eyes are soft, and his dark and unruly hair glints in the sunlight. "Repeat after me, Kath!"

I nod, placing my bottle down on the grass. "Sure. It's not like I have anything to lose." Kingsley competed earlier, and just knowing he's here in the crowd somewhere is making me break out in a cold sweat.

"My name is Katherine Hamilton. I'm the daughter of Charles Hamilton. My father built an empire, and I am my father's daughter!"

I laugh, nervously wringing the bike handles. I had to replace the handlebar grips, and the bike has required some repair work here and there, but apart from that, it's still the very same bike Kingsley gifted me when we were eighteen.

"Come on," Marcos says. "Try it."

"Jesus," I laugh, shaking my head and rolling my eyes. "Fine. My name is Katherine Hamilton. Charles Hamilton is my father, and I am my father's daughter."

"Not quite," Marcos grins. "But close."

I fall silent as I wring the handlebars again. I look up at Marcos, and my eyes blur with tears. "Thank you."

I don't think he knows what it means to me to be here today. Not just at the competition, but everything else too. He gave me something to focus on and throw all of my attention to when I was in a bad place. Most importantly, he didn't give up on me. He believed in me when I struggled to do the same.

He smiles softly. "Thank me when you win."

I search the planes of his face. He's deeply tanned after the countless hours he's spent outside with me. "I want to thank you now. I was in such a bad place, Marcos! Every decision I made..." I wipe away a tear. "They led me down a dark road. I was lost. I thought it would lead me to happiness, but in the end, it opened up a big dark chasm in my chest. Geoffrey saw it. He tried to pull me back from the edge so many times." I look up at the clouds overhead. "I like to think he's here today." I swipe at my tears and attempt a smile. "The last eighteen months have been hell, quite frankly."

Marcos laughs. He grilled me hard every minute of every day. Military boot camp has nothing on Marcos.

"Every single minute has been worth it."

He nods and scans his eyes across the crowd before focusing back on me. "It's been my pleasure, Kath."

I nod too. No more words are needed. I think Marcos knows that he dragged me out from a very dark place and gave me something completely new to focus on. If life has taught me one thing, I thrive when I have a goal to work toward, and this has been the ultimate goal. Many would say it's impossible, but I say it's only a matter of willpower. I needed this for me. I needed to prove that I could drag myself out of that dark hole, and I did. For the first time in a very long time, I can finally feel the sun warm my skin again.

"You're up next." Marcos pulls me in for a hug, propping his chin on my head. "Blow this competition wide open!" We rock for a moment before he steps back.

I grab my bike and grin. "See you on the other end, coach."

---

Kingsley.

I throw the bottle down on the grass and grab another one. Luke, my coach, won't stop talking.

"You're in for the win again. You nailed that last trick, man. It was even better than in the training sessions."

I nod distractedly, wiping sweat off my forehead. It's an unusually hot day in this part of the country.

When I go to throw the second water bottle down on the grass, I pause.

"You're scheduled for an interview with DIG BMX on Wednesday. I told them it might be tight with the competition the day before, but they—" He nudges me on the shoulder. "Kingsley, are you listening?"

"Kath?" She's walking towards me. It must be her.

"Kath? Who?" Luke asks, but I ignore him. "Hey man, where are you going?"

It's definitely her. I would know those eyes and that smile anywhere. She's more tanned than usual, but it's her.

*It's her.*

Before I can grasp what is happening, my feet carry me over to her. She's walking with someone, a tall Latino man I have never seen before. "Kath?"

She looks up and stops short, eyes bouncing between mine. We're standing close.

"Hi, Kingsley."

I swallow thickly. My brain has still not caught on. "You're here..."

She sucks her lips between her teeth to suppress a smile. "I told you I would come for your title."

The guy next to her covers up a laugh with his closed fist. "I'm just going to..." He gestures to the side of the ramp. "I'll be over there, Kath."

I'm at a loss for words as she searches my face for the longest time. What is she doing here?

"How are you, Kingsley?"

Her eyes are so much bluer than I remember. "I'm okay."

She lowers her gaze, and I dip my head because fuck it, I need those eyes on me. "How are you?"

She blushes, wiggling her fingers on her left hand in front of my face. "I'm divorced."

I stare blankly at her ring finger where Hunter's engagement and wedding ring used to sit. How did I not know? "I'm sorry?" I cringe. How fucking awkward can I be.

Katherine laughs, and it's just as beautiful as I remember. It's a tinkling sound that carries on the breeze. She brushes away strands of hair stuck to her lip balm. "Don't be. I'm not."

She starts walking, and I stand there for a couple of

seconds, unable to understand what the fuck is happening. I scramble after her. "Where are you going?"

She side-eyes me with a smirk. "I'm going after your title."

I halt in my steps. "My title?" I rush after her. It's only now that I notice the bike and the helmet hanging off the handlebars. It's the bike I gave her. "What's with the bike?"

She throws her head back, laughing. "I'll speak to you in a bit, alright? My turn is up."

"Wha—"

They're announcing her name on the speakers. This time I stop dead in my tracks. She's going to compete...

*"I'm going to beat you in a competition one day, Kingsley. It's on my bucket list."*

～

Katherine.

I approach the ramp, smiling so big it hurts. My nerves from earlier are forgotten, and the only thing I can focus on is the stunned look on his face. Marcos winks at me as I lean the bike against the ramp and fasten my helmet. The crowd doesn't intimidate me anymore.

"Katherine Hamilton!" Kingsley calls out behind me.

My fingers falter with the strap. I slowly turn and look over my shoulder. Kingsley stands with his hands in his pockets. His head is slightly inclined to the side, and his smile is sinful.

"Ask me!"

My heart jolts in my chest, and I duck my head to hide

my smile. I can't believe we are doing this now. I lift my gaze and ask, "Have you ever been in love, Kingsley?"

His smile widens. He watches me for a moment longer before chuckling. "Yes, Katherine Hamilton. I have!"

I want to sob with happiness. I have waited so many years to hear him say those words to me.

I sink my teeth into my bottom lip to suppress my blinding smile as I reach up and fasten my strap. "Well then, Kingsley. Let me beat your ass in this competition, and then I'll come down and kiss you!"

The spectators around us laugh. I'm sure my soul glows with happiness.

When I'm at the top of the ramp, I take a moment to sweep my eyes over the crowd. So many faceless people watching and waiting.

"This is for you, Geoffrey!" I whisper as the clouds part, and the warm summer breeze lifts my hair off my shoulders.

I find Kingsley in the crowd. For one short moment, it's just us. He smiles, and I breathe a soft laugh. I kick off the ground, fly down the ramp, and jump through the air.

# EPILOGUE

The morning sunlight is streaming in through the blinds. I stretch on the bed like a cat and roll my head to find Kingsley awake and watching me.

His brown eyes crease at the corners as he smiles. "Good morning, sleepyhead."

I push his face. "Go away with that stupid grin. It's too early!"

He chuckles and shifts on the bed until I feel his warm lips on my swollen belly. "Your mommy is a sleepyhead."

The sight of his pillow-creased face, tousled hair, and his lips on my pregnant belly while he talks to our unborn son is too heartwarming not to appreciate.

He crawls back up and takes the quilt with him, careful not to put his weight on my stomach. Hiding us underneath the blanket, he makes me laugh and squirm as he nips my neck with his teeth.

"I have something for you." He rolls off and opens the bedside drawer. "I wanted to make a big event of it. Make it special, you know...?" He rolls back over and reaches for my hand. "But then I thought, no. We don't work like that. We make the small moments extraordinary. We always have." He slides a diamond ring on my finger. "Like this one right now." His piercing eyes search mine. "Will you spend the rest of your life with me, Katherine Hamilton?"

I stare at him, then at my ring, and then at him. "Kingsley…"

He brings my hand up to his lips, placing a soft kiss atop the ring. "Make me the happiest man on earth?"

"My past…" I whisper because I don't have a filter. Still, a small part of me doesn't feel deserving of this moment. And of this man.

He thumbs my ring and moves down to kiss my belly, lingering with his warm lips on my skin. His eyes meet mine. "Your past made you, Kath. You have to embrace it and let it go. I have." He crawls back up my body and kisses me softly. "Marry me!"

"Yes."

He smiles against my lips. "Really?"

I laugh through my tears. "Yes, Kingsley. A thousand times, yes!"

His mouth comes down on mine, and he throws back the quilt, making me moan his name as he sinks into me with a groan. Our hands clasped above my head on the pillow.

*The End.*

# COUNTER BET

## CHAPTER ONE

Emily.

I line my lips with my favorite red lipstick, then glance at my latest painting on the easel. I stayed up until the early hours, mixing colors to get the right shade, but I'm still not entirely happy.

I place the lid back on the lipstick, eyeing the result in the mirror. My makeup is flawless as always.

"Are you ready, Emily? Rick is waiting," my mom calls from downstairs.

I breathe a tired sigh as I run my fingers through my blonde hair. Here's to another year of pretending to be so goddamn perfect all of the time. Today is the first day of my senior year, and while the thought of putting high school behind me should excite me, it doesn't. It terrifies me. I play my role perfectly at Hedgewood High. I'm the head cheerleader with the perfect grades and the clean-cut boyfriend who also happens to be the star quarterback.

Cliché, you say?

That's because it is.

I'm not ready for everything to change next year. I don't know why it fills me with so much dread? I'm already unhappy, so a new start should be positive, but I feel comfortable behind my mask. I'm at the top of the hierarchy.

People see what I let them see, and the anxiety beneath the surface is kept behind lock and key where no one can see it except for me. Mostly though, I think I'm bored. Life is predictable in every sense of the word.

I grab my bag off my bed, leave my room, and skip down the steps to find my boyfriend ruffling my little sister's hair. She's three years old and cute as a button.

Rick is dressed in a pair of light blue jeans paired with a white Henley. His letterman jacket lies on the kitchen table.

He glances at me, then smirks as he crouches down to whisper in my sister's ear. Her adorable giggles fill the room.

"What are you two whispering about?"

My little sister pokes her tongue out and runs off.

I watch her little piggy tails bounce. "I sometimes think you like her more than me."

Rick's hazel eyes dance with mischief as he wraps me up in his big arms and leans down to nuzzle my neck. "Are you jealous, baby?"

He smells delicious with his freshly washed hair and the new cologne I bought for his birthday.

"Hands off my daughter, Rick!" My dad booms in a loud voice as he walks into the kitchen.

Rick jumps back in surprise. "Yes, sir. Sorry, sir."

My dad rolls his eyes. "How many times have I told you to stop calling me sir? It makes me feel old."

"Sorry, sir," Rick says, a wide grin on his lips.

My dad chucks him on the back of the head, earning a disapproving glance of my mom.

She puts my freshly pressed cheer uniform in my bag. "Try not to ruin this one, sweetie."

I bite back my retort. Technically, Rick ruined my last one, but she doesn't need to know that.

"Are you ready?" I ask Rick, gesturing to the door, pushing his broad back to get him moving when he snatches a freshly cooked waffle.

∽

Rick parks in his reserved spot next to the front steps of the main building. It's one of the many perks of being the star quarterback and having a father who's one of the most successful lawyers in town.

Our dads are close colleagues and work for the same firm. Needless to say, they were over the moon when Rick asked me out after school two years ago, and I said yes, not because he sets my soul on fire but because it's the most logical decision.

"Are you okay?" Rick asks with a sidelong look in my direction as he cuts the engine. "You're quiet."

I unfasten my seatbelt and plaster on my most convincing smile. "I'm great."

Rick looks unconvinced but doesn't comment. We exit the vehicle, and he puts his arm over my shoulder as we make our way over to our friends. As always, Rick is oblivious to the longing looks girls throw his way. Or he simply doesn't care.

"Hey, man," he says to his best friend, Jamie. They do

some weird handshake and shoulder thump while Hailey pulls me into a bone-crushing hug like we didn't see each other yesterday.

I laugh through a mouthful of her hair.

"He fucks like an animal! I can hardly walk," she whispers, looking pointedly at Jamie.

I follow her line of sight. Jamie, the school's star receiver, looks pleased with himself as Rick and the other guys laugh at one of his rare jokes. He reaches up and sweeps his unruly blonde hair off his forehead. I can see the appeal, but he's a notorious player.

"I called it, didn't I?" My smile is boastful. They flirted with each other for the better part of last year, but they both refused to act on it until summer. I now know more about Jamie's cock than I care to admit, thanks to Hailey.

We make our way into school. The hallway is bustling with students and bleary-eyed teachers who look anything but happy to be back after their summer vacation. Rick keeps close to my side with a possessive hand on my hip as Jamie talks about the upcoming football season.

I tune out, lost in my own thoughts. My workload this year will be even more challenging with cheer practice and art classes. I need to keep my head level.

∽

I move the pasta around on my plate as Hailey launches into the latest gossip. Interestingly, this stuff fascinates her so much when I literally can't care less about who sucked whose dick and pulled what girl's hair. Sometimes, I feel like an outsider looking in. Still, I appreciate the normality of my friends laughing and gossiping in the lunch hall.

A football flies over my head. Rick catches it, then passes it on to Jamie. I push my tray back, leaving my food untouched. Unease twists my stomach for reasons I can't pinpoint. It's been happening a lot lately.

Rick pulls me onto his lap and kisses me until I'm light-headed. I don't pull away. He angles my head to the side and trails kisses over my jaw. His cock hardens in his jeans, poking me in the thigh.

I scan my eyes across the bustling lunch hall. My mask is still intact. But only just.

Students laugh with their friends, and teachers look fed up at being back at work even though it's only lunchtime. An empty coke can flies across the room.

Rick grabs my ass, nipping my skin with his teeth.

Am I the only one who feels empty inside?

I feel eyes on me. Not the everyday envious glances from other girls or appreciative looks from boys. Someone is observing me.

I shake off my self-deprecating thoughts and sweep my gaze across the room until they collide with a set of kohl-rimmed blue eyes.

*Dallas Garcia.*

She's new to the school. I don't know much about her. Only that she hangs out with the emo kids and is a regular in detention.

I swallow past the thick lump in my throat while she continues studying me as if she can see right through me. It makes my skin itch.

"Let's get out of here," Rick whispers in my ear, then steals another kiss.

I avert my gaze from Dallas' penetrating eyes and kiss him back, ignoring the unease knotting my stomach.

There's a crack in my façade.

~

Mr. Greenwood stands at the front, pointing to his barely legible handwriting on the whiteboard. There's a dried coffee stain on his wrinkled shirt, which is also missing a button.

My eyes drift over my shoulder.

Dallas pops gum and taps her foot to the beat playing in her earphones while typing on her phone. I count at least three piercings, one in her nose and two in her eyebrow. Both of her arms are covered in tattoos.

"Dallas!" Mr. Greenwood sighs, pinching the bridge of his nose.

Steph, Dallas' best friend, nudges her shoulder. My eyes drop to Dallas' legs beneath the desk. Creamy skin peeks out through the holes in her ripped black jeans.

She pulls out her earplugs and frowns at Steph, who nudges her head to the teacher.

Mr. Greenwood holds out a detention slip. "I'm running out of detention slips, Dallas."

She slides out from behind the desk, grabbing her bag off the back of the chair. Her scuffed black chucks are so unlike my expensive heels.

She puts the detention slip in her bra, then grins at Mr. Greenwood. "Better get some more then."

I stare after her. She's everything I'm not, and it's intriguing me. What's it's like to simply not care? I've lived my whole life under the spotlight. Always had expectations of me.

Hailey nudges me. "Are you okay? You seem distracted."

"I'm fine." But she's right. I *am* distracted. When the bell rings, the notebook in front of me remains blank.

*Want to read more? Download now. Counter Bet is available for free with kindle unlimited.*

# ACKNOWLEDGMENTS

I'll keep this short and sweet. Releasing a new book is always exciting and nerve-racking, so I want to thank everyone who has supported me on this journey. Paula for reading everything I write and injecting me with a healthy dose of bravery. Chris, for taking hours out of his day to edit what I write. My hubby, for being supportive, even when I lock myself away for hours on end to write. You, the reader, for taking a chance on me. This story is very close to my heart, so it's my hope that it made you smile, laugh, and maybe shed a tear or two. It would mean the world to me if you left a review. I always love to hear from my readers, so follow me on social media for news and updates on my upcoming releases. Let's chat :)

Much love,
Harleigh.

# ABOUT THE AUTHOR

Harleigh Beck lives in a small town in the northeast of England. She has three children and a hubby who's supported every crazy idea that's popped into her head throughout the years. She also has a black and white cat who never ceases to surprise her with the weird and wonderful places he finds to sleep. Since she was a little girl, she's been writing stories, and her teachers complained to her mum that they had to bring her stories home on the weekends. New writing ideas tend to strike at the most unlikely times, like when she's at work or queuing in the supermarket. When she's not writing, you'll find her head down in a book, munching on something undoubtedly unhealthy. She mainly reads romance, and her favourite books are high school romances and dark romance. She has lots more books planned, so be sure to follow her social media for updates.

Printed in Great Britain
by Amazon